LANA NEWTON grew up in two opp
Union – the snow-white Siberian tow?
domed Ukrainian capital, Kyiv. At the
Australia with her mother. Lana and h.
Coast of NSW, where it never snows and is always summ.

Lana studied IT at university and, as a student, wrote poetry in Russian that she hid from everyone. For over a decade after graduating, she worked as a computer programmer. When she returned to university to complete her history degree, her favourite lecturer encouraged her to write fiction. She hasn't looked back, and never goes anywhere without her favourite pen because you never know when the inspiration might strike.

Lana's short stories appeared in many magazines and anthologies, and she was the winner of the Historical Novel Society Autumn 2012 Short Fiction competition. Her novels are published by HQ Digital, an imprint of HarperCollins UK.

Lana also writes historical fiction under the pen name of Lana Kortchik.

To find out more, please visit http://www.lanakortchik.com
Facebook: https://www.facebook.com/lanakortchik
Twitter: https://www.twitter.com/lanakortchik

Her Perfect Lies

LANA NEWTON

ONE PLACE. MANY STORIES

HQ
An imprint of HarperCollins*Publishers* Ltd
1 London Bridge Street
London SE1 9GF

This paperback edition 2020

This edition is published in Great Britain by
HQ, an imprint of HarperCollins*Publishers* Ltd 2020

ISBN: 9780008364861

For Sal, the bravest of the brave

Part I

Chapter 1

A stranger watched her from the mirror. Grey eyes, pale lips, blonde – almost white – hair, as if bleached by the sun, a face she felt she had never seen before. The only thing she knew about this stranger was her name.

Claire. They said her name was Claire.

They told her other things, of course – things she found hard to believe. She was famous, touring around the world with the largest ballet company in the country. The nurses talked about her as if they knew her. One had even seen her perform, in faraway Australia of all places.

Through mindless hours in her hospital bed, she imagined herself on stage in front of thousands. *Impossible*, she would whisper, the stranger in the mirror nodding in agreement. Yet, there were pictures and videos to prove it. She peered at herself in the photographs, as Odette, Sugar Plum Fairy, Cinderella. Dazzling costumes, elegant posture, long limbs. Was it really her? She looked at the twirling doll on the screen of her phone until her eyes hurt. *Impossible, impossible, impossible.*

Tchaikovsky's *Swan Lake*, like a clap of thunder, filled the room. Unfamiliar, and yet, she felt she ought to know it, as if she had heard it a thousand times before. Every time she willed her body to move, her feet would slide into a ballet position like it was the most natural thing in the world. What her mind had forgotten, her body remembered. Pirouettes, jetés, and pliés came to her in time to Tchaikovsky's eternal creation, each as perfect as a summer rain.

Today was a special day. The nurses seemed excited for her. She felt she should be excited, too. Staring in the mirror, right into the stranger's eyes, she forced her face into a smile and widened her eyes, but instead of happy she looked scared. She was exhausted, as if she had lived a thousand lifetimes, none of which she could remember. Splashing her face with cold water, she brushed her hair and tied it in a high ponytail. Reaching for her bag, she applied some makeup. Black for her eyelashes, pink for her cheeks, red for her lips. The last thing she wanted was to look like she was part of this grey hospital room.

The London sky outside wasn't grey but a vivid purple. She watched the last traces of sunlight disappear, and then, out of nowhere, the rain came. It battered the lone oak tree outside, and the leaves thrashed in the wind. Over the music she could hear their rustle. This sky, this oak tree, the room she was in, the cafeteria down the hall – these were the boundaries of her world. Beyond them, she knew nothing.

The music stopped and she turned sharply away from the window. She could sense his gaze. The man standing in the doorway was tall, and she felt dwarfed by him. They stared at each other in silence for a few seconds too long – Claire, her cheeks flush with rouge, eyes filled with fear, and her husband, impeccably dressed, unsmiling, unfamiliar.

'Hi, Claire.' The man took a few steps in her direction.

'Hi, Paul.' In two weeks she had seen him twice. Now he had finally come to take her home.

'Feeling better today?'

She didn't know how to answer his question. Better than two weeks ago? Yes. But better in general? She couldn't remember what that felt like. 'I still get headaches. But my back is almost healed.'

4

She peered into his face. There were wrinkles around his eyes and dark stubble on his chin. She didn't have it in her heart to tell him he was a stranger to her. But he was looking at her as if she was a stranger, too. His eyes remained cold.

'Do you have everything?' he asked.

'I just need to say goodbye. Wait here for me? I won't be long.'

She made her way down a busy corridor, navigating gurneys, trolleys and people. She had made this trip many times before, could probably do it with her eyes closed – a left turn, twenty uncertain paces, another left, down two flights of stairs and a right. The door she wanted was hidden behind a pillar, tucked away from prying eyes. You could easily walk past and not even know it was there. Today it was wide open, as if inviting her in.

It was quiet in the room, no music playing, no television murmuring in the background, no eager visitors with their chatter and flowers. Only the heartbeat of the machines, like clocks counting down the seconds, and the ventilator puffing, struggling, breathing in and out. If nurses or doctors spoke in here, they did so in hushed voices, as if they were afraid of disturbing the man on the bed. Which was ironic because all they wanted was for him to wake up.

Outside the window was the hospital car park, a noisy anthill of activity, with ambulances screeching and cars vying for spaces. The rumble of engines was a muffled soundtrack to the man's artificial existence. She felt grateful for the oak tree outside her room, for the peace and quiet. She would have hated having nothing but cars to look at. But the man didn't care. He was asleep.

Sitting on the edge of the bed, Claire took his hand. After two weeks, this gesture had become a habit. Day after miserable day she would do it on autopilot, looking into the man's face, studying his lifeless features. Today she could swear his eyelids were moving. She wanted to ask the doctor if it meant anything. Fluttering eyelids – was it a sign? Was he about to wake up? Or was it her imagination showing her what she wanted to see?

5

'Your father, is it?' A nurse crept up behind her silently, like a cat. She looked a little like a cat too, scruffy and ginger, her eyes cagey. She paused next to the man's bed, removed the chart from its folder and checked the monitors. 'You look just like him.'

The man's skin was grey today, more so than usual. His face was gaunt, his body a skeleton on the white sheet.

'Yes,' said Claire. 'I'm waiting for him to wake up, so he can tell me about my life.'

If the nurse was surprised, she didn't show it. 'Are you a patient here?'

Claire didn't answer but turned away from the nurse and towards her father. The woman's mouth opened as if to repeat her question, but at the last moment she seemed to change her mind. Her eyes darted over Claire's face as she made a few notes on the chart and placed it back. 'I hope he pulls through,' she said finally. 'I'll pray for him. And for you.'

She was already out the door when Claire called out, 'Can he hear me? If I talk to him, can he hear?'

The ginger head reappeared in the doorway. 'They do believe so. I mean, after all the research they've done. Speak to him, tell him you love him. It will help.' The nurse nodded as she spoke, as if for emphasis. Her eyes filled with compassion.

Claire squeezed the man's fingers. Ever so slightly she shook him, pushed his shoulder with her tiny fist, willing him to open his eyes. His hand felt cold in hers, a dead weight pulling down. She brought it to her face and saw her tears fall on the calluses of his palm. *These hands held me when I was a child*, she thought. *These lips, now motionless, read bedtime stories and kissed me goodnight.* How could she have forgotten all that? It didn't seem possible. Memories like that were part of one's DNA, only gone when life itself was gone. She leant over, pressing her lips to his forehead. 'Wake up, Dad,' she whispered. 'I need you.'

She had spent the last two weeks feeling guilty. Guilty that she was awake, while her dad was unconscious. That she could walk, look out the window, enjoy the pale sunlight and the meagre hospital food. And now she felt guilty she was leaving this place, returning to what once had been her normal existence, while he was stuck in this bed, not yet dead, but not quite alive either.

On the way back she walked slowly, delaying the inevitable, not ready to leave the familiar for the unknown.

Paul was waiting in her room. 'Time to go,' he said and his lips stretched into a smile. Even to her confused, drug-addled mind, it looked forced. Glancing away, she nodded quickly and reached for her bag. Her whole life, all two weeks of it, packed into a small travel case. Paul walked out without touching her. As she waited for him to talk to the doctors and sign the paperwork, she felt sweat drops on her forehead. Her throat was dry.

The nurses came to say goodbye. As she hugged them, she cried like she was parting with the only family she had.

In the car Paul was silent. The only sound was the swish-swish-swish of windscreen wipers as they sped through the rain. There was so much she wanted to know. *How did we meet? How long have we been married? Do we make each other laugh? Are we happy?* She didn't ask any of those questions. Instead, she said, 'Where were we going?'

'What?' Paul startled as if she woke him from a dream.

'Dad and I – where were we going on the day of the accident?'

'I don't know. I wasn't there.'

Shadows loomed outside the car window – trees, houses, lamp-posts. Claire watched them whiz past at forty miles an hour. She could make out manicured lawns, flowers and driveways. Some windows were dark, others brightly lit. She imagined a different life inside each one. Perhaps a married couple sitting down to dinner before retiring to bed to read and fall asleep in each other's arms. Or a grandfather listening to his grandson play the piano.

'Do I have any other family?' she asked as they turned onto a motorway. There were no more houses, no more lights, only dark skies and even darker trees.

'There's your mother.'

'She never visited me at the hospital. Why is that?'

For a moment he looked confused. 'I was surprised when I didn't see her there. I expected her to be by your side at a time like this.'

I have a mother, she thought. Squeezing her eyes shut, she searched for a recollection. If she reached deep enough, if she focused hard enough, would she be able to see her mother's face? That wasn't something one could easily forget. Not even someone like her. Swallowing the sudden lump in her throat, she dug her nails into the soft skin at the back of her wrist. She wondered what her mother was like. Had she taken her to ballet classes when she was little? Had she stayed up late baking cupcakes for her birthdays? Did she look just like her, only slightly older?

'Any brothers or sisters?'

'You're an only child.'

Before she could ask another question, the car screeched to a stop outside a two-storey house. In the headlights she could see a sprawling lawn and a white staircase curving up to a set of French doors. It was not a house; it was a mansion. As she gaped at it, wide-eyed, Paul opened her car door. She emerged, slipping on wet gravel. He caught her mid-fall but almost immediately let go.

Bright lights snapped on suddenly along the front of the house, startling her. 'Motion sensors,' explained Paul. He carried her suitcase up the stairs and there was nothing left for her to do but follow into the life she knew nothing about. The rain lashed the side of her face as she walked, and the droplets ran down her body, filling her shoes with water.

When they reached the front door, she heard whimpering. Surprised, she glanced at Paul, but he was busy fumbling for the keys. Finally, he unlocked the door, letting her in. As soon as she stepped over the threshold, she was under attack. Something enormous crashed into her, making her cry out in terror. She lost her footing and fell, at the last moment grasping a wall. A large beast wrestled her to the ground, its heavy breathing in her ear. Barking excitedly, it slathered her with a long, wet tongue. Catching her breath, she ran her fingers through the fur. When Paul turned on the lights, she saw the beast was only a dog. It was a large Labrador, with a long tail and droopy ears.

'Down, Molokai,' said Paul. Instantly the dog leapt off but continued jumping on the spot, its yellow tail dancing.

'Molokai?' The word stirred something in her, a distant memory that wouldn't rise to the surface. It wasn't a word she recognised, and yet it sounded familiar, as if a dozen threads of her life were intertwined in those three syllables. In frustration she looked at the dog and the dog looked back, its mouth open in a smile.

'Molokai is an island in Hawaii,' explained Paul. 'That's where we honeymooned.'

'Oh. How old is she?'

'*He* is five.'

Carefully she rubbed Molokai behind his ear. Something told her dogs loved that. This one certainly did – as soon as Paul's back was turned, he jumped all over her again. 'That's a nice welcome,' she muttered, not sure what to do next.

'Yes, he's very friendly. Sometimes too friendly. If ever there are burglars in the house, he'll probably lick them to death. He loves you the most.'

Looking into the dog's dark eyes, Claire suspected the feeling was mutual. For a moment she felt a little less lonely.

'Come in,' said Paul. 'No point standing in the doorway like an unwanted guest.'

But that's how I feel, she wanted to tell him as she walked into the living room. Like an unwanted guest who had confused date and time, ending up in the wrong place when she was least expected. Luckily, Molokai was by her side. Her hand on his neck, she stared at the high ceiling and the marble floors. In the far corner of the room she spotted a white cat. It glanced at

Claire for a few seconds and ran off as fast as it could, hiding behind a curtain. Looking up, she noticed an enormous crystal chandelier, all baubles and fake candles. It was the ugliest thing she had ever seen.

'Your pride and joy,' said Paul. 'You bought it in Italy.'

Choosing to ignore this information, Claire perched on the edge of a sofa. Paul watched her for a few seconds. 'No need to look so overwhelmed. This is your home. Make yourself comfortable. Hungry? There are sandwiches in the fridge.'

'You made me sandwiches?' She was touched.

'Our housekeeper did.'

'We have a housekeeper?' Why did she find that so surprising? The housekeeper seemed to go hand in hand with the marble floors and the sprawling staircase. 'How can we afford such a big house?'

'Your mother bought it for us.'

'My mother is rich?'

'Old family money,' he explained.

Although food was the last thing on her mind, Claire sat down at the dining table with Molokai at her feet. She could feel his cold nose on the bare skin of her leg. Paul didn't eat, nor did he look at her, staring at the newspaper instead. She could tell he wasn't reading. His eyes remained steady, far away. Like jigsaw puzzle pieces that didn't quite fit they sat in awkward silence on opposite sides of the table.

Soon there was nothing left of the sandwiches but a few pickles. She didn't like the salty taste on her tongue.

'You don't want those? They're your favourite,' said Paul. 'You always ask for extra pickles on everything.'

Uncertainly she poked a pickle with her fork. 'They taste like seawater.'

'That explains why you like them. You love the sea.' There was a fleeting smile on Paul's face and this time Claire could swear it was genuine. 'You look exhausted,' he added. 'Why don't I show you to your room?'

Gratefully, she followed him up the stairs to a spacious room decorated in beige. It was tidy but for a worn-out silk robe on an armchair. The king-size bed looked so enticing, Claire was tempted to fall in and lose herself under the covers, wet clothes and all.

The room was quiet – no traffic, no voices and only a muffled whisper of leaves reached her through the open terrace doors. She peeked through the curtains but couldn't see beyond the darkness.

'My room is across the corridor. If you need anything, anything at all, just knock.' He kissed her good night. His lips on her cheek were arctic. He might as well have been kissing a distant aunt.

'Wait,' she said. He paused in the doorway. She cleared her throat. 'My mother. What's her name?'

'Angela. Angela Wright.'

'And my father?'

'Your father's name is Tony.'

And with that he was gone, shutting the door and taking Molokai with him. Claire barely had the energy to change into her nightdress, but despite her exhaustion, sleep wouldn't come. She closed her eyes under her beige covers and concentrated on the sound of rain hitting the windowsill, repeating her parents' names quietly to herself and hoping to remember something, anything, about them. The events of the day played over and over in her mind until she heard the phone ring, and then Paul's voice. A minute later there was a knock on her bedroom door.

'Someone just called from the hospital,' Paul said. 'Your father is awake.'

Chapter 2

The human mind . . . what a fragile thing it was. One minute your life had meaning. You had a past, a present and a future that was anticipated and planned for. You went to work, saved money, paid into your pension. You got married, travelled the world, fell in love, had babies, pizza every Saturday and takeaway Chinese every Friday night. And then, just like that, without any warning or indication, your mind could turn its back on you, leaving you in a void. Knowing who you are, where you are in life, all gone like an early morning fog. Without that knowledge, what was left?

One day at the hospital, Claire had overheard the nurses chatting over their cups of coffee. If you could be anyone else for one day, who would you be, they mused as they took careful sips of their flat whites. Wouldn't it be wonderful, to live someone else's life for a day, to be them, to feel like them? A movie star, perhaps, or a famous singer. A cattle drover in Australia. To live a life as far removed from yours as possible, wouldn't that be something? That was how Claire felt – like she was living someone else's life. But it wasn't wonderful. She felt like she was drowning and no one was there to save her.

With a start she woke up and for a moment didn't know where or who she was. The strange room, the luxurious bed, the expensive furniture – none of it looked familiar. And then she remembered – she was home.

Sitting up, she rubbed her eyes. Spotting a silk robe draped casually over an armchair, she threw it on and stepped out of bed. She crossed the room in small, tentative steps and pulled the curtains open. The rain of the night before was gone. All she could see was the blue of the skies and the green of the trees. She wished she was outside, walking in the park, window shopping or having a coffee in one of the many cafés lining the nearby streets. She didn't want to be in the alien house that was supposed to feel like home but didn't.

Glancing at the clock, she noticed it was only nine in the morning. Another three hours until Paul drove her to the hospital to meet her father. How was she going to fill the time? A part of her wanted to fast-forward these three hours, while another part of her, a shy and retreating part, wanted to hide. *It'll be okay*, she told herself. *I might not remember him but he is my father. He loves me. We love each other.* Last night when the hospital had called, she'd wanted to rush to her father's side right away. But she had to wait. There were no visiting hours in the middle of the night.

She could hear a soft whimpering outside. Molokai, she thought. And she was correct – the dog leapt into her arms, whining happily, as soon as she opened the bedroom door. She ran her hand through his fur and was rewarded by a thousand kisses. 'Look at you, you're all muddy. Have you been out for a walk? No, not on the bed.'

Miraculously, the dog obeyed. Accompanied by Molokai, she set out to explore. There was an en-suite bathroom in her bedroom. She marvelled at the size of it – it was twice as big as her hospital room. All marble and granite, it was decorated in the same colour scheme as the bedroom. Absentmindedly stroking a cotton towel, she wondered whether she had picked out this colour.

There were two bathroom sinks next to each other. Did she

once share this room with her husband? For a few seconds, as she peered at her reflection in a hexagonal mirror above the sinks, she thought about her marriage. There was so much she didn't know.

The freestanding bathtub in the middle of the room – for it was a room in its own right – looked so tempting, she wanted to climb straight in and feel the water on her body. But for now, the shower would do. She undressed behind a waterfall of crystal-like beads and eagerly turned the shower taps. For ten minutes she stood under cascades of warm water, while Molokai patiently waited outside the glass door.

Afterwards, while the dog bounced around like an overexcited toddler, she sat in front of a tall mirror in her bedroom. One after another she opened five bottles of perfume, spraying a little bit of each on her wrists and neck and regretting it instantly. The smell was overwhelming and made her gag.

The house was quiet. No cars driving past, no voices from the park. She didn't know where Paul was. His car wasn't in the driveway. Tying the cord of her robe together, she left the room. There were three other doors on this floor and, holding her breath, she opened each one. Two of the rooms contained no personal touches and seemed unoccupied. The last of the three clearly belonged to Paul. It was untidy, with clothes all over the floor. The room looked like Paul – masculine brown wood and dark furniture. She stood in the doorway, feeling like a child locked in an unfamiliar house with no way out. It was unsettling and more than a little scary.

She didn't want to snoop on Paul. It felt too much like encroaching on the private life of a stranger. She shut the door to his bedroom and walked down the marble staircase. Although she remembered the majestic living room from the night before, it still took her breath away. Suddenly she felt confused, like she was lost in the woods and didn't know what direction to take. Everything in this house seemed alien and she couldn't believe this was where she lived. Shivering, she walked into the kitchen. Just like she expected, it was spacious, with what she assumed must be all the latest appliances. In the fridge, she found a dozen sandwiches similar to the ones she'd had the night before. Reaching for a ham sandwich, she ate it as quickly as she could and then looked through cupboards. In amazement she stared at fruit she didn't recognise, delicate crystal glasses, porcelain plates and every flavour of tea imaginable. She found some cat food and refilled the cat's bowl, wondering whether it was hiding somewhere, too nervous to come out.

Her strength restored, she explored further, walking from the kitchen to the dining room to another guest room. They had a sauna, a swimming pool and an air hockey table in the basement. Finally, she spotted an old-fashioned piano in the drawing room. Tired now, she slid into a chair in front of it and ran her fingers over the keys. The most beautiful sounds escaped from under her fingertips and she paused for a moment, lifting her hands and staring at them as if she had never seen them before. Then she resumed playing. It wasn't *Swan Lake* or any of the music she'd heard in the hospital but a melody she didn't recognise.

'What do you think, Molokai? Did you know I could play the piano?' she asked the dog, who wagged his long tail in response.

As Claire contemplated this newly discovered ability, somewhere inside the house a phone rang. She stopped playing and stood up, nervously clutching her hands to her chest. What was she to do? Did she answer the phone? Or let it go to voicemail? Slightly unsteady on her feet, she walked towards the sound and watched the phone like it was an explosive device about to go off. Eventually it stopped ringing and Paul's voice could be heard asking to leave a message. 'Claire, it's me, Gaby. Call me back as soon as you get this. I need to see you.'

When the person on the other end hung up, Claire returned upstairs. She felt safer there. There were no phones she could see, no unfathomable voices coming through the speakers.

Back in her bedroom, she opened the wardrobe. Walking inside

15

– yes, the wardrobe was big enough to walk inside it – she examined rows of designer clothes, shoes and underwear. It was like being in a department store. She went through every drawer, rummaged through dresses and looked behind shoe racks. Who needed what seemed like a hundred pairs of shoes? And all these clothes . . . most of them looked like they had never been worn.

Suddenly, Molokai leapt off the bed and growled. Seconds later she heard the doorbell. Unsure of what to do, she froze with a shoe in her hand. Molokai ran through the door and soon his excited barking could be heard from downstairs. She followed on legs that seemed to have turned to jelly.

From behind the front door, she heard a woman's voice. 'Hello, anyone there?'

'One second,' said Claire, throwing a quick glance in the mirror and wondering whether she was dressed appropriately for a visitor. Through a gap in the curtains she could see a delivery truck parked on the opposite side of the road. Concluding it was just a courier and breathing out in relief, she fiddled with the lock. It was complex and she couldn't open it. 'I'm sorry, I don't have the keys for this door,' she called out. 'Are you delivering something? Can you leave it outside, please?'

'Claire, it's me, Gaby,' she heard in reply. 'Can I come in?'

Claire recognised the voice from the answer machine. To her surprise, a key turned and the door opened.

A stunning brunette was standing in the doorway. She looked like she had just walked off a movie set. There was a hint of something foreign about her – the Mediterranean tinge to her skin, the deep caramel to her eyes. A leather skirt hugged her slim hips. There was a bouquet of flowers in her hands.

'Oh my God, look at you!' she exclaimed, drawing Claire into a hug and almost crushing the flowers. Claire struggled but only for a second – resistance seemed pointless. 'It's so good to see you! You have no idea how worried we were.'

Claire extricated herself from the embrace, mumbling, 'It's good to see you, too.' She didn't know what else to say. Unlike Claire, Molokai seemed to know exactly who the woman was. A chewed dog toy – a plastic duck with its head missing – miraculously appeared in his mouth and he presented it to the visitor. His tail was wagging.

The brunette ignored the decapitated duck but gave Molokai a distracted stroke. 'These are for you,' she said. Her eyes twinkled as she shoved the flowers into Claire's hands. 'They're orchids.'

Intimidated by the woman and the flowers, Claire wished she had brushed her hair instead of dousing herself in all that perfume. *I must smell like a bouquet of flowers myself*, she thought. But the woman didn't seem to mind.

'You don't remember me, do you?' The brunette shook her head with disapproval, as if talking to a child who was struggling with her homework. 'It's me, Gaby. Your best friend.'

As Claire stood in the doorway gawking, Gaby made her way into the dining room. She seemed to know her way around Claire's house much better than Claire did.

'You have the key to the house?' Claire asked to break the silence.

'Of course I do. You and I are like sisters. I went to school with Paul. That's how we met.'

While Claire arranged the flowers in a vase she had found, Gaby walked into the kitchen and poured two glasses of red wine. A sudden thought occurred to Claire. Didn't a person tell their best friends everything? If that was the case, Gaby would have all the answers she was so desperately searching for.

Gaby handed Claire her wine. Taking a careful sip, Claire put her glass down.

'You don't like it?' asked Gaby. 'It's your favourite.'

Claire found it hard to believe. Her taste buds seemed unacquainted with the sharpness of the wine. She was desperate for a sip of water to get rid of the bitter taste but didn't want Gaby to think less of her. She felt a little intimidated by her old self, who would have enjoyed the wine and known what to say to this beautiful stranger.

In the first week at the hospital, many people dropped in to see her, faces and conversations she could hardly remember now, so confused and drugged up she had been back then. Little by little, however, the stream of visitors dwindled, before finally disappearing altogether. There was only so much one-sided conversation even a good friend could take. Only so much small talk with someone who did nothing but sit in her bed, staring into space, not knowing what to say, not knowing who she was.

What if she couldn't live up to the person she had once been? And how could she, if she remembered nothing about her? 'I'm not sure I'm allowed wine. I'm on all sorts of medication.' She pushed the glass away.

'I'm sorry I haven't been to see you in hospital. I've been away for work. My first time in Japan, what a fascinating place . . .' Gaby spoke fast, and her cheeks looked flushed. 'Yesterday we went to that amazing Thai place you love. What is it called?' She looked at Claire expectantly. 'Oh yes. Thai Basil. Tina, Ruth and Betty were there. We were talking about you. Let me tell you, I was absolutely beside myself when I heard. I wanted to cut my trip short, of course, but there was still so much to do. And I thought, you're already in hospital. Paul and your mum are there. There's nothing I can do.'

'My mum wasn't there.'

Gaby's eyebrows shot up in surprise but she didn't comment. Instead, she told Claire all about Nijo Castle ('I've never seen anything like it!) and Mount Fuji ('We went on the most amazing boat.' *A boat on the mountain?* Claire wanted to know. But apparently there was the most amazing lake there, too.). Finally, Gaby lowered her voice and said, 'I'm sorry about your dad.'

'My dad's awake. He's going to be okay. Paul is taking me to the hospital to see him later.' Impatiently she looked at the clock. Another two hours to go. 'Have you met him? What is he like?'

'Paul?'

'My dad.'

'I've met him a few times. I thought he was quite the flirt.'

'He was?' asked Claire, wondering if Gaby was making things up, embellishing to make her stories more exciting. She seemed just the type to do something like that.

'All completely innocent, of course.'

'Of course.'

'He seemed besotted with your mother. I remember wondering if I would ever meet anyone who loved me that much. The guys I meet . . .' She shook her head. 'Never mind. So, are you telling me you don't remember—' Gaby leaned forward and lowered her voice to a whisper '—anything? Not even your birthday party last month? Come on, no one could forget that night.'

Dejectedly Claire shook her head. 'No,' she said quietly. 'No, I don't.'

'Wow,' Gaby whispered, staring at Claire like an entomologist studying a particularly rare beetle. 'What does it feel like?'

'It just feels . . .' Claire thought about it. 'It feels blank.'

'Sometimes I wish I could forget my life.' Gaby seemed lost in thought for a moment, then shrugged. 'Enough about me. You have to promise you are looking after yourself. It must be so terrible. I can't even imagine.'

Now it was Claire's turn to shrug. 'Tell me something about me. A story to jog my memory.'

'How about some photographs? Let me have your phone.' Gaby grabbed Claire's phone and pressed a few buttons. 'Here is your Facebook page. You must have thousands of photos up there.'

She scrolled through pictures, telling Claire funny anecdotes about all the people in them. Claire had spent hours in the hospital staring at the photos. But it was one thing looking at faces of strangers and quite another listening to Gaby bringing these strangers to live. 'This is Tiffany,' Gaby was saying. 'You went to ballet school together.' Tiffany was wearing a tight-fitting business suit, as if she had just stepped out of a job interview, but her posture, her body, the way she carried herself betrayed a dancer.

'She's beautiful.'

'You call her the cow behind her back. And sometimes even to her face.' Another photo popped up. 'And this is Kevin. He tried to kiss you at your birthday last year. And when you turned him down, he kissed three other people just to prove it didn't mean anything.'

'Three other women?'

'Not all of them women.' There must have been shock on her face because Gaby laughed and added, 'Dancers, what can I say?' She had a good laugh, loud and infectious. It lit up her face and made her eyes twinkle. Suddenly Claire felt like a ray of light had illuminated her otherwise dark universe. She had a friend. She was no longer alone.

When a photo of a blonde woman in her fifties appeared, Claire exclaimed, 'That's Mum!'

'You remember?'

'I just knew.' But she didn't know how she knew. She pondered it for a moment, wondering if it was a memory or just intuition. Her mother was looking straight at Claire from the screen, her light hair pulled away from her face, her arms around the man Claire had spent hours watching at the hospital.

'This is her with your dad at a barbecue a few years ago.'

Angela looked tiny next to Tony. She seemed lost in his embrace, and he hovered over her, holding her close as if he wanted the whole world to know she was his.

Claire couldn't stop looking at her mother. She was so beautiful, her eyes so kind, her features delicate. Suddenly she found herself unable to speak or smile at Gaby or think of anything else. Tears filled her eyes and she didn't know why. To change the subject, she asked, 'What about me and Paul? Are we happy?'

Gaby seemed thrown off balance by her question. She emptied half her wine glass before she replied, 'If you need to ask, the answer is probably no.'

'We're not happy?' As if Paul's cold smile and distant eyes hadn't already alerted Claire that something was wrong.

'Let's just say, you have some issues.'

'What kind of issues?'

'It's not my place to tell you.'

'If you won't tell me, no one else will.'

Gaby stepped from foot to foot, as if she wanted to be anywhere but here, having this conversation with Claire. 'Maybe that's for the best. I have to run, anyway. I'm always late, to everything. How do I look?'

Claire assured Gaby she looked fine, better than fine. But what she wanted to do instead was ask her friend not to go because for an hour in her grim morning she had laughter and joy. Gaby almost made her forget that she had forgotten her whole life. And for a brief moment with Gaby she felt hopeful. 'Will you come back to see me?'

'Of course.'

When the door closed behind her friend, Claire went up to her room. Climbing into bed and hugging Molokai, she reached for her mobile phone. It was as if her fingers once again had a life of their own. They knew exactly what numbers to press to unlock the phone. She looked through every photo until she came across the one she was looking for. Stroking her mother's beautiful face with her fingertips, she struggled not to cry. Her mother was smiling at her as if telling her everything was going to be okay.

Claire loaded her contact list, hoping to find her mother's number. And there it was, listed under Angela, ten digits that just a few short weeks ago she had probably known by heart. She stared at the number, blinking rapidly, reading it out loud, rolling every syllable off her tongue, hoping it would trigger a shadow of recollection, a glimmer of hazy remembrance.

Her whole body trembling, she pressed the call button. The phone rang and rang.

* * *

As Claire followed her husband across the hospital car park and through the front entrance, she realised she was petrified of the real world. She had spent a morning in that world and felt out of place, an outsider looking in. But at the hospital she was at home. As if this was where she belonged. Others had childhood memories, heartwarming and sweet, sometimes bitter, but always there to remind them that once there had been a different life, a different journey. They had memories of weddings, anniversaries and holidays by the sea. All Claire had was this place, with its closet-sized rooms, grim corridors and overworked staff. Nothing had changed here since the day before. It was still grey, shabby and depressing. So why did it feel so infinitely comforting to be walking down the familiar corridor?

No one expected her to be herself here, she realised. No one expected her to be anything. She could just *be*. Wake up in the morning, eat her meals, wrinkling her face in disgust, have her meds. She didn't have to make decisions because they were made for her, by the doctors and the nurses. And that was what she missed when she stayed inside her beautiful mansion wearing her designer clothes, living someone else's dream life but feeling like a prisoner.

She wished she could go back to her old room and remain like before, confined within her small world where nothing threatened her peace. She wished she could sit by the window, watching the oak tree outside, longing for a different life but not forced to go out there and live it. Could she stay with her father instead of going back to the alien house with a husband who treated her like a stranger? Of course, her father was a stranger to her, too. But she'd spent so long watching him, studying his face for clues, memorising his every feature, she felt she could open her mouth and recount every little detail of his life. His life was on the tip of her tongue, at the edge of her subconscious.

On the drive to the hospital, she had asked Paul what her father was like. 'He's not the friendliest man in the world. I don't think he likes me much,' he'd said. 'But he's your father. He loves you.' His answer wasn't what she wanted to hear, and it didn't match the inner picture of her dad she had painstakingly created over long hours of watching and thinking, so she put Paul's words to the back of her mind, to that place where her other memories were hiding.

But now, as she was about to face the man who had known her since the day she was born, the man she remembered nothing about other than the shape of his nose and the curve of his mouth, she wondered why her husband would say something like that. Didn't Paul and her dad spend time together, discussing football and weather over a pint of beer? Were there no family barbecues, Christmases and birthdays where sausages sizzled on the grill and intoxicated confidences were exchanged late into the night? Or maybe Paul not getting along with Tony was completely natural. Fathers didn't always like to share their little girls with their husbands. And husbands were often intimidated by their fathers-in-law.

As she turned the handle and pushed the door to her father's room, she tried to calm her beating heart. She didn't want the nurses at the reception area to hear it but how could they not? The thumping in her chest was deafening. It was like church bells ringing in her ears.

Her mind was filled with snippets of imaginary conversations with her father. Would she know what to say? Would he know what to say? Would they be able to pick up where they had left off, even though she couldn't remember anything? Her relationship with her father, was it instinctive? Was it in her blood, in his blood? Did it transcend crashing cars and lost memories? She didn't want small talk with her father. She wanted him to tell her who she was.

The door wouldn't give in. She pushed and pushed.

'Here, let me help,' said Paul, pulling the door lightly, making her feel silly and a little light-headed. 'Good luck. I'll wait here for you.'

'You aren't coming in?'

'I'll give you two some privacy. In the meantime, I'll speak to his doctor.'

A part of Claire was relieved she was about to face her father alone. She felt a little less nervous meeting him unobserved. She didn't want their relationship to be judged by an outsider, even if that outsider was her husband. She wanted to be alone with her dad, to find her own way back to him, to let him find his own way back to her.

On tiptoes she walked in, sliding her feet as if she were on stage, performing a pas de deux she hadn't yet mastered. She paused in the doorway, watching the man on the bed just like she had so many times over the past two weeks. Only this time everything was different. This time he was awake.

She wondered if she would always remember this moment. Everything in her life was about to change. Or, rather, a little bit of her old life was about to come back.

From where she stood she couldn't quite tell whether he was sleeping. Not a part of him moved and his breathing was calm. Without the ventilator inhaling life into her father's lungs, the room seemed quiet and lifeless. Tony was tall and broad-shouldered, a bear of a man, but he appeared frail, propped up on his pillows and leaning to one side. He didn't seem to hear her. She took a few steps forward.

He looked like an old man laid out on a white sheet, his stubble making his face look grey, his eyelids trembling like butterfly's wings. Her heart pricked with pity.

'Dad,' she called out softly. She sounded high pitched and unsure of herself. Was she being presumptuous, calling him that? It didn't feel unnatural. Quite the opposite, the word slipped out easily, on reflex. Yes, she didn't know anything about him, but he wasn't a stranger. He was blood. Shaking a little, her legs unresponsive as if they were filled with cotton wool, she crossed the room and perched on the edge of his bed.

He didn't stir. His eyes were closed. Just like all those other endless days in the hospital, she studied him in silence, trying to memorise the features that she had known since birth but that were completely unfamiliar to her. A straight nose, bushy eyebrows, wide cheekbones, a mop of grey hair that needed a comb.

Suddenly, unlike all those other times she had sat here, he moved his arms in his sleep. Claire got up, her cheeks burning. She needed to cool down, feel cold water on her face. Slowly and uncertainly, as if she was learning how to walk, she made her way to the bathroom attached to his hospital room and leaned on the sink, watching her face in the mirror.

'Good afternoon. How are we feeling today?' came a loud voice. Claire peeked through the creak in the door and saw a doctor leaning over Tony. He wore a white coat over his business suit. There was a cold smile on his face, a smile of someone who was paid to care but didn't.

'Never better,' croaked Tony. He sounded hoarse, like he was recovering from a bad cold.

'That's good to hear. If it's alright with you, I am going to ask you a few questions, just to see if your memory has been affected. Take your time to answer. There's no rush. And don't worry if you can't remember something. It's completely normal in your condition. Can we start with your name?'

'Wright. Tony Wright.'

'Very good, Tony.' A machine gun fire of questions followed – what was his address, his date of birth, his occupation, his marital status, how long had he lived at his address, how long had he held his driver's license, did he have any children, any pets, what did he enjoy doing. Her father responded in a lifeless voice but without any hesitation.

And finally, 'Do you know what happened on the day of the accident?'

Tony spoke through gritted teeth. 'I was in the car. That's the last thing I remember.'

'I expect the police will want to speak to you later today. They've been waiting for you to wake up.'

From the bathroom, Claire heard the bed creak. 'Why?' asked Tony.

'There's been a serious accident. Two people got hurt.'

'Two people? I crashed into the motorway divider. No one else was involved.'

'Your daughter Claire was with you.'

A few seconds ticked by before Tony answered. 'That's not true. I was alone in the car.'

Claire wished she could see her father's face but from where she was hiding, it was impossible. Was his memory affected, just like hers? Was he confused, just like her?

'Don't worry, the police are treating it as an accident. I will tell them you don't remember. You've been through a lot and—'

'I remember perfectly well, Doctor. There was no one in the car with me.' His voice rose as if he was angry. At the doctor? At the never-ending questions? Claire felt sorry for her father. What he needed was a rest, not an interrogation.

As if he could read her mind through the bathroom door, the doctor said, 'I'm sorry for disturbing you. Please try and get some rest.'

'Wait, Doctor. I can't feel my legs. Why can't I feel my legs?' Tony's voice quivered.

Five seconds passed before the doctor replied. Claire knew how long it took because her gaze followed the silver-plated hand of the clock on the wall. In that time the doctor shuffled uncomfortably, averted his gaze, coughed. He didn't meet Tony's eyes when he said, 'Your spine was severely damaged in the accident. We did all we could but . . .'

'I can't walk?'

'I'm very sorry. With time and extensive physiotherapy there's a chance, a small chance—'

'Is there anything you can do? Operate, do something, fix it.'

'We tried our best but the damage was quite severe, I'm afraid.' The doctor was moving away from Tony. Imperceptibly, little by little, he was shifting towards the door. 'There was nothing we could do.'

'Nothing you could do?' Tony sounded close to tears. Claire felt close to tears herself.

'I'm very sorry, sir.'

The doctor left without another word. Claire glanced at the door, at her father's back, at his heaving shoulders. She wondered if she could slip out without him noticing. Although she wanted to comfort him, to take him in her arms and make it all go away, she knew it was impossible. And she didn't want to meet him for the first time when he was sobbing uncontrollably on his bed and all she felt was helpless and lost.

Soon his crying subsided and his breathing became regular. Claire tiptoed past him to the door, turning the handle softly. She was about to walk out when she heard his voice. 'Hello, Teddy Bear.'

His voice was soft like a caress. She turned around. Tony had pulled himself up in bed and was watching her intently. With his mop of grey hair and bushy eyebrows, his crooked nose, like an eagle's beak, and his narrow cheekbones, he looked moody, as if permanently disappointed with life – until he smiled. His smile transformed his face and made him appear attractive and kind. It made Claire's heart feel lighter.

'Hi, Dad. How are you feeling?' She stepped from foot to foot, not sure what to do with her hands, then closed the door and walked back to his bed.

'I've been better.' He laughed like it was a joke only he could understand. 'Come over here and give your old man a hug.'

She leaned closer and he scooped her up in his arms, effortlessly pulling her to him. 'Be careful,' she said. 'I'm heavy.'

'Oh yes, as heavy as a feather.'

As she relaxed into his arms, she thought he was surprisingly strong for someone who was bedridden and unable to move. He smelt of hand sanitiser and soap, hospital smells she found familiar and reassuring. His heartbeat was a comfort against her chest. For a few seconds he didn't let go. And she didn't want him to.

'Ask me again,' he said, finally releasing her.

'Ask you what?'

'How I'm feeling.'

'How are you feeling?' she repeated like an obedient daughter.

'After a hug like that? Like a million dollars!' He winked and patted the bed next to him, urging her to come closer. His fingers wrapped around hers, squeezing tightly. 'So what did I miss?' he asked, smiling brightly. He had a good smile. It was kind. It inspired trust. Paul had got it all wrong, she thought. Her father wasn't unfriendly. He was warm and welcoming.

'I wouldn't know. After the accident, I lost my memory. I was in the hospital with you for a long time.'

'What accident?'

'Our accident.'

'I know they keep saying you were with me. But they are wrong. It was just me in the car that day.'

'But if I wasn't with you . . .' She hesitated. 'What happened to me?'

'I don't know, darling. Did you say you lost your memory?' His eyes appraised her, taking her in. She was glad she had made an effort with her appearance. Her hair was tied back into a bun as if she was about to perform on stage. Heavy mascara made her look older, more mature. A layer of powder concealed the dark shadows under her eyes, making her appear less vulnerable. But her father seemed to look right through the mask. The look of concern on his face made her heart beat faster, happier. 'Have they done any tests? What's the prognosis?'

'All they do is tests. I'm convinced one guy is writing his PhD paper on me. I don't mind, as long as he helps. But all he seems to care about is the sound of his own voice.'

'So it could be a while?'

'No one really knows.' She didn't want to talk about herself anymore. To change the subject, she asked, 'What happened on the day of the accident? Were you speeding? Tired?'

'Why do bad things happen to good people? In my line of work, I have to believe in luck. And every now and again luck turns its back on you.'

'In your line of work? What is it that you do?' She felt silly asking this question, as if she was an impostor, pretending to be this stranger's daughter. And yet, she knew she was his daughter. She could feel the pull, the connection between the two of them, a lifetime of memories waiting to be discovered.

'I take calculated risks for a living.' He fell quiet, as if lost in thought. It was almost like he didn't want to tell her. He cleared his throat before saying, 'I run the family business for your mother. When your grandfather was alive, I was his right-hand man. Then I took over from him. But enough about me. How have you been?'

She shrugged. 'Like a fish out of water. I don't remember anything about myself.' To her horror, she started to cry and couldn't stop.

He pulled her close, enveloping her in his arms. Instantly she felt better. 'I wish your mother was here,' he said. 'She'd know what to do.' There was a wistful expression on his face. *He must miss Mum so much*, she thought. How could he not, when even Claire missed her and she didn't even know her.

'Where is Mum? She hasn't visited us in hospital. I was wondering . . .'

'She had to go away for a couple of months.'

'Away where?' How could she be away at a time like this?

'She's in California, looking after her elderly aunt.'

'Tell me something about her. What is she like?'

'Your mother is the kindest person I know. Everyone loves her. When she's around, she makes you forget all your sorrows. The day I met her was the luckiest day of my life.' His eyes were dreamy, as if he was no longer in the drab hospital room but somewhere far away where there was no sorrow, only joy. 'Would you like to see a photo of her?'

'More than anything.'

'I always keep one in my wallet. It's on the table over there.' Claire passed the wallet to her father. His hands were shaking, from nerves or maybe because he was unwell, and he dropped the wallet. The contents spilled out all over the floor, his bed and his lap. Claire helped him collect coins, bank notes, loyalty cards for shops and cafés, a lighter, a silver chain – and a family photograph of the three of them. Earmarked and yellow around the edges, it looked like it had been repeatedly unfolded, examined and re-folded. 'This was taken on a holiday in Paris. You were 15.'

With reverence Claire held up the photograph to the light. Her 15-year-old self was wearing a pair of shorts and a T-shirt, and her hair was a shade lighter, a touch longer and curlier. But it wasn't herself she wanted to see. As she looked at her mother's face, once again her eyes filled with tears. It was like looking at herself, only two decades older. Her mother had the same slim build, the same light hair pulled back into a bun. She radiated joy, while the Eiffel Tower was a misty silhouette behind her. Claire wondered if the joy was genuine. Didn't everyone look happy when posing in front of the Parisian icon? Her father didn't. He seemed gloomy, as if Champ de Mars in autumn was the last place he wanted to be.

'Your mother loves her shopping, especially in Paris. And you love the museums. Every day it was a battle between the two of you, trying to decide where to go and what to do. I never took sides. No matter where we went, I'd get bored and complain. You called me a grumpy old man. You'd ask why I bothered to go away in the first place. I'd tell you it's because I wanted to be with you. And you'd say, "but if you want to be with us, does it matter where we are? So quit your complaining and enjoy the three-hour shopping spree or the five-hour tour of the Louvre."'

'We look like a happy family.' And they did. They looked like they wouldn't be out of place on a Hallmark card.

'We are. I've always made sure of it.'

Claire felt her heart soar. Yes, she didn't remember the people in the photograph. She knew nothing about their relationship with one another, their life together, their hopes and dreams. But she had a family. She was a part of something bigger than herself. There was meaning to her life, even if she didn't know what it was.

'You can keep the photo if you like,' said Tony.

'Are you sure? What about you?'

'I have it in here.' He pointed at his heart.

Affectionately Claire squeezed Tony's hands and stood up. 'I wish I could stay longer.' She realised how much she meant it. 'But Paul needs to get back to work.' She hugged him goodbye and added, 'I know you're putting your brave face on for me. You don't want to upset me. But I need to know. How do you really feel?'

He was silent for a while. She couldn't see his eyes. He was hiding them from her. When he finally looked up, she saw the truth. She saw sadness and pain as if something inside him was broken. Tony had a smile on his face but it wasn't a happy smile. It broke Claire's heart. 'I feel like I'm living my worst nightmare. If only I could stay asleep forever,' he murmured.

'I'm so sorry, Dad. I'm sorry you feel this way.'

'Don't be. God has a plan for all of us. We all go through dark times. Every once in a while, we find ourselves standing over an abyss. The darkness is mesmerising. It pulls us in. Some people will want to jump. Others will find the strength to move away from the edge.'

'Do you want to jump?' she asked in a tiny voice.

'Only time will tell.' As she was about to walk through the door, he added, 'Next time you visit, bring me something to read.'

'Of course. I'll see you later, Dad.' I love you, she wanted to add but didn't dare. It seemed to her that she had only met him

31

for the first time today. And yet in her heart she felt like she had known him her whole life. If only she could remember. As she looked at him in silence, she felt so sad, but also warm inside. She was no longer a raft adrift in the ocean, a blank slate of a life with no past, no present and no future. She had her father. She was loved. She belonged.

* * *

Claire stepped outside her father's room and into the waiting area, nauseous and dizzy, as if she was not on firm ground but on a ship swaying on stormy seas. When she looked up, she saw two police officers walking down the corridor towards her. A man and a woman, they looked like twins in their identical uniforms, both ginger and short, their faces tired and drawn, as if they had seen too much in the line of duty. Claire faintly remembered being questioned by them shortly after the accident. But she couldn't recall what they had asked, nor what she had said to them. She couldn't even remember their names. The first week at the hospital had been a blur.

They smiled at her in recognition and nodded in unison, then marched into her father's hospital room without much ado or so much as a knock. Claire retraced her steps, stopping outside her father's door, peeking through the gap.

The police had their backs to her but she could see her father's face. What if he could see her too? Even though he wasn't looking at her, his eyes on the police officers, his face stretched into an uneasy smile, Claire shifted her body slightly to the left, so that she was no longer by the door but leaning on the wall next to it. Nurses and doctors rushed past her, visitors and patients walked by at a more leisurely pace. None of them paid the slightest attention to a pale young woman with her hands clasped nervously and her eyes wide. She could no longer see her father or the police officers but she could hear them. The man introduced himself as

PC Stanley. The woman said her name was PC Kamenski. Claire was surprised they had different surnames. They looked so alike, she expected them to be related.

'Is this a good time? You seemed like you were sleeping,' said the woman.

'I was trying to. Couldn't sleep last night,' said Tony.

'We can come back later if you want to rest.'

'I've rested for two weeks. It's been a regular holiday resort.'

The cops laughed uncomfortably. 'Is it okay if we ask you a few questions?'

'That's what you're here for, isn't it?' Her father sounded exhausted, and suddenly Claire felt a wave of anger so strong, she almost gasped. Why couldn't the cops see how ill he was? Why wouldn't they leave him alone? Didn't they have real crime to solve and real criminals to catch?

'Can I start with your full name, please?'

He told them.

His date of birth, address, occupation, marital status.

He told them.

And finally, 'Where were you on the fifth of March at four o'clock in the afternoon?'

'That was the day of the accident. I believe I was driving. But you already know that or you wouldn't be here.'

'Were you drinking that day? Taking drugs?'

'Why don't you ask my doctor? They would have done a blood test.'

'Please answer the questions, sir,' said PC Stanley in a voice that sounded tired rather than annoyed.

'No, I wasn't drinking. Or taking drugs.'

'Who was in the car with you?'

Tony didn't say anything at first and then coughed, clearing his throat and asking for a glass of water. Claire felt her body lean forward involuntarily, waiting for his answer. She held her breath.

'There you are,' she heard a loud voice behind her. Turning

around sharply, she saw Paul approaching her form the direction of the doctor's office. She almost groaned out loud. She desperately wanted to hear what her father had to say but at the same time she didn't want Paul to see her eavesdropping outside Tony's hospital room. What would he think? She moved away from the door and smiled at Paul. He asked, 'How did it go with your father?'

'Wonderful. I have no memories of him but I feel like I've known him my whole life. Did you talk to the doctor?'

He nodded. 'Your father will need extensive physiotherapy. He has to work hard if he wants to walk again. His recovery might take a long time. He was upset and confused when he woke up. Pulled his IV out, scared the nurse. But he seemed to recover quickly. He remembers who he is, remembers what happened, which is extraordinary.'

'Poor Dad. I wish I could have been there for him when he woke up.'

'Are you ready? I have fifty minutes for lunch before I need to get back to work.'

Paul was already walking towards the exit and Claire trailed behind him, trying to keep up, when out of the corner of her eye she saw the police officers leaving her father's room. 'Can you wait for me for a minute? I want to speak to the police.'

She caught up with them near the reception. They seemed desperate to leave the hospital and who could blame them? When they saw her, they slowed down but didn't stop. She walked with them. 'Do you have a moment? I want to ask you something.'

'Of course, anything,' said the woman.

They found some empty chairs in a waiting area outside a room that wasn't her father's. Claire was glad. She didn't want a nurse to wheel Tony out in his wheelchair only for him to see his daughter speaking to the police. For some reason she felt he wouldn't like that. PC Stanley and PC Kamenski moved from side to side, trying to get comfortable. Although lacking in height, they were both wide-shouldered and looked out of place on the small hospital chairs, like grown-ups sitting in toddler seats. The woman took out a notebook and scribbled something down. Claire noticed her glance at the clock above their heads. There was only one question she desperately needed to ask. But she didn't know how to bring it up, so she coughed and cleared her throat, just like Tony did moments earlier, and said something else entirely. 'I'm concerned about my father. How did he seem to you? Was he confused? Having problems remembering?'

'On the contrary. He seemed quite sure of himself.'

'If you are concerned, why don't you talk to his doctor?' asked PC Stanley. He, too, glanced at the clock. Of course, thought Claire. It was lunchtime for them. The last thing they wanted was to be stuck in a hospital waiting area, talking to her.

'Thank you. I will,' said Claire. The police officers rose to their feet. Before they had a chance to say goodbye, she added, 'One more thing. I'm not quite sure I was in the car on the day of the accident.'

'Did you remember something?' Both of them were staring at her now, all thoughts of lunch seemingly forgotten.

'Not really. It's more . . .' She hesitated. She couldn't tell them the truth. She didn't want to contradict anything her father might have said to them. 'It's just a feeling I have.'

'You are still confused. It's understandable,' said PC Kamenski softly.

'Are you sure I was in that car?'

'Positive. I pulled you out myself.'

Claire tried to imagine her fragile, broken body trapped in the back of a car on the side of a motorway somewhere. Tried to imagine the pain and the fear, police sirens blaring, strong arms yanking her out, and couldn't. In her mind she couldn't see anything other than this hospital waiting room, her father's immobile body in a bed down the corridor, herself alone and afraid and searching for answers. Maybe her father was right. Maybe she hadn't been in that car after all.

PC Kamenski was looking at her with suspicion and Claire felt tears perilously close. She almost opened her mouth and told the police officers everything. All her fears and misgivings and how confused she was. But she doubted they wanted to hear.

The man stepped from foot to foot impatiently. The woman closed her notepad. 'If you remember anything, please don't hesitate to call. Here is my direct number,' she said, reaching into her pocket and placing a card in Claire's hands.

Long after they were gone, Claire stared at the card but couldn't see the writing from the tears in her eyes, couldn't hear her husband's voice from the noise in her head. She was lost in a maze with no way out.

* * *

On the way home, Paul suggested lunch at Claire's favourite restaurant, Thai Basil. Having heard of it from Gaby and hoping it would trigger a memory, she agreed. Thai Basil was a red oasis in grey and rainy London. The furniture, the walls, the carpets, even the ceiling were a variation of that colour. Dotted around the room were porcelain elephants with their trunks pointing up – for luck, Paul told her. Claire relaxed into her ruby cushion, fighting to stay awake. Suddenly the day had become too much. Too many new faces and places, too much new information to process.

Taking a deep breath to stave off the panic, Claire closed her eyes and thought of her father. Immediately she felt better. The warm feeling she'd experienced earlier was back. He was just as confused as she was, even though he tried not to show it. And just like her, he clearly had trouble remembering the accident. She wasn't alone, and neither was he.

'I didn't realise ballerinas ate Thai food,' she said to her gloomy husband when the starters arrived. Although everything looked delicious, she didn't seem to have much of an appetite.

It surprised her. Other than the sandwich in the morning, she had had nothing to eat, so nervous was she about meeting her dad. The sandwich was a distant memory now.

'Your diet consisted of grapefruit and Thai once a month, for which you punished yourself at the studio for days,' replied Paul.

'Sounds healthy.'

'It wasn't.'

'I was being sarcastic.'

'Oh.'

They were seated at a corner table, away from the other diners. Pouring some tea, she said, 'What do you do for a living?' Once again, she felt silly asking this question. She felt like she should already know the answer.

'I'm a heart surgeon at the hospital.'

'Which hospital?'

'Yours.'

She wanted to ask him why she had only seen him twice in two weeks if he worked at the same hospital where she had been a patient. But she didn't want to upset him. They sat in silence for a while. She shifted uncomfortably in her chair, while Paul absentmindedly checked his phone and glanced at his watch, as if he would rather be anywhere but sitting across from her at a restaurant table. Frantically she searched her mind for something else to say but couldn't think of anything. Finally, Paul said, 'Try these spring rolls. You love them.'

'They're delicious.'

'Have another one. Have them all if you like.'

'What about you?' She pulled the plate closer.

'I prefer this satay chicken.'

She picked up a stick of satay chicken, took a quick bite, took a bite of the spring roll and looked at him like he was a madman. Paul filled both their plates with stir-fry.

'Tell me about our marriage. Are we happy?' she asked when the food was gone – all but the fish cakes which she didn't like.

'Very,' he said.

'We don't have any . . .' Claire hesitated, trying to think of the exact word Gaby had used. 'Issues?'

'Of course not. What makes you think that? We are one of those rare couples who never argue.'

'Tell me stories. Something to jog my memory. How did we meet?'

He squinted his eyes as if appraising her. Then he said, 'The night I first noticed you, you literally danced into my life. I saw you through the window of your dance studio. You were practising the same sequence of steps over and over. I was transfixed. I think I forgot where I was going. It took me four days to find the courage to talk to you. Four evenings of watching you from the street like a common criminal.'

'What did you finally say to me?'

'Can I bum a cigarette?'

'You asked a ballerina for a cigarette? What did I say?'

'You said you didn't have one but you could ask the janitor at the studio. And you did. Then I had to smoke it in front of you. I didn't even smoke. It was horrible.'

'But worth it?'

'Absolutely. Six years later we were married.' He spoke of what was possibly the most romantic memory of his life with a detached expression on his face, as if reciting a poem he had been forced to memorise.

'And what is our life together like?'

'It's wonderful. We are very much in love.' He glanced at the clock. 'I wish I could stay longer but I have to rush.'

Perplexed at this change of subject, Claire watched his face as he paid the bill and led her outside, opening the car door like the perfect gentleman she knew he was. When they were slowly navigating the London traffic, she asked, 'Do you know what happened on the day of the accident?'

'You went to visit your parents that morning, like you do

38

every Saturday. You were going to meet some friends for lunch afterwards. I don't know how you ended up in the car with Tony. As far as I know, you'd made no plans with him.'

Paul dropped her off outside their house, and when she was about to walk through the front door, she turned around. He was still there, his hands on the steering wheel, the engine running, watching her intently, as if making sure she got home safely. She wondered why he felt the need to do that. It wasn't like she was going to run away the minute his back was turned. She smiled at herself, at how silly that sounded, then waved and he waved back, before finally turning the car around and speeding away.

Chapter 3

From her balcony on the first floor, Claire watched as night bus after night bus pulled up opposite and groups of drunken passengers spilled out, stumbling, laughing and shouting. Claire envied them, wishing she too could be merry and carefree. It was past midnight and she'd spent most of the night staring at her mother's face in the photograph, searching for answers. Eventually, she must have drifted off because she dreamt her mother stepped out of the picture and leaned over her. Angela's lips moved but Claire couldn't hear the words. She leapt up in her chair and looked around, half expecting to see her mother. But she was alone. All was quiet, and only the wind made the leaves whisper.

She returned to bed but couldn't sleep, and at eight in the morning she got up. Gliding like a ghost from room to room, she felt like an actress hired to play a part of a stranger she had never met before. She questioned everything – the way she moved, the way she talked, the way she stood. Would the old Claire pause by the mirror as she made her way downstairs and study her face for a few seconds too long, as if she didn't know it? Would she stand under the hot shower for five minutes, ten, fifteen, hiding from the world?

Waiting for her on the kitchen table was a note from Paul. Her heart quickened.

Breakfast in the fridge, someone from the hospital is coming to check on you at 9.30.

Gasping, Claire rushed back upstairs to get dressed and brush her hair. Only when she was satisfied with her appearance did she look inside the fridge where she found an omelette, a wilted tomato and a jar of olives. Ignoring the tomato and the olives, she ate the omelette cold.

A nurse was coming to see her. She wondered if it was someone she knew. It would be nice to see a familiar face. Claire wanted to know when her memory was coming back. She couldn't get her life back if she didn't remember anything about it. And she couldn't fix her marriage if she didn't know what was wrong between Paul and her. He might have told her they were the happiest of couples who never argued but she didn't believe him. A happy couple didn't behave like them, not touching, barely talking and not sharing a room. A loving husband would have visited her more often as she lay in her hospital bed, trying to make sense of who she was. Suddenly nauseous, she leaned on the edge of the dining table and closed her eyes, counting down from fifty to one, just like the nurses had taught her.

On twenty-five, she was breathing easier. On seven, the doorbell rang.

The man standing outside was dressed in a business suit and held a folder in his hands. He was small and wrinkled, and his prune-like face was stretched into a smile. He introduced himself as Dr Johnson.

'A doctor? I was expecting a nurse,' she said, clasping her hands nervously.

'Is that why you won't let me through the door?' The doctor's smile grew wider.

Claire realised she was blocking the doorway. 'I'm so sorry,' she exclaimed. 'I don't know what I'm thinking. I'm not myself these days.' She stepped aside and the doctor walked in.

'That's why I'm here. To make you feel more like yourself.'

'You think it's possible? Will I remember everything? How long will it take? I didn't realise doctors made house calls.' Claire was talking fast, tripping over her words. She paused and studied the doctor, who made himself comfortable on the sofa.

'That's a lot of questions. We usually don't make house calls, you're right. But I'm a friend of your husband's.'

'You knew me before the accident?'

Dr Johnson nodded but didn't say another word, hiding behind his folder.

'I'm so sorry. I forgot my manners, among other things. You must think I'm awfully rude. Would you like something to drink?'

A dismissive wave in reply. It was clear Dr Johnson didn't believe in small talk. He got straight down to business. 'So, Claire, I understand you returned home from hospital yesterday?' As if for emphasis, his finger pointed at something in his file.

'The day before yesterday.' Claire sat down opposite the doctor. With his small glasses perched on the tip of his nose, he looked like he had all the answers. Surely he would be able to suggest something, give her a magic pill that would help her remember. All she had to do was ask, and he would fix her. That was his job, wasn't it?

Dr Johnson looked up. 'How are you finding it so far? Overwhelming, I would imagine.'

'That's an understatement, Doctor.'

'Don't worry, it's a normal reaction in a patient with memory loss when returning to their normal life. Have you been feeling unusually agitated lately?' When Claire nodded, he continued, 'Again, completely normal, nothing to worry about.' He wrote something on the chart. 'What about headaches?'

Claire rubbed her aching temples. 'Not as bad as before.'

'Have you been feeling confused? Disoriented?'

'I don't remember who I am. Of course I'm disoriented and confused.'

'That's—'

'Perfectly normal. I know. Most of the time I feel afraid. Like something bad is about to happen. I think it's my meds. They make me paranoid. Sometimes I wonder if I should stop taking them.'

Dr Johnson appraised her for a few seconds before replying, 'I wouldn't recommend that.'

'No, of course not. Forget I said anything. And please don't mention it to my husband.'

Dr Johnson nodded. 'Let's do some short-term memory tests, shall we? To check your progress.'

What progress, Doctor? she wanted to say. But before she had a chance, three pictures appeared in front of her, with names written underneath. Dr Johnson instructed Claire to look at them for a few seconds and then flipped the cards over. On the other side were the same images without the names. Claire had to pick the names out of a long list. Some of them were similar to one another, with a difference of one or two letters. There was a number next to each name. Claire didn't know what the numbers meant, nor did she ask. She wanted the test over and done with. She wanted to be alone, so she could go through the photo albums and find another photograph of her mother. But she did her best to match the names to the pictures, on the off chance that by some miracle it would help recover her memory.

Dr Johnson nodded at every answer, his face impassive. It was impossible to tell what he was thinking. Finally, he took the pictures of people away, only to replace them with pictures of vegetables. Claire had to memorise them and then pick names from a long list. 'Verbal new learning,' he explained.

'And what do you expect me to learn from this, Doctor?'

'You don't need to learn anything. I need to assess how well you're doing.'

Not only did Claire manage to answer every question but she recorded a close to perfect score. Better than 90 per cent of Dr Johnson's patients. The doctor looked unimpressed when he told her that. 'You're doing great, Claire.'

'You think I'm doing great, Doctor? Then why do I feel so . . .' She couldn't think of the right word. *Empty, lost, desperate? All of the above?*

'You don't feel like yourself. It's understandable and to be expected. You have what's known as post-traumatic amnesia. It's generally caused by a severe head injury.'

Claire nodded while suppressing the desire to laugh in doctor's face. *Tell me something I don't know.* But what she said instead was, 'These other patients of yours. The 10 per cent who did better than me on the tests. Have they recovered? Can they remember?'

'Some of them.'

'So what's the prognosis?'

'The good news is, this type of amnesia is usually temporary.'

Claire perked up. This was good news indeed. 'How long?'

'The human mind is incredibly complex. You could wake up tomorrow and remember everything. Or it could take years.'

'Or it could never happen?'

'It's impossible to tell. You were unconscious for a long time. That could affect the duration of your amnesia.' Claire must have looked disappointed because something resembling pity appeared Dr Johnson's face. Pity was not what she wanted to see. She looked down into her hands. The doctor continued, 'All we can do is stay positive. Do you have a strong support network? Family, friends?'

Claire thought of Paul's cold eyes as he collected her from the hospital. She thought of her missing mother. 'I have my father. And my best friend.'

'That's a good start. You'll need all the support you can get. Try to immerse yourself in familiar activities. Anything could trigger your memory, anything at all. People, experiences, sounds. Scents can work particularly well.' Dr Johnson stood up.

'Is there anything else we can do?'

'There isn't much, unfortunately. No reliable treatments at this stage, I'm afraid.'

'What about unreliable? Hypnosis, maybe?'

'Some people believe hypnosis can help. But they are in the minority. We certainly don't recommend it. The mind is a tricky fragile thing. It's best not to influence it with something so intrusive.' The doctor shrugged apologetically. 'There is no foolproof solution. Find out what you've enjoyed before the accident. These experiences might act as a catalyst, and before you know it, you'll remember.'

Claire wished she knew what she had enjoyed before the accident. She made a mental note to ask Gaby. And then it occurred to her – she loved to dance! Yes, that was it. 'When can I go back to work?' Suddenly it felt like the perfect solution. She had been dancing since she was a little girl. What could be more familiar? She thought about how easily she seemed to remember the movements. If only she could dance again, her mind might catch up with her body.

'You were a ballet dancer, were you not?'

Claire nodded, for the first time feeling excitement and anticipation warming her from the inside like burning coals.

'Not yet. No strenuous exercise. Although you're physically strong, mentally you're extremely fragile. As you improve over time, you can start challenging yourself – slowly. Remember, baby steps.'

'I can't stay here, cooped up in this house, not knowing what to do with myself.'

'It might be frustrating at times, but rest is what you need right now.'

'Please don't tell Paul I want to go back to work. I'll tell him when the time is right. I don't want him to worry.'

Dr Johnson nodded. 'I'll visit once a month to see how you're getting on.'

'Oh,' said Claire, suddenly nervous. What was the point, if there were no treatments and no definite prognosis? If there was nothing they could do, why even try? 'How will it feel when I start remembering? Will it all come back at once?'

'It's more likely you'll experience islands of memory. You'll remember certain things, perhaps those that have made the most impact on you in the past.'

'What about everything else?'

'Once you start remembering, it's a good sign. Other memories will follow.'

'And what if they don't?'

'That is also possible. No one can tell for sure. The human mind—'

'Is complex. Yes, you've said.'

'Remember, stay positive. In the meantime, I want you to start a diary. Write down anything that comes to mind. Ideas, memories, thoughts. Anything could help.'

He said goodbye, leaving Claire standing in the doorway, watching his retreating back, unsure what to do next. After he disappeared, she did as she was told – she found a blank notepad and sat by the piano. As her hands played a melody she didn't recognise, she thought of something to write in her new diary.

What did the doctor say? Thoughts, memories, ideas? After two hours, there was only one question in Claire's notebook, written in a square childish handwriting:

What happened on the day of the accident?

* * *

In the afternoon, Claire played the piano until she could no longer see from the tears in her eyes. As Tchaikovsky's *1812 Overture* filled the room, she could sense memories within her reach but when she tried to grasp them, they melted away like fresh snow in spring. Being here, in this house she didn't remember, looking at the stranger in the mirror and knowing nothing about her filled her with dread she couldn't understand or control. She didn't know what it was she was afraid of, but she was afraid nonetheless. If only her father was here. He would know exactly what to say to make her feel better.

The moment her piano fell silent, Claire heard a noise. Molokai bounced up in the air and barked, disappearing into the living room. Claire slid off her chair and softly tiptoed after him. The living room was empty but she could sense a presence. She wasn't alone. There was someone in the house.

The dread was no longer a low current running through her. Suddenly she could think of nothing else. Would Molokai be able to protect her if . . . if what? If there was an intruder in the house? If she had a secret enemy she knew nothing about? Her head was spinning and the walls were closing in on her. She couldn't see anything around her. All she could do was scream.

'Don't be alarmed, Miss.' She felt pair of strong arms lifting her off the floor. 'I'm Nina, your housekeeper.'

Claire opened her eyes cautiously and saw a round woman dressed in a pair of tracksuit bottoms and a T-shirt, carrying a mop. She looked like she was in her thirties but could have easily been younger or older – she had one of those faces that seemed ageless. The woman was staring at Claire with her mouth open. She was the one who looked alarmed.

'I'm sorry,' said Claire. 'I don't know what came over me. I'm so sorry.'

She longed to put her head on the woman's chest and cry her heart out. There was something maternal about her.

'Oh no, Miss. Don't be sorry. You have panic attack. You not well. I know you have memory problem. Mr Paul tell me. But I know how to make you feel better. You come and sit. I make you something.' The woman sounded foreign. Claire could hardly understand her.

Nina led Claire to a chair and, after making sure she was comfortable, proceeded to the kitchen. Claire heard the fridge door open and close, the sound of a knife on a cutting board and then a loud noise of a kitchen appliance, perhaps a juicer or a blender. Relieved and a little embarrassed, she put her head into her hands and tried to slow her breathing but her heart was racing and she felt dizzy and nauseous.

Five minutes later, Nina emerged with a glass of juice. 'Your favourite. Apple, watermelon, kale, ginger. It will make you good as new.'

To make Nina happy, Claire took a sip, her hand shaking so badly, the glass rattled against her teeth. She forced her voice to sound normal. 'So, Nina, where are you from?'

'Scotland.'

'You don't sound like you're from Scotland.'

'Well, I am. But before then, Russia. I left to escape cold.'

'You went to Scotland to escape the cold?'

'Nowhere as cold as Russia,' explained Nina. 'Not even Scotland. We have snow nine months a year.'

Nina wiped the table, while Claire carried her empty glass to the sink and started washing it. 'No, no, I do that,' said Nina, rushing to Claire's side and wrestling the glass from her as if she was afraid she would instantly lose her job if Claire as much as lifted a finger.

'I don't mind helping,' said Claire.

Nina looked at her like she couldn't believe her ears. 'You sit, relax. I'm very sorry for your accident. You not yourself, Miss.'

'What do you mean?'

'You even look different. Expression in your eyes, it change.'

Intrigued, Claire asked, 'What was I like before?'

'Honestly? You walk around like world owe you favour. This is first time you speak to me.'

'How long have you worked here?' It occurred to Claire she didn't like the sound of her old self very much. What kind of person didn't speak to someone who cleaned and cooked for her?

'I am with you and Mr Paul three years now. Since you move

48

into house.' Nina's cheeks jiggled as she dried the glass with a tea towel. Her face was plump, like she had eaten too many Russian blinis. 'So it is true? You not remember anything?'

Since she'd woken up in hospital, Claire had seen this reaction many times. It was a mix of pity and curiosity. She wanted none of it. She cleared her throat and asked, 'Nina, did you ever meet my mother?'

'Of course I meet her. She come every week.'

Claire stared into space, lost for words. 'What is she like?' she muttered.

'You not know what your mother is like?'

Claire looked at the stain on the floor where Nina had spilled a bit of juice. 'She went away for a while. I haven't seen her since the accident. And since I don't remember anything . . .'

'I cannot believe your mother go away at time like this. She loves you so. You always complain she crowd you, call you too often. Every time you sick, she move in. You hate it.'

'She sounds lovely,' whispered Claire.

'Your mother is beautiful gentle person. Always nice words to say to me. Even let me borrow her dress.' Sitting next to Claire, Nina added, 'The only one she not like is Mr Paul. Do not worry. When your mother come back, she make everything better.'

'Wait, what did you say?'

'When?'

'About my mother and Paul?'

'They no get along. I always see them argue.'

'Argue about what?' exclaimed Claire.

But Nina didn't seem to hear. She was chattering away, while her mop never stopped moving. 'I think it is matter of mind. Your brain protects you from traumatic memories. But if strong mind, you can overcome.'

'You mean, like mind over matter? If I try hard enough, I'll get my memory back?'

'Exactly.'

Claire wondered if perhaps Nina was right and all she had to do was force herself to remember. In vain she probed the void inside her head. No matter how traumatic the memories, she wanted them back. Every single one.

Nina stopped in the middle of the kitchen, put her mop down and said, 'What you want for dinner, Miss Claire? I go to market. I cook.'

'Anything, Nina. I don't mind. And thank you.'

While she waited for Nina to return from the market, she opened her walk-in wardrobe and examined row after row of designer clothes in awe. She tried on a gorgeous Dior dress and a high-heeled pair of Jimmy Choo shoes. The dress made her look sophisticated, glamorous like a movie star, messy hair notwithstanding. This beautiful house and expensive clothes, was it really her life? She felt like an impostor as she posed in front of the mirror.

Then again, what did she know about herself?

Judging by the photos Paul had shown her and the Amazon jungle of flowers in her hospital room, she was a woman who had many friends. She was popular, social and liked to entertain. She was a woman who danced for a living. That required discipline and determination. She must have been hardworking and dedicated. She was a woman who wouldn't even speak to her housekeeper, as if she was beneath her.

Shuddering, Claire turned away from the mirror.

To take her mind off her dark thoughts, she decided to search her room. Her chest of drawers was filled to the brim with personal belongings. Old envelopes, cinema tickets, coins, all clues to who she was, all in disarray. The drawers were at odds with the rest of the house – like an island of chaos in her otherwise perfect universe. She rifled through various items that had once defined her life but no longer meant anything to her. There were dozens of old programmes featuring Claire in a white tutu, graceful like a swan and just as delicate. 'Claire Wright as Cinderella', she read.

'Claire Wright as Sugar Plum Fairy'. She spent a long time looking through each programme, touching the photos, feeling them through her fingertips.

And then, under the old cinema tickets, under the brochures and programmes, she came across a brown envelope. Intrigued, she peered inside at what seemed like an official document. One by one she pulled the papers out of the envelope and spread them on her bed. 'Divorce on the ground that the marriage has broken down irretrievably,' the papers said. Claire read it a couple of times, her brain refusing to process what it saw at first. Did she and Paul file for divorce? Although the names on the documents confirmed it, she didn't want to believe it.

So Gaby had told her the truth. They did have issues. But why would Paul lie to her? Why would he say they were happy together when clearly they weren't?

Claire shoved the papers under her bed as far as they would go and sat on the floor, her back against the wall. The silence was deafening. She felt the dizziness again, the darkness closing in on her, the scream rising in her chest. She didn't want to be alone. What she needed was to hear a friendly voice, to talk to someone who cared. She forced herself to get up and change back into her casual clothes, then she walked downstairs and called her father. He didn't answer for a long time. She almost hung up.

'What are you doing?' she asked when she finally heard his voice. 'You sound like you've been sleeping.'

'I wish. Right now I'm playing chess with myself.'

'You are? And how is it going?'

'Very well. I think I might be winning.'

'That's good to hear. Have you eaten?'

'They gave me porridge. Gruel for breakfast.'

'I hope they're looking after you.'

'Today they took me to the common room. It was like having a picnic on Brighton Beach. Wish you could remember those. We would go every August, just the three of us. We would dress up in our summer best. Your mother would prepare baskets of delicious food. We'd spread our blanket on the pebbles and race each other to the water. Then we would play badminton and cards.' His voice sounded far away, lost in a dream.

Claire felt relief flooding her body. The darkness retreated. Tentatively she smiled. 'Let me guess. You always won?'

'Of course. Unless we played charades, in which case your mother won. She was quite the actress. I often tell her she missed her calling. She should be on TV.'

'Hope you made friends in the common room. Someone to play chess and share your porridge with.'

'I won't share my gruel with anyone but you. When are you coming over?'

'First thing tomorrow.'

'Can't wait!'

She thought of her dad as she played the piano, hoping her brain would catch up with her fingers and remember this melody, or that one, or the next. And she thought of her husband, who told her they were in love, when he hadn't once smiled at her or showed her any affection or even seemed concerned. She tried not to think of the divorce papers signed by both of them that were now hiding under her bed. Soon, Nina returned from the market. Claire concentrated on the noises in the kitchen, on oven door slamming, pots clanking and water running. Anything not to think. Finally, Nina's dishevelled head appeared in the studio. 'Food ready. Your favourite chicken fajitas. You need anything?'

'No, no,' said Claire. 'I'm okay, Nina. Go home and relax.'

In the afternoon, she swam in the pool and sat in front of the TV, finally falling asleep to the reruns of *Bless This House*. When she woke up, Paul was home. Absentmindedly he inquired about her day but didn't seem interested in her response. His back was turned as he took his coat and boots off. All she wanted was to ask him about the documents under her bed.

Would he tell her the truth? He had already lied to her once. 'I found . . .' she began.

But Paul wasn't listening. 'Have you taken your medication today?'

Suddenly he was leaning over her, making her feel small and vulnerable. Drowsy and disorientated, she tried to get up so she wouldn't have to look up into his face when she spoke to him. 'Of course.' Did the doctor tell him she didn't want to take her medicine anymore? She shuddered.

'Next time, wait for me to get home.'

'What do you mean?'

'I want to see you take it.'

She thought she had misheard. 'You want to see me take my medication?'

'That's right.'

'You don't trust me to do it? I'm a grown-up, Paul. I can take care of myself.'

'You've been through a lot. I need to make sure you're okay.' He didn't look at her when he said that. Picking up a plate, he loaded it with food and locked himself in his study. Claire turned the lights off and sat in the dark, waiting for him to come out so she could ask him about their impending divorce and how it fit into his story of a perfectly happy marriage. At ten o'clock, when there was still no sign of him, she went to bed. She hadn't touched the fajitas.

Chapter 4

The common room at the hospital was filled with flowers and balloons, wall to wall, as if it was decorated for someone's birthday. As if at any time, a cake would arrive, followed by a clown. But there was not a smile in sight, and not a happy face. Just the opposite: the patients sitting on either side of Claire as she waited for her father to appear looked conquered by life and done with the struggle of it all. They looked just like she felt – tired and hopeless and deflated.

Matt from neurology shook and stared. He couldn't talk and couldn't walk unassisted. He introduced himself to Claire, kissing her hand like she was the queen.

Steve was missing a leg. He spent ten minutes lamenting the fact it was his right leg and not his left. *How will I go back to work? How will I earn a living?* Steve drove a taxi in the West End, something he'd done for forty odd years, he told Claire. He could imagine a life without a leg but not without his taxi.

A man from the psychiatric ward, who didn't introduce himself and didn't even glance at Claire, talked loudly to no one in particular. He was convinced he was a Russian prince, kidnapped after the Revolution. He couldn't recall his name or speak Russian but Claire thought he looked old enough to remember the Russian

Revolution. Claire tried to focus on his voice, which was loud enough to drown all the other noises in the room but not loud enough to drown the thoughts in her head. She was thinking about her husband looming over her last night, his voice loud and threatening. When he was in the room with her, she felt tense, like he posed a danger to her that she couldn't remember but was aware of on some subconscious level. When she was with him, she didn't want to say or do the wrong thing in case he disapproved of her. But was it really his approval she wanted? Or was it more than that? Was it possible that she was afraid of him?

Finally, after she'd waited for ten minutes, a nurse wheeled Tony in. Matt, Steve and the old Russian prince had long returned to their rooms. Claire and her father had the common area to themselves.

She hugged him hello, wanting to give him comfort, but it was she who felt comforted when he held her close. 'You won't believe the treats I have for you,' she said, placing her large backpack on the table and undoing the straps. Her face lit up in anticipation, as if the treats were for her and not for him, and she showed him boxes of food prepared by Nina and half a dozen books.

'You need Vitamin C, so I brought a kilo of oranges.'

'Will Vitamin C help me walk again?'

'A pomelo. I found it in the kitchen at home. It's supposed to be good for you.'

'What in the world is a pomelo?'

'I had to ask Nina. Apparently, it's a citrus fruit from Southeast Asia. Tastes a bit like a grapefruit.'

'Nasty and sour? No, thank you. Next time bring me some good old apples instead. Granny Smiths, my favourite.'

'I'm glad you asked,' she said, pulling out a bag of apples. He nodded with approval. She reached inside her bag one more time. 'And here I have something truly wonderful.'

'As wonderful as the pomelo? Impossible.'

'Mock all you want. But this is Nina's special Napoleon cake. It's like heaven on a plate. You've never tried anything like it.'

'It must be heaven if it's named after the short French Emperor.'

'Apparently it takes two days to make one Napoleon cake. And Nina baked one just for you.'

'If she baked it for me, why do I only get one slice? Where is the rest of the cake?' He smiled, winking. After Claire placed the stickers with his name on every box and placed the food in the fridge at the end of the corridor, she got comfortable in a plastic chair next to him. There was a spark in his eyes that hadn't been there before, as if a little bit of his vitality had returned.

'Tell me something I don't know,' she said wistfully. 'That covers just about everything, doesn't it?'

Gently he covered her hand with his. 'You'll remember. It'll happen before you know it. And in the meantime, I'm here for you. We can build new memories together.'

Claire watched the man in front of her with wonder and affection. Here he was, smiling at her, giving her hope, when it was him who needed support. Her chest swelled with feeling as she squeezed his hand. After a moment of silence, she said, 'I wanted to talk to you about the accident.' His smile vanished and his eyes narrowed. Without a word he waited for her to continue. She cleared her throat. 'I spoke to the police and . . .' How did she bring it up without accusing him of lying? 'You've been through a lot. It's understandable that you are still confused about what happened that day.'

'I'm not confused. I remember everything perfectly.'

'The woman . . .' Claire tried to remember her name and couldn't. 'She told me she pulled me out of the car herself.'

'She's lying.' Tony closed his eyes and turned away from her. For a moment he looked like he was about to fall asleep in his wheelchair. Claire wanted to shake him awake, to force him to look at her and answer her questions. Why would the police lie about something like that? And if they were telling the truth, did that mean her father was the one lying?

If, as she suspected, he was suffering from partial memory

loss, she knew from experience he would feel disoriented and confused. But here was the thing that bothered Claire. Her father didn't seem disoriented or confused. He seemed absolutely, 100 per cent, certain of what he was saying.

* * *

Claire sleepwalked through the rest of her morning, staring at books and the television screen. But if someone asked her what she had been reading or watching, she wouldn't be able to say. The window was open, trickling pale late-autumn sunlight all over the room. In the park, children were chasing one another, joyous and carefree.

Finally, she pushed the books away and turned the TV off, jumping to her feet. She couldn't stay here all day, aimless and unsure of herself. Hour after hour passed, day after day, and still she wasn't any closer to finding the answers. She needed to do something that would shed light on who she was.

'Nina, do you have a moment?' she called out. When the housekeeper appeared, Claire asked if she could take her to the ballet studio.

'I wish I could,' said Nina, wringing her hands. 'But Mr Paul . . . he say you no go to ballet studio.'

Claire wasn't sure she understood correctly. 'Paul asked you not to take me to the ballet studio?'

'Yes. He say too soon.'

A chill ran through Claire. She remembered how her husband had made her feel the night before when he demanded she take her meds in front of him. This feeling was back again now – like someone was watching her and she couldn't escape. Like she was a fly trapped in Paul's web. 'I'm not a prisoner here, Nina. I can go if I want to.'

'I'm sorry, Miss Claire. Paul fire me if I take you. Also we have guests tonight. Lots to do.'

'Guests? What guests?'

'You are having the Peters coming. Mr Paul not tell you?'

Claire tried hard to hide her alarm. Why wouldn't Paul tell her they were having guests? And who were these people? The last thing she wanted was to spend her evening pretending. Smiling to strangers like she was fine, like her life hadn't been erased whole. Even if these strangers had once been friends. Angrily she reached for her phone. She was going to call Paul and tell him she was not up for a dinner party. She had just returned home from the hospital. She hardly knew who she was. What was he thinking?

As she was about to press the call button, she heard the doorbell.

Claire opened the door to a fresh-faced and happy-looking Gaby, who was dropping in on her way to the gym. She was like a breath of fresh air, all smiles and air kisses. Claire felt relief wash over her like a tidal wave. Gaby was just what she needed to inject some joy into her life, if only temporarily.

'You're having the Peters over?' Gaby squealed in excitement, while Claire poured her friend a glass of wine. Red, her favourite. 'Wish I could be here. Haven't seen them since . . .'

'Since when?'

'Since he left her for someone else and then returned two weeks later like nothing had happened.'

'And she forgave him?'

'What choice did she have? She's almost 40,' Gaby said as if that explained everything. 'And you know what those doctors are like.'

'No, I don't. What are they like?'

'Can't resist a pretty face.'

'Do they have children?'

'Not yet. Although she's desperate to get pregnant, so he never leaves her again. It hasn't worked, and all she does is check his phone every time he goes to the bathroom. Pathetic, really.'

'Why does she stay with someone who doesn't love her? What's the point?'

'Because she loves him?' Gaby spoke with confidence, as if she was an authority on the Peter's marriage. 'Often, when we love someone, we assume they love us back and ignore all the evidence to the contrary. We just can't imagine it any other way.'

'What about trust? Commitment?'

'What's trust? Nothing but the lies we tell ourselves to be happy in our relationships. You forgive, you trick yourself into believing, you convince yourself it's you he wants to be with and not her.'

Claire had a strong feeling Gaby was no longer talking about the Peters. She thought of the documents she had found in her room. 'Were Paul and I getting a divorce?'

Gaby's face became guarded. Claire sensed she didn't want to talk about her marriage to Paul, even though she was more than happy to discuss the Peters' moments earlier. 'You'd have to ask Paul,' Gaby said finally.

'I'm asking you. You are my friend. Paul is a stranger, distant and cold. Sometimes I feel like I'm terrified of him and I want to understand why. Honestly, he is the last person I would ask.'

Gaby hesitated. 'Paul is not the easiest person in the world to live with,' she said. 'He can be a bit . . .' She seemed to look for the right word. 'Controlling,' she added.

Claire remembered Paul's face, cold and unsympathetic. She remembered his voice when he spoke to her. As if she had done something unforgiveable and he despised her for it. She thought of him ordering her around, like she was a schoolgirl he was responsible for but didn't much like. Of not being able to go back to work, even for a visit. Controlling was an understatement. 'I see,' she said quietly.

'You put up with it for ten years but finally you'd had enough. You told me you couldn't take it anymore. You filed for divorce and asked him to leave. He was moving out and then the accident happened.'

'So he pretended it never happened? That we were happy and in love?'

'Is that what he did?' Suddenly Gaby looked so sad. Claire felt bad for upsetting her. Her friend breathed in smiling and happy, and here Claire was, with her problems, ruining Gaby's day. 'I'm sorry. Let's not talk about it anymore.'

'No, I'm sorry. I wish I could tell you something different.'

'You haven't told me anything I didn't already know.'

When Gaby left, Claire turned the music on, so loud that Nina came running from the kitchen to make sure everything was okay. Claire chose a Gucci dress for the evening and when their guests arrived, she was glad she had made an effort. The Peters looked like they were on their way to the opera. They seemed perfect together – Greg with his height and broad shoulders, slightly rotund around the middle like a retired wrestler, and Maggie, a tiny butterfly and just as pretty, like a fluffy meringue in her pink dress. They laughed, they were friendly and carefree. They refilled each other's glasses of wine and piled each other's plates with food. They smiled lovingly at each other. As if nothing was wrong.

Claire almost doubted Gaby's story. Except, every once in a while, the wife would look at her husband for a fraction too long, as if trying to read between the words. She would take his hand in hers, as if afraid to let go. And every once in a while, the husband would pull his hand back with an apologetic gesture.

Over Nina's lasagne and exotic avocado salad, which was an instant success, as well as a mango juice for Claire and a bottle of red wine for everybody else, after the pleasantries had been exchanged and the weather discussed, Greg said, 'Nice choice of music. How did you ever agree to this, Claire?'

'What do you mean?' Claire was enjoying Freddie Mercury's mesmerising voice.

'I thought only classical music was permitted inside these walls.'

Maggie said, 'Queen *is* a classic. And if it isn't, it should be.'

'I agree,' said Claire. 'I think the music's beautiful.' Turning to Maggie, she added, 'Paul tells me you're a photographer.' It was the first thing she had said all evening. If the guests noticed how quiet she was being, they didn't mention anything.

'Paul tells you correctly. I travel the world taking pictures of wild animals. It's the best job in the world.'

'It sounds incredible. But you must be away a lot. Does Greg come with you?'

A shadow crossed Maggie's face. 'He can't take the time off. You know what doctors are like. So I'm trying to cut down on travelling. Do more work locally.'

'Are there many wild animals to photograph here in London?'

'Not as many as I'd like. Instead I take family portraits, do a wedding every few weeks. It keeps me busy.' Maggie sounded like a caged animal herself.

'I'd love to see some of your work.'

'I bought your latest African coffee table book,' said Paul, interrupting the animated discussion he was having with Greg about the latest advances in open heart surgery he had learnt about at a conference in Vienna.

'I'm glad someone has,' said Maggie.

'More juice, darling?' asked Paul, turning to Claire. He was the perfect husband, kind and attentive. His arm was draped around the back of her chair and a smile never left his face. He was putting on an Oscar-worthy performance for the sake of his friends. Claire wanted to scream.

'This lasagne is gorgeous,' said Greg. 'Did you make it yourself?'

'Our housekeeper did.' She fought a sudden impulse to apologise for not having prepared the food herself. Would the old Claire feel this way? Somehow she doubted it.

'Finding a good housekeeper is an art,' said Maggie. 'And I should know, I've fired two of them in the last six months.'

'Finding them is easy. It's keeping them you seem to have a problem with.' Greg turned away from his wife and towards

Claire. 'She's fired the last one for wanting to take Easter off to spend with her grandchildren. And the one before for being too young and wearing a short skirt around the house.'

'I bet you wanted to keep that one.' Maggie stared into her lasagne with a face like a sour grape.

'She was good at her job.'

'What job are you referring to exactly?' She flashed a killer look at her husband as 'Killer Queen' blasted from the loudspeakers.

'So, Maggie, out of all the places you've been to, which was your favourite?' asked Paul, clearing his throat and refilling everyone's glasses.

'Definitely Australia. It's a fairy-tale land if there ever was one. So much beauty everywhere you look, a photographer's paradise. I think I left my heart in Australia and I'm planning to return one day to find it.'

'Did you know Australia is home to the most venomous snake in the world?' asked Greg. 'The inland taipan. Its bite can kill eighty people.' He said it with wonder, as if he longed to get bitten by an island taipan.

'That's why I'd never go,' said Paul. 'Everything on the continent is out to kill you. The sharks, the snakes, the spiders. I'm happy in the safety of my home in London, thank you very much.'

'Most Australian flora and fauna is unique. It can't be found anywhere else in the world. Isn't it fascinating?' said Maggie.

'I'd move there in a flash,' said Greg, 'if it wasn't for our elderly parents. Just imagine the expanse, the wilderness. For thousands of miles, there's nothing.'

'You say it like it's a good thing,' said Paul with a smile. 'Why would I travel all that way to see nothing?'

'You've been to Australia, Claire. What did you make of it?' asked Greg.

'Have I?' With three pairs of eyes staring at her, Claire wished she was invisible. She didn't want to make small talk, answer pointless questions, smile to people she felt she'd never seen before.

What she wanted was to speak to her mother. She had tried her number time and time again over the last couple of days but Angela never answered.

'I'm so sorry!' Greg looked mortified. 'I completely forgot. Of course you wouldn't remember.'

'Trust my husband to put his foot in it,' muttered Maggie.

'You went with your ballet company last year,' Paul said to Claire. 'You said it was the most beautiful place in the world.'

'Have you thought of going back to work?' asked Maggie. 'I popped in yesterday with some proofs of the last performance and everyone was talking about you.'

Claire stared right at Paul and said, 'Soon, I hope. I get bored sitting around the house all day.'

If Paul understood the anger behind her glance, he didn't let up. Averting his gaze, he stood up. 'Everyone ready for dessert? Nina makes the best cheesecake in London.'

The guests nodded happily and Claire jumped up, almost knocking her chair over, eager to escape to the safety of the kitchen where she could be herself, where she could let down the mask and no one would see.

'No, stay here, talk to Maggie. You've done enough. Greg and I will bring the cake,' said Paul. Claire sat back down, shaking.

Paul and Greg disappeared into the kitchen, and Claire was left alone with Maggie, who chatted excitedly about people Claire didn't remember. After five excruciating minutes she got up and said, 'I'll just go and check if the men need any help.'

On the way to the kitchen, she felt her phone vibrating in her pocket. Locking herself in the bathroom and trying to stop her hands from shaking, she reached for it. It was Gaby, wanting to know how it was going. Assuring her everything was fine, Claire said goodbye and then dialled her mother's number, listening to the long signals.

She wished she could stay hidden away in the bathroom forever. But the Peters were waiting, expecting nothing less than a flawless pretence from Claire, just like the two of them were pretending they had a perfect marriage, like Paul was pretending he had a perfect marriage. Claire splashed some water on her face and made her way back to the dining room, like she was walking a tightrope, tense and trembling, her fake smile firmly in place.

Soon the dessert was gone, and so was the coffee. One bottle of wine turned into two, then three. The news came on TV and the dark living room lit up with mute images. Greg mentioned how attractive the female news presenter was, while Maggie turned away in disgust. Claire remained mute like the TV, sipping her juice and nodding in all the right places, like a puppet following other people's lead. What was everyone talking about? She had no idea. All she could think of was her father alone in the hospital. All she could hear was her husband's voice when he demanded she take her meds in front of him. It was after midnight already. What time did these things usually finish?

When the couple finally left, she gathered the plates and the glasses, carrying them to the kitchen sink. Her headache was back, and she felt dizzy as if she hadn't slept in days.

'Leave it, Nina will clean up in the morning,' Paul told her.

But she couldn't leave it for Nina to clean – even though she suspected it was exactly what the old Claire would have done.

Soon she was ready for bed, out of the Gucci and into her favourite comfy pyjamas. She could hear Paul in his room, talking on his phone (at midnight?), turning the light on, pacing. She crossed the corridor and stood in the doorway to his bedroom, suddenly nervous. Paul was still wearing his shirt. His tie was loose around his neck. His shoes were off, his hair messy. 'Paul? Can I ask you something?'

He looked up expectantly but didn't say a word.

'I wanted Nina to drive me to the ballet studio today but she refused.'

He didn't seem fazed by that. Like his keeping her as a prisoner in the house was nothing out of the ordinary. 'I asked her not to take you. I don't think you are ready.'

'Shouldn't it be up to me?'

'Clearly not. All I want is for you to get better. The doctor said to take things slowly. And that's what you will do, whether you like it or not.'

Back in her room, she slid to the floor and slumped against the wall, her head resting against it. Her heart was beating like a trapped bird against its cage. She could hardly breathe. Was she having another panic attack? But no, she was not going to scream. She didn't want to give Paul the satisfaction. The last thing she wanted was to prove him right and show him that she wasn't well enough to make decisions for herself. She wondered how her father was doing in the hospital, whether he felt like her, sad and alone. She reached for her phone. She needed his voice to pull her away from the abyss, to remind her she was not alone.

And then she noticed that her phone was blinking. She had a new voicemail message.

'Claire, this is Mum. How are you, darling girl? Daddy told me what happened. I'm frantic with worry. I will call you again tomorrow.'

Chapter 5

In the middle of the night Claire woke up screaming. Shaking and in tears, she shot up in bed. Her right hand throbbed like it had been caught inside a mouse trap. She must have hit it on her bedside table. Dark shadows danced a terrifying tango around her, and suddenly the walls came alive, threatening to swallow her. There were blotches of light, too, appearing as if out of nowhere only to disappear a few seconds later. Her voice died down to a whisper and in silence she sank back into her pillows.

Suddenly she was in Paul's arms, and he held her close, whispering, 'It was just a bad dream. It's alright, just a bad dream.' He switched on the little lamp on her bedside table, peering into her face. She recoiled from the light, whimpering like a frightened animal. 'Look at you, you're terrified. It's okay, you're safe now, nothing to worry about.' His pyjamas were on inside out, as if he had pulled them on in a hurry.

She flinched away from him and he let go of her, retreating to the edge of the bed. Relaxing into her pillows, she wanted nothing more than to believe that everything was fine, that it was only a dream, to feel safe again and to forget her fear. But it was impossible – the dream lingered at the back of her mind like a ghost. It felt so real, this nightmare, as if it wasn't a dream at all but a terrifying memory.

'Do you remember what you dreamt of?' Paul asked and she shook her head. But as if through a mist, she could still see it – an angry man, her alarmed anxiety, a sudden violence. If she closed her eyes, she felt she could reach out and touch her vision.

She didn't want to talk about her dream, didn't want to ever think of it again. She asked, 'Tell me about my mother. What is she like?'

'She's the kindest person I've ever met.'

'That's what everyone says.'

'That's because she's wonderful to everyone around. She has respect for everybody.'

'What did she do? For work, I mean.'

'Many years ago she was a music teacher. She didn't need the money. I think she donated everything she made and more. But she's passionate about her music and she loves children.'

A music teacher! That explained Claire's ability to play the piano like it was second nature, without a conscious effort on her part. '*Was* a music teacher? What about now?'

'She doesn't really do anything anymore. Just stays at home. She always looks so sad when I see her, like she's got a huge weight on her shoulders.'

'Tell me something about her. A memory that stands out.'

'She taught me how to dance.'

'She did?'

He nodded. 'I was so nervous about our first dance as husband and wife. I'd never danced in my life and here I was, about to do it with a professional ballerina. What would people think when I stepped on both your feet? Your mother taught me how to foxtrot. She said it was the easiest sequence of steps you could ever learn. If you can walk, you can foxtrot, she told me. And our first dance was beautiful. My sister said we looked like Beauty and the Beast on the dance floor.'

Through her tears Claire smiled. 'That's a beautiful memory. So you had a good relationship with my mother?'

'The best.'

'You didn't argue?'

'Your mum has never argued with a living soul.'

She watched him intently, trying to read the expression on his face. He was sitting on the edge of her bed, large, tall, his hair wild. His smile never faltered and his eyes never looked away. He sounded absolutely sure of what he was saying and she wanted desperately to believe him. She would have, if only Nina didn't sound absolutely sure of what she had said, too.

'I didn't have time to tell you earlier but I spoke to your father's doctor today. They can't keep him in hospital any longer. There's nothing else they can do for him. He suggested facilities—'

'Facilities?'

'He'll need professional care for the rest of his life.'

'We could hire someone. Have him live with us,' she suggested, her heart filling with hope. She would give anything to have her father home. If Tony was here, this desperate dark hole inside her would disappear. Her father would fill it with love and laughter. She would never feel alone again.

'Is that what you want?'

'Absolutely. The thought of him all by himself in that hospital room . . . It breaks my heart.'

'I'll start looking for a nurse.'

'Thank you,' she whispered, grateful and a little less afraid.

* * *

The next morning, the nightmare still haunted Claire. Even though her beautiful house was filled with sunlight, all she could see were shadows. Slowly she creeped from her bedroom to the shower and back, her head low, her eyes down, petrified of things she couldn't remember or understand. Her hands trembled, her palms were sweaty, and every sharp sound startled her, even the peaceful noises of playing children in the park. She needed to hear the voice of one person who loved her unconditionally. She called her father.

'Did I wake you?'

'Of course not. You and I are early risers. It's your mother who likes to sleep in. I bet you've been up for hours.'

'You bet wrong. I've been asleep until half an hour ago. What are you up to today? Still playing chess?'

'Reading. I've finished the book you brought.'

She thought of the large volume she had left at the hospital only yesterday. 'Were you up all night reading?'

'It made a nice change from being up all night staring at the ceiling. Bring me something else to read.'

'What would you like?'

'I was thinking the Bible.'

'Won't the hospital have a copy?'

'I don't want just any copy. You borrowed your mother's Bible a couple of years ago. See if you can find it for me. It's a very special book.'

'I'll have a look. What's for breakfast today?'

'Guess.'

'More gruel? Well, you won't have to eat gruel for much longer. We're bringing you home, Dad.' She wished she was there to see his face. Maybe she should have waited to give him the news in person. But she didn't want him to go on one minute longer than necessary thinking he was in the hospital to stay.

His voice broke when he said, 'You are?'

'Of course we are. Paul and I will look after you. You don't have to worry about anything.'

'Thank you,' he whispered. He sounded like he was about to cry.

Fighting her own tears, she said, 'We'll come and visit you later today, okay, Dad?'

She was ready to hang up when she heard, 'Claire?'

'Yes?'

'Don't worry about the Bible.'

'Why?'

'All my prayers have already been answered.'

Claire had been right – hearing her father's voice was the best medicine. It was as if he was here, next to her, ready to protect her from anything, even the horror of her dream. But once he was gone, so was the illusion of safety. The house was filled with terror. Everywhere she turned, it was waiting for her. In the kitchen where she tried to eat but couldn't. In the living room where the TV was on but its sound scared her. Even in the studio, where she played the piano but the music she produced was sinister and heavy to her ears. She couldn't stay in this house, walking from room to room aimlessly, afraid to sit still, so she threw on a jacket and a scarf, put her shoes on, grabbed her keys, made sure Nina wasn't there to stop her and ran out of the door.

Although it was cloudy and wet, the daylight blinded her and the sounds startled her. She realised she had never been outside alone. Not that she could remember, anyway. Overwhelmed for a moment, she stood still, taking in the noise, the rush hour traffic, the buses slowly peeling off the curb and the motorcycles racing past. It was like a different universe, moving to its own mad tempo, with people brushing past, cars honking, shop signs flashing. Before she could change her mind, she started jogging down the street, as if running away from something. As she ran, darting in and out of the crowd, narrowly avoiding bumping into people, she forced herself to read every street sign she could see. If she could fill her head with nonsense, she would have no space for feeling. And that was what she wanted most of all. Not to feel.

There was a Waitrose and a chemist, and next to it was a jeweller, and next to the jeweller was a bakery. Beside the bakery was a psychologist's office. As soon as she saw it, Claire slowed down and came to a complete stop. Dr Matilda Brown, she read. Hypnosis, hypnotherapy, regression therapy. The woman on the sign was smiling invitingly. *Come in*, she seemed to say, *and I'll solve all your problems.* Wouldn't that be nice, to have all her problems solved at once? Claire hesitated only for a second before pushing the door open.

A world that was a far cry from the grey outdoors greeted her in Dr Matilda's reception room. It was almost unbearably warm. Claire found herself undoing her scarf and unbuttoning her jacket. A thick smell of incense tickled her nose until she sneezed. The incense sticks were artfully arranged in a vase on the floor.

'Can I help you?' came a disembodied voice from behind the curtain.

Claire strained her neck to see the person talking. Seconds later the beads parted and a small woman emerged. Claire recognised her as the therapist from the sign. Before her courage left her completely, she said, 'I'm here to see Dr Brown.'

'I'm Dr Brown. Do you have an appointment?' The therapist offered Claire her hand to shake. It felt warm and welcoming, just like her office. 'No? Let's see. How soon would you like to come in?'

'As soon as possible.'

'I can see you now, if you like. I had a cancellation. Otherwise I could fit you in next week.'

'Now would be great.'

'Please follow me.'

The therapist took Claire to a room behind the purple beads. It was sparsely furnished, with only a couch and an armchair facing each other. The smell of incense wasn't as strong here. The room was filled with natural light and Claire could hear a quiet murmur of music.

'Please, take a seat,' said the therapist.

'Thank you, Dr Brown.' Claire relaxed into the couch, fighting a sudden impulse to close her eyes. It was the music, she realised. It made her eyelids droop.

'Please call me Matilda. Would you like a cup of tea?'

'Black, please.'

'I don't keep anything with caffeine here, I'm sorry. Hypnosis

71

works best when you're relaxed and not agitated. I can offer you some camomile.' Claire nodded, terrified at how forward she had been, coming here so suddenly. She wondered if it was too late to turn back. Therapy meant talking about your life. And that was the last thing she wanted to do.

Matilda returned minutes later with a steaming teapot and two cups, placing them on a small table by the armchair. 'It's dreadfully cold outside, isn't it? I wouldn't want to be out and about.'

'It is,' agreed Claire, even though she hadn't noticed. Her fingers were drumming a nervous rhythm on the edge of her cup.

'What would you like to talk about today?'

Claire opened her mouth to speak but couldn't say a word. To her dismay, she felt tears streaming down her cheeks. It was too much for one person to bear, all the tension of the past week and a half, the heartbreak and the uncertainty. All she could do was sob under Matilda's understanding gaze.

'Here, here,' said the therapist, stroking her hand. 'You take all the time in the world. Sip your tea. It'll help you relax.'

Claire tried to compose herself. 'I'm sorry, I'm such a mess.' She took a sip of camomile. Matilda was wrong – it wasn't calming at all. It would take more than tea to make her feel like herself again. Claire took another sip, just in case a miracle happened and it made her better, before placing her cup on the table.

'You look like you could do with a shoulder to cry on. That's what I'm here for. Feel free to tell me anything.'

'Hypnosis . . . can it help recover lost memories?' asked Claire, stalling for time, putting off the inevitable. If she could ask Matilda questions, she wouldn't have to talk about herself. And then her time would be up and Matilda would be rushing her out of her office to make way for her next patient. Claire would be able to return home and . . . and what? One thing she knew for sure. She couldn't go on as before or she would go mad.

'Over time I believe it can, yes. Our mind is extremely powerful. Even when we think we've forgotten something, chances are it's still there, under the surface, waiting to be found. Is there a particular event you'd like to remember?'

'Only my whole life.' Another sip of the hot tea, soothing music playing in the background. 'What's the difference between hypnosis and hypnotherapy? I thought they were the same thing.'

For a few seconds Matilda watched Claire carefully. Everything about the therapist seemed unhurried and relaxed, just like her music and her tea. 'Hypnosis is an altered state of consciousness. It's the drowsy state that precedes falling asleep, deep relaxation of body and mind. Hypnotherapy is the application of hypnosis.'

'Is it like they show on TV? When people do bizarre things on stage and have no recollection of it afterwards?'

'It's nothing like that. When you're under hypnosis, you are not under anyone's control but in charge of your own emotions. You bypass your conscious mind and can speak to your subconscious mind directly. And often, with analytical hypnotherapy and regression therapy, a patient can remember something his or her mind has supressed.'

'Regression therapy, isn't it something to do with past lives?' Claire vaguely remembered reading about it in one of the medical magazines at the hospital. She remembered thinking what nonsense it was.

'It can be used to access childhood memories or remember previous incarnations. You do believe in reincarnation, don't you?'

'I wish I knew what I believed in. Truth is, I've forgotten everything about myself. Do you believe in reincarnation?' asked Claire, thinking there was hope for her after all. If people could remember their previous lives, what was stopping her from remembering her current one? All she had to do was close her eyes and listen to Matilda's voice. Matilda would guide her through the maze of her past.

'It's a tricky question. I've had patients experience vivid visions and emotions under hypnosis. Some were convinced what they saw was indeed their previous lives. But it could just as well have been an image from their subconscious mind, something they've seen or read, as a child perhaps. Something that had made a deep impression, only to be forgotten later.'

Claire felt her shoulders cave in, her eyes on the carpeted floor. It seemed even Matilda didn't have the magic pill.

'Why don't you tell me what's on your mind?' asked Matilda, making a few notes. 'How can I help?'

'I was in an accident. I only remember what happened afterwards. Everything else is blank.' She told Matilda about waking up in hospital, meeting her husband for the first time, about her home and her father.

'You have bad dreams that scare you and you think they could have something to do with your past?'

'Could it be possible?'

'Anything is possible. Why don't you lie down on the couch and make yourself comfortable? I would like to try an introductory session of hypnosis. We won't go too deep and won't look for answers just yet. Today is more about you familiarising yourself with the process of hypnosis, learning to trust me and your inner voice. How does that sound?'

Claire did what she had wanted to do since the moment she walked in – she stretched out on the couch and closed her eyes. The music was a little louder now, like a wave hitting the shore, rhythmic and comforting. And so was Matilda's voice. 'I want you to find a comfortable position, either sitting or lying down. Make sure your back is straight and your neck is supported. Feel free to move around at any time if it will make you feel more comfortable. Your subconscious mind is always active, absorbing thoughts and images. Become aware of your breathing. Take a couple of slow deep breaths. And now, as I count from ten to one, you will feel your body relax and your mind empty of thoughts. Ten . . . You feel every muscle in your body relaxing . . . Nine . . . Let go of stress and ignore fleeting thoughts or images . . . Eight . . . You drift in and out of consciousness . . . You are more and more relaxed . . .'

By the count of six Claire felt her body become heavier, as if it was filling with warm liquid. She had to make a conscious effort to stay awake. It was a scary feeling, this sensation of emptiness. It implied letting go of control, allowing someone else in.

'If I ask you a question, feel free to answer or simply nod. Are you comfortable?'

Claire nodded.

'Your mind is blocking your memories but that doesn't mean they're gone. Sometimes our mind plays tricks on us to protect us. Your memories are still there, and with time and patience you can access them again. You *will* access them again.'

How much time? Claire wanted to ask but couldn't make her lips move.

'Now I want you to imagine yourself in a happy and peaceful place where you feel safe. This might be somewhere you visited before or somewhere you just imagined. It could be at a beautiful beach or at home. Anywhere you like, as long as it's peaceful and safe. Take your time and when you can think of your happy place, I want you to tell me about it.'

With her eyes closed, Claire tried to imagine what it would be like to feel happy. The truth was, she didn't know. She only knew what it felt like to feel lost and confused.

'There is absolutely no rush,' she heard Matilda's measured voice. 'This happy place doesn't have to be real. You can create it in your mind. Think of somewhere beautiful and tranquil, somewhere where you would be safe. When you have found your happy place, nod and we will continue.'

Claire tried to think of rolling hills and peaceful forests. She tried to think of rivers that ran into the ocean, enormous and green and far away. She thought of her father's smile and of the way he made her feel. Of coming home and meeting Molokai. Of laughing with Gaby. But instead of happiness, a wave of panic swept over her. Suddenly, she couldn't breathe. She could see the shadow from her nightmare, looming over her. She could sense its presence. She bit her lip to stop herself from crying out and shot up on her couch. 'I'm sorry, I can't do this. I have to go.'

As fast as she could, she scrambled to her feet and ran out of the room, not turning back to see the look on Matilda's face. What a terrible mistake it had been to come here. She needed to forget her dream, not dredge it out into the open. Instead of facing her demons, she needed to run away from them. She couldn't think of her nightmare without feeling like the floor was about to open up and swallow her whole.

Faster and faster she walked past the shops and the buses, as if afraid Matilda would chase after her and force her to come back. As she was nearing home, she felt her pocket vibrating. Someone was calling her from an overseas number her phone didn't recognise. She stared at it without blinking and then pressed the green button.

'Claire? It's Mum.' Her mother's voice was distant and faint, as if there was an ocean between them. But it was loud enough to fill Claire's heart with hope.

'Hi, Mum.' Claire stood in the middle of the road, while cars swerved around her. She was crossing and forgot where she was going. When car brakes screeched and a man's head appeared in the window, shouting 'Get out of the way!', she waddled off the road on unsteady legs and leaned on the wall of someone else's house.

'I called as soon as I could. How are you feeling?'

'I'm fine. Where are you?'

'Thank God! I've been so worried. I had to go away for a little while. Your Aunt Judy isn't feeling well. Your dad told me what happened. What are the doctors saying?'

'Nothing much. When are you coming home?' This conversation baffled her. She thought she would know what to say to her mother, just like she had known what to say to her father when she'd first met him. But it wasn't quite the case. Maybe if she could see her mother's face, touch her mother's hand, she would feel differently.

'Soon, darling. Tell me everything. How have you been?'

'Not great. I can't remember anything. It's been . . .' She couldn't find the right word. Terrifying, soul-destroying, lonely? She didn't want to upset her mother but she didn't want to lie to her, either.

'I wish I could be there for you. I feel awful. I wish I could take you in my arms, make you feel better. My little girl.'

'I wish you were here too. I keep having these dreams. And afterwards I feel afraid. Threatened. Someone is chasing me. Someone wants to hurt me. It's terrifying. I am not myself. I can't sleep. I can't eat.' Her head in her hands, Claire was sobbing into the phone.

'They are just dreams, darling. Probably because of the accident. I wouldn't worry about them if I were you.'

'They feel so real.'

'Some dreams are like that. You need to concentrate on your recovery. Get plenty of rest, get better and soon you will remember everything. And before you know it, I will be with you.' Angela continued to talk about how much she was missing her daughter, how Aunt Judy was driving her crazy with her unreasonable demands, and how she wished she could drop everything and get on the next plane to London. 'But I can't. The old dear doesn't have anyone else. She's all alone.'

So am I, Mum, Claire wanted to say. *So am I.*

'I have to go, darling. Aunt Judy is waiting for her meds.'

'Wait, Mum. I came back and I know nothing about my life. I have so many questions. I need to know about my marriage to Paul. Are we happy?'

'As happy as anyone could be in a marriage, I suppose.'

Would no one give her a straight answer, not even her mother? 'I don't know what that means, Mum. What about you? Do you have a good relationship with Paul? Do you ever argue?'

'I don't want you to worry about that. It's not important. Your health is what's important.'

'But I want to know.'

'You've been through enough. You need to rest and do what makes you happy. You deserve that.'

'Nothing makes me happy,' Claire muttered, bewildered.

'What, darling? I can hardly hear you. The line is terrible.'

'I didn't say anything.'

'Listen, darling, I have to rush. I'll call you later, okay?'

'I'm scared, Mum. I have no one to talk to.' But Angela was already gone.

* * *

In her heart, Claire had believed Angela was a magic potion that would instantly cure her. She believed the moment she heard her mother's voice, she would feel better. But it wasn't quite the case. Having spoken to Angela only briefly, Claire was left wanting more. The more she thought about their conversation, the more questions she had. She dialled the international number that had come up on her phone over and over again but no one answered.

The next morning, Claire was in bed when she heard a knock on the door. Although she wasn't asleep, or maybe because she hadn't been able to sleep well at night, it was a struggle to sit up and force her eyes open. The door handle turned before she had a chance to tell the person on the other side to come in. In the dim morning light she saw Paul's silhouette looming in the doorway. She felt a shiver of cold foreboding. What was he doing here so early? But when she glanced at the clock, she saw it was almost midday. What was he doing at home? It must be Saturday, she realised. The thought of being alone in the house with him all day made her want to scream.

'Are you okay?' asked Paul. 'You look like you've seen a ghost.'

'I'm not feeling well,' she mumbled, wishing she could put her head under the pillow and pretend she was asleep, so she wouldn't have to see him.

'Two police officers are here. They want to talk to you.'

'To me?' Where was that pillow that could hide her away from the world?

'Yes. Something about the accident.'

Shaking, she followed Paul to the living room. The two police officers were already there, looking comfortable on the couch, as if they belonged there, as if they were welcome. Claire suspected they were used to marching in uninvited. Their uniforms opened doors.

When they saw her, they stood up and invited her to join them, motioning towards the couch, like it was their house and she was the guest. She did what they said and sat down, as far away from them as possible.

'We are sorry to intrude on the weekend,' said the woman, not looking sorry at all. What was her name again? It was Polish, maybe? Claire tried to visualise the card she had placed in her bedside table after having spoken to them at the hospital. PC Kamenski and PC Stanley, she remembered. The ginger twins. She was surprised the names came to her so quickly. If only she could remember the rest of her life as easily.

'That's fine. You're not intruding.'

'We have a few questions about the accident.'

'I wish I could help you,' Claire said. Paul was hovering nearby with a cup of coffee. She lowered her voice. 'But I still don't remember anything about the accident.'

'Nothing at all?' The woman seemed disappointed. The man was making notes in his notepad and looked indifferent.

Claire shook her head.

'We spoke to your father. Something in his account doesn't add up,' said the man, studying her coldly.

He waited for Claire to say something. She cleared her throat. 'My father is confused. He's been through a lot. He might be suffering from memory loss himself. He doesn't remember me being in the car with him but that doesn't mean . . .'

'On the contrary. Your father told us he was taking you horse-riding. It's a family tradition the two of you share.'

'He told you that?' She watched them in silence for a few moments, wondering if they were playing some kind of a game to get her to confess . . . to what? What they were saying was impossible. Tony was adamant she wasn't in the car with him. Why would he tell the police something different?

'Your father told us you were in the front seat of the car, next to him. That you were talking about a holiday you were planning as a family when he lost control of the vehicle,' said PC Kamenski.

'And?'

The woman didn't reply but studied Claire's face as if looking for clues.

'Were you in the front seat, Mrs Wright?' asked PC Stanley.

'I told you. I don't remember. I assume so. Why wouldn't I be?'

'Do you often travel without your seatbelt on?'

'I don't know. I'm sorry.'

'Why would your father tell us you were in the front seat next to him when we pulled you out of the back seat? Can you think of a reason?'

Claire could feel the blood rushing away from her face. She could feel her cheeks paling, her heart beating, faster-faster, like wings ready for take-off. 'I don't know. I don't remember,' she repeated.

Paul burst into the room, stern and foreboding. He towered over the police with his arms crossed. 'Excuse me, officers,' he said. 'My wife's been through a lot. She hasn't been well. I think it's best if you leave.'

They got up to their feet 'That's okay. We have no further questions. Goodbye, Mrs Wright.'

She muttered something in return; she might have waved, she wasn't sure. For the first time that she could remember, she was grateful to her husband.

'Are you okay? Would you like to go up to your room? I can make you a cup of tea,' Paul said when they were finally alone.

Claire turned towards the window and watched the police car screech out of their driveway. Then she turned to Paul and said, 'Take me to my parents' house.'

Chapter 6

Her heart beating like a nervous butterfly, Claire stood outside a tall white fence. If she rose to her tiptoes, she could peek into the front yard. She thought the house she shared with Paul was a mansion, but her parents' house in an exclusive part of North London was a small castle. With its brown brick and black roof tiles, it looked dark and ominous, and yet, it possessed a certain charm. Petunias and daffodils spilled out of their pots in a cascade of colour and the lace curtains in the windows looked handmade. The garden looked beautiful, even though the flowers looked like they needed water, their wilting heads nodding in the wind. Claire could see apple trees, blueberry bushes and a lone gooseberry shrub.

'Is this where I grew up?' Even in her warm jumper, Claire felt chilly and uncomfortable. She could sense her past lurking inside.

Paul nodded. 'This is where you lived until we got married.'

Claire touched the gate she had known since she was a child, undid the latch she must have opened a million times before, willing herself to remember through the tips of her fingers. To her surprise, the gate was unlocked. Gingerly, she stepped onto the carpet of overgrown grass, while Paul looked inside the rusty letterbox and retrieved a stack of letters. 'Doesn't look like anyone's been here in a while,' he said.

'Of course not. Mum's away and Dad's in hospital.'

Old newspapers littered the pathway. The curtains were tightly drawn. 'I wish we had the key,' said Claire, walking around the perimeter of the house, peering into every window, hoping to catch a glimpse of the world inside. 'Shouldn't we at least water the flowers?'

Next door, a dog barked. A door slammed somewhere and a dishevelled head appeared over the hedge that separated the two properties.

'Hello, Claire,' said the head. It had dark hair with grey roots and belonged to an elderly lady.

'Oh, hello,' replied Claire. The lady had an advantage over her. She appeared to know Claire well, while Claire had no idea who she was talking to.

'Haven't seen you in ages. Where have you been hiding?' Without waiting for a response, the woman continued, 'Are you looking for your mother? She's not here.'

'I know that. We were just passing by.'

'Do you know when Angela is coming back? She asked me to water her plants. She said she didn't trust your dad to do it.' The neighbour pointed at the dry roses and daffodils that were begging for water. 'That was three weeks ago,' continued the neighbour, shaking her head in disapproval. 'She said she was going away for a week.'

'A week? Are you sure?'

'She would never leave Felix for longer than that.'

'Felix?'

'The cat.' The neighbour threw a suspicious look in Claire's direction. 'She said a friend was looking after him.'

'How long have you lived here?' asked Claire to break the awkward silence that followed.

'Why, fifty-odd years.' The neighbour practically climbed over the fence to look at Claire. She was wearing gardening gloves and an apron. 'You know that.'

'Of course.'

'Are you okay? You don't look so good. Last time I saw you, you barely had time to say hello—'

'I'm fine,' said Claire. 'Just fine.' Suddenly she wanted to leave, all thoughts of watering the flowers forgotten. Only one thing stopped her – this woman must have known her since she was a child. There were a thousand questions she wanted to ask. If only it didn't mean answering questions in return. Nervously she said, 'Do I have any childhood friends still living here?'

The woman's eyes widened and she almost dropped the small spade she was holding. 'Childhood friends? What are you talking about? You didn't move here until you were 16.'

'16? Are you sure?'

'Of course I'm sure. Like I said, I've lived here fifty-odd years. Is everything okay? You really don't seem like your usual self.' Eyebrows raised, she glanced from Claire to her husband. 'Is everything—'

Claire interrupted the neighbour before she had a chance to finish her sentence. 'I just remembered, we have to go.' Turning around, Claire ran towards the gate without as much as a backwards glance. She didn't stop until she reached the car.

On the drive to the hospital to visit her father, she curled up in her seat like a kitten, not saying a word, her chin resting on her knees. Paul was mute too, and gloomy. Only when they turned off the motorway and approached the hospital did she ask, 'What made you think I grew up there?'

'That's what you said. You told me childhood stories about the house. How your mum let you have the biggest room in the house when you were five. How you decorated the room together. How you would watch the dogs play in the park outside your window. How much you wanted a puppy. That's why I bought Molokai for our wedding anniversary.'

'Why would I tell you something that wasn't true? Is it possible the neighbour was lying?'

'I can't see why she would. What does she have to hide?'

Did I have something to hide? wondered Claire.

It was midday when they reached the hospital. Suddenly, the sun disappeared and it started to rain. The car park was flooded, and by the time Claire ran to the door under the ineffective cover of a newspaper, her shoes filled with water. It was an uncomfortable feeling, as if every step she took, she was going to slip.

In silence they made their way down the familiar corridor towards Tony's room. *If all goes well*, thought Claire, *this might be my last visit to the hospital.* The thought left her conflicted. On one hand, she wanted to bring her father home. On the other, this was still the only place where she felt safe.

The door to her father's room was open. A blonde woman emerged, pushing a tray table in front of her. Not glancing at the visitors, she made a right turn and started to walk away. 'Wait,' cried Claire. 'Why are you taking Dad's lunch? It doesn't look like he's finished it.' The truth was, it didn't even look like he'd started it. The hot dish still had its lid on, the butter was unopened, the bread roll uncut, the orange juice untouched.

'Tell me about it. It's a daily battle with him. He hasn't eaten in days.' The nurse threw her hands up in the air dramatically, as if Tony not eating was the most exciting thing that had happened to her all week.

Claire had always suspected her father's optimism was just an act. And here, on the hospital tray, was the proof. 'What about the food I brought for him?'

'Check the fridge in the kitchen. I bet it's still there.'

The woman was right. All the boxes Claire had lovingly packed remained in the fridge, unopened. The fresh orange juice she had squeezed, Nina's Napoleon cake, the pelmeni, the sandwiches and the chocolates.

Claire stormed into her father's room, pulling the door so hard, the handle left an angry red mark on the palm of her hand. At the sight of him she wanted to cry. He looked painfully thin, old before his time. She stood back as pleasantries were exchanged between the two men, the weather discussed, the health, the news and the football scores. Finally, Tony turned to her and said, 'Hello, Teddy Bear. You're awfully quiet today. Come and give your old man a hug.'

He didn't just look frail. He felt frail in her arms. It was like hugging a bag of bones. 'We brought you some food,' she said. 'There's some spaghetti Bolognese, and a Russian meat dish that's impossible to pronounce but I can assure you it's delicious. As always, Nina's outdone herself. Did you eat the cake? The pelmeni?'

'I ate it all. Thank Nina for me. The cake was to die for.'

Why was he lying? He wasn't just hiding the food he hadn't eaten, Claire realised. He was hiding how he truly felt. Was he putting on a show to protect her from the truth? She was a grown-up, she could take it.

'You didn't eat anything, did you?' Her hands were on her hips. She knew she looked angry but didn't care.

'There might be a tiny bit left. They feed me like a pig for slaughter. You should have seen the meatballs and mashed potato I had for lunch.'

'Is that what it was? It was hard to tell, with the lid still on. Don't lie, Dad. I spoke to your nurse.' Tony blinked and looked away. Suddenly he seemed so sad. She felt bad for speaking to him like that. 'You've lost so much weight. I worry about you,' she added softly.

'Please, don't. It's not me you should worry about.'

'How will you get better if you don't eat?'

'I won't get better. Whether I eat or not. So what's the point?'

'The point is, you need your energy. To recover, to walk again. You need your strength.'

'Stop kidding yourself. I'll never walk again. It's not meant to be.'

Wasn't meant to be? What was he talking about? 'Only four more nights and you'll be coming home where I can keep an eye on you.'

'Four more nights. It's like counting down to Christmas.'

'I wouldn't be too excited if I were you. I'll be there to make sure you work hard and eat well. We are hiring a nurse and a physiotherapist. No more lounging around.'

'Is that what I'm doing?'

'No more feeling sorry for yourself. No more skipping meals. You'll miss this place before I'm done with you.' Fighting back tears, she smiled.

'I can hardly wait.' He smiled back.

They stayed through the remainder of the visiting hours, playing cards and watching TV together. Before they were about to leave, Claire asked, almost like an afterthought, almost like she didn't care, 'Dad, when did you say Mum was coming back?'

'In three months or so.'

'We spoke to your neighbour. She's looking after Mum's flowers. She said Mum was supposed to be back two weeks ago.'

'Old Sue? She'd forget to wake up in the morning if that dog of hers didn't bark at the sun as soon as it came up. Please, don't worry about anything. Promise?'

'Only if you start eating better. Promise?'

Claire followed Paul to the car, and when he opened the passenger door for her, told him she had forgotten her purse in Tony's room. That wasn't strictly a lie. She did leave her purse under her father's bed because she needed an excuse to come back to his room alone. She was hoping Paul wouldn't walk with her all the way from the carpark and she was right. He said he would wait in the car. Ignoring the rain lashing her face, she ran back towards the hospital entrance, past the reception, down the corridor and into her father's room. Tony was on his bed with his eyes closed. He looked like he'd fallen asleep. Claire coughed and he opened his eyes. His face lit up at the sight of her. He started to speak but she interrupted. 'I need to ask you something and I want you to tell me the truth. Why did you lie to the police?'

'I told them what they wanted to hear. The sooner they leave us alone, the better.'

Shivering in her clothes, wet from the rain, Claire whispered, 'They said they pulled me out of the back seat.'

Tony narrowed his eyes and his lips stretched into a thin line. It was a while before he spoke. 'Now that doesn't make sense, does it? Why would you be in the back seat and not in the front with me?'

Chapter 7

Claire tried her best to fill her days with light to forget about the darkness. She swam in her Olympic-size swimming pool, back and forth and back again, her athletic ballerina body slicing the water like a knife. She danced in her sunlit studio until every bit of her ached, hoping the physical pain would make her forget everything else. She played with Molokai and laughed at his antics. And still, the darkness wouldn't leave her. Every length of the swimming pool and every pirouette in front of the mirror, it accompanied her like a trusted and loyal friend. It was in her dreams and in her waking hours, so vivid, like a recollection of something terrifying and grim. The darkness was in the absence of her mother and the unanswered questions that haunted her.

One day, Paul returned from work and said, 'I know you are running out of your meds.'

'I am?' She hadn't noticed.

'Here, I got your refill for you.'

'Thank you,' she said, absentmindedly taking the pills and putting them in her bag. 'What are these? They look different from my normal pills.'

'Just a different brand.'

The sky had been ominously bleak for days, threatening rain.

Finally, on the day her father was due to come home, thunder clapped and lightning struck, as if in jubilation or threat. At eight in the morning, her mother called her. Through hurried small talk, there was one question that tormented Claire. She had to ask, couldn't *not* ask but she waited till the last moment, when she knew her mother was about to hang up. 'Mum, where did I grow up?'

'Why, London, of course.'

'Your neighbour told me it was somewhere else.'

'Old Sue? Don't listen to her, darling. She's as mad as a March hare. If you had your memory, you'd know. How is that going, by the way?'

The subject thus changed, they talked about Claire ('No improvement? I'm so sorry, darling, I wish I could be there.') and how much Angela longed to be home with her daughter and how difficult it was, looking after Aunt Judy. 'The old bird is driving me crazy. Yesterday she made me drive to the supermarket three times because she couldn't decide what she wanted for dinner. All I do is scrub and clean and look after her, without as much as a thank you.'

'Why don't you hire someone to do it?' After catching a glimpse of her parents' house, Claire was surprised her mother would clean and cook herself. It wasn't like she didn't have the money.

'I haven't even thought about it, darling. It's not something I would normally do.'

And then her mother had to go and Claire was left feeling more confused than ever.

In the afternoon, she stood by the window and waited. Longing to see her father as soon as possible, she had called the hospital three times to find out what time they were bringing him home but no one could tell for sure. So she stood and watched the road until her feet ached and her vision became blurry. Staring at the empty driveway battered by the rain, she trembled in anticipation. Once her father was home, she would no longer be alone. She wouldn't have to fill her hours with mindless tasks, jumping every time her phone rang. Tony would be there to share everything. All her fears would disappear and her heart would be light. And that was what she was waiting for by the window that afternoon. For her fears to disappear under her father's loving smile.

When she saw the ambulance turning the corner and driving up to their house, she sprinted down the stairs two steps at a time and then slowed down, her heart racing. She didn't wait for the doorbell, opening the door to two burly men in white and Tony on the stretcher between them. When she saw him, her day was no longer dreary. Suddenly it filled with colour, as if he were the sun that came out from behind a cloud and made everything sparkle. Claire greeted Tony happily, hovering over him, giving directions, holding his hand as she led the way to a guest bedroom. How she wished he could stand up to greet her, so she could hug him properly. He looked as lost as she felt. All he managed was a wave and a weak smile.

His new room was conveniently located on the ground floor. If he wanted to, he could wheel himself to the kitchen, to the terrace, the home cinema, the indoor swimming pool. Claire was excited when she told him that, until he pointed out the obvious – in his condition he should probably stay away from the swimming pool.

'We'll have great adventures together,' she said. 'I'll take you to the park if it ever stops raining.' That put a smile on his face. She knew it had been a long time since he'd been outside.

When he was settled and the orderlies had left, Claire clucked over him like a chicken over its young. *Are you hungry, Dad? Do you want me to open the window? Do you want me to read to you? Do you want to watch TV? Can I bring you something to drink? What can I do? What do you want? How do you feel? Are you sure you don't need anything?*

He hid under his quilt, even though it was warm in the room. The bedding was a light shade of pink that probably had an exotic name, like blush or taffy. The bedroom had a girly feel to it and didn't suit him. 'How about a vodka martini? We'll have a celebration.' He smiled to show he was only joking. 'I'm fine, darling, thank you. Just stay here with me while I sleep. I could do with a rest.'

Feeling his calloused hand in hers, hearing his voice, seeing his weary face filled her heart with joy. He was finally home.

When he woke up in his taffy bed, she was by his bed, reading a book. He looked rested and happy to see her. His smile was genuine and kind. 'Still here?' he asked.

'Of course. Molokai and I are keeping you company.'

Tony glanced at the Labrador retriever peacefully curled up by his feet. He nodded with satisfaction. 'Every happy home needs a dog.'

'I tried to get him to come out and play but he won't leave your side. Dogs are good judges of character. He can sense a good person.'

'He can sense a dog person. I love dogs, always have. They're better than most people. Loyal.'

'Molokai is definitely that. They don't get more loving than him.'

'A dog is the only creature that loves you more than it loves itself. Unlike people, they are wired for unconditional love.'

'Did I have a dog growing up?'

'Unfortunately, your mother is a cat person. I'm still trying to convince her dogs are much more fun. She can't see past the fur and the barking.'

'Who is looking after your cat?'

'A friend is fostering him until your mum gets back. She doesn't trust me to feed him.'

'Of course not. You're a dog person.'

She brought some lunch – a sandwich for him, some fruit for herself. She didn't have much of an appetite. Nor, it seemed, did Tony; he ate listlessly, as if he was only doing it to please her. He seemed far away, lost in thought. 'You know what I'd like right now?'

'What?'

'A bath!' His eyes twinkled. She could smell the hospital on him – the disinfectant, the soap and the dirt. 'When does the nurse start?' he asked.

'Not until tomorrow. But I'm happy to give you a bath.'

He shook his head. She could tell he didn't want to be a burden. Even if helping him would make her happy. Even if having her help him would make him happy. It must have been killing him, the helplessness, relying on other people in every little thing.

'I'm happy to,' she insisted.

'If you're absolutely sure.'

Claire ran his bath and helped him into his wheelchair, pushing him to the bathroom. And what a bathroom it was – fit for a king. 'Don't make it too hot. I prefer my bath cold and energising.'

'Let me undress you, Dad.'

'Leave the underwear. There are things a daughter shouldn't see.'

'You can't have a bath in your underwear.'

'I'll take it off myself. I'm not completely incapable. Just lift me up.' She helped him up and into the bathtub. 'I'm so sorry. I feel terrible. It's too hard for you. You look so frail and tiny.'

'I'm a ballerina. My body is ten times stronger than it looks.'

He sat back, sighing happily, as if feeling cool water on his body was a pleasure he had long forgotten. 'More bubbles, please. To protect my modesty.'

'Were you like this with the nurses at the hospital?' Suddenly she wanted to cry with relief. Her father was home. She was needed. She was loved.

He relaxed into the bath with a smile on his face. 'I remember bathing you when you were a baby. How innocent you were, how helpless. And look at us now. I'm just as helpless myself.'

'But not as innocent?' she joked, massaging shampoo into his head.

'It's the circle of life. Still seems like yesterday, you know? You were the sweetest child. Daddy's little girl. I remember the first time I held you. You were crying and no one could settle you. Not the midwife, not even your mother. I picked you up, rocked you ever so gently and sang to you. Sang the only song I knew. You stopped crying immediately and looked up at me with those big blue eyes of yours. That was the moment I fell in love with you. I think your mother has always been a little jealous of the bond between us. We were thick as thieves, you and I. Always off on adventures. Always up to something.'

'Which song did you sing? Sing it to me now.'

He hummed the melody and for a moment looked thoughtful, as if searching for words. 'Down in the valley, the valley so low, hang your head over, hear the wind blow.'

'You have a beautiful voice.'

'That's what your mother used to say. She called it my magic voice. The minute I started singing, you stopped crying. Why are you crying now? What's wrong? What did I say?'

'Happy tears,' she said, wiping her face. 'It's good to have you home, Dad.'

'It's good to be home.'

Chapter 8

Tony's nurse arrived the next morning at eight o'clock sharp – the grandfather clock in the living room was still chiming when the doorbell rang. Helga was stout, German and spoke as little as she could possibly get away with. But when she did speak, it was textbook English with only the slightest trace of an accent. She informed Claire she was a year away from her retirement and needed the money. It seemed Helga was counting the seconds till the day she could dedicate her life to grandkids and azaleas. Claire hoped it didn't mean she would neglect her duties but Helga seemed more than capable. She was definitely not a pushover. Even Tony had to take notice and listen. Before she even unpacked, she gave him a bath and fed him breakfast – and he ate every bit without an argument. Claire was impressed, warming to Helga instantly, even though she felt like the nurse was usurping her private time with her father.

'Your physiotherapist starts tomorrow. He'll be here three times a week,' she told her dad after the bath and the breakfast.

'Don't want any physiotherapy,' he grumbled. 'What's the point? It's not like I'll ever walk again.'

'Physiotherapy is important,' said Helga in her no-nonsense voice. 'Especially for someone who doesn't move. It's vital to have some form of physical exercise. It improves blood circulation and strengthens the muscles. It will help you regain balance and motor skills in affected areas.'

'Don't see the point,' repeated Tony like a belligerent teenager. But his voice lacked conviction.

Nina, who had come to pick up Tony's tray, said, 'Water drop sharpens stone.'

Everyone looked at her in confusion. 'What does that mean?' asked Tony.

'Means little by little you can get great results. Is a Russian expression.'

'Never heard it before in my life.'

'That because you not Russian,' replied Nina.

'This physiotherapist better not be a man. I don't want a man touching me.'

But it was a man and his name was Andrew. He spent an hour massaging and stretching Tony's muscles, and by the time he was done, the two of them were the best of friends. Afterwards, Tony was glowing. 'I bet all the ladies love you,' he said to Andrew. 'You have the magic touch. You made an old man feel like a newborn baby.'

Tony and Claire did their best to carve out a semblance of a normal existence out of the train wreck of their lives. One day, about a week after Tony had moved in with them, he told Claire to bring him a Rubik's cube. She had found one in Paul's study. 'You know how to solve it?' she asked, impressed.

'I don't. But you do. Give it a go. It might jog your memory.'

She didn't believe him at first but he was right. When she took the cube, it was as if her fingers suddenly had a life of their own. They turned and twisted, and soon the little squares fell into place. She wished she could solve the puzzle of her life just as easily.

Sometimes Claire noticed a trace of sadness in Tony's eyes. She didn't want to see it but there was no hiding from it. At moments like that, she would laugh twice as loud, joke twice as much. Anything to chase the clouds away. And it worked. He always had a smile on his face just for her.

Claire's nightmare had become more and more frequent. Violent, disturbing, blood-chilling, she could always count on it, and soon she grew to expect it. In her dream, she was hiding in a tight space, a cupboard perhaps, holding her breath so *he* wouldn't hear. She wasn't alone in the cupboard. There was someone else with her. Who was this other person? What was he doing there? She didn't know but she clung to him as if her life depended on it. And then gradually, in slow motion, the door would open, revealing a pale light. And the shadow would loom over her.

Claire would shoot up in bed, her mouth open in a silent scream, hands flailing. What she wanted more than anything every time she had the dream was to shout at the top of her lungs, to roar with fear, let all her terror out, so it would no longer haunt her. But she had to stay quiet, otherwise *he* would come. When she closed her eyes, she could still see him, the shadow from her nightmare.

She would still her trembling hands by clutching them into fists and bringing them close to her chest. 'I'm home,' she would whisper. 'I'm safe. It was just a dream.' There was no need to wake Paul or disturb her father. What would they think if every night she woke up screaming and in tears?

When her night light went on, the shadows retreated. 'See, just a dream,' she would tell herself. 'You're safe here.' She wanted to hear a human voice, even if it was her own. But instead of calming her, the sound of her talking to herself scared her even more.

Because she needed someone to talk to, preferably a stranger who wouldn't judge or wouldn't compare her to her old self and feel sorry for her, Claire had found herself back in Matilda's office one day. Since then, it had become her safe haven, the only place where she could be herself. Only here could she allow the mask to fall away. The mask of a loving daughter and trusting wife whose life wasn't hanging by a threat. Once the mask was gone, maybe her true face would be revealed. What that face was, she didn't know yet. But that was the whole point of these sessions, to learn who she truly was.

She would recline on the therapist's couch, close her eyes and listen to the voice that never failed to lull her into an illusion of calm. Claire stopped associating the voice with the woman sitting in the armchair behind her. It had a magical feel to it, as if it belonged to no one. It was the voice inside her head, telling her what to do and how to feel. Today was no different. She felt herself drifting-drifting-drifting, until she became dizzy and light-headed.

'Tell me about the nightmares.'

'They are terrifying.' Claire was on the brink of sleep, barely able to speak. She slurred her words and didn't care.

'Did you have another one last night?'

'Last night and every night.'

'That's good. Your mind is trying to tell you something. How do you feel when you experience them?'

'Afraid but also curious. I want to know what happens and at the same time I don't. What if it's something so terrible, I'm better off not knowing?'

'You're the only one who can answer that question, Claire. Do you want to live in ignorance? Or do you want to face your demons?'

Claire wanted to tell Matilda she was battling her demons every day. How many more could she handle?

'Either way, I always wake up.'

'I want you to find yourself in your dream. Experience it fully. Tell me what you feel.'

Claire didn't want to experience the fear and the panic and the pain. But she couldn't fight the voice. She had to do as she was told. 'I feel afraid.'

'Anything else?'

She tried to focus.

'Whenever you're ready. There is no rush. Concentrate on your dream. Let it come to you like it does every night.'

'Darkness. It's dark, like there is no light in the world. Like all the hope is gone.'

'Are you alone in the darkness?'

'I don't know. I feel threatened, like someone is chasing me.'

'This someone, can you see their face?'

'I can't. But there's a struggle. Someone is trying to hurt me.'

'Good, stay there. Stay with this feeling.'

'I can't,' Claire whimpered, shaking.

'You are doing great. You're being so brave, you're doing just fine. What do you see now?'

'I'm hiding in a cupboard, peeking out.'

'What do you see?'

'I see a man.' Claire sobbed. 'His hands are clasped into fists. He's violent, unkind. He wants to hurt me.'

'Can you see his face?'

In a voice she didn't recognise Claire whispered, 'I can't. I don't know.'

'You're safe,' said the voice. 'No one is going to harm you. Now take a deep breath and find yourself back in this room. As I count up from one to ten, let all the images fade. One . . .'

Claire felt violated as a deep memory was yanked to the surface. The memory she wasn't yet ready for, would never be ready for. Although she couldn't recall the specifics, she remembered a feeling. And this feeling was fear. Someone had done bad things to her in the past.

She thought of Paul leaning over her every single evening as he handed her the meds. She thought of not being able to go to the ballet studio because he had forbidden it, pretending to have her best interests at heart. She thought of his smile that never reached his eyes. And suddenly she knew without a doubt who the shadow from her dream was.

Chapter 9

Every morning as soon as she woke up, Claire made breakfast for her father. An omelette, not grey and unpalatable like at the hospital but runny and yellow, just the way he liked it. According to Nina, the trick was to add a little bit of water. It gave the omelette a fluffy texture, made it light and delicious. For lunch, she often served the Russian blinis made by Nina or pancakes she had attempted herself. Claire loved them with strawberry jam and Nutella, and so she would pile them up on her father's plate because she wanted him to have something sweet. She had wrestled the responsibility of feeding him from Helga. Literally wrestled a tray from her one day. Long gone were the days when he would refuse to eat. He devoured the omelettes and the pancakes, but especially the blinis, telling her how good they were, how good she was for bringing them. Because he loved the food, Claire felt he loved her a little bit more. And that made her happy.

One afternoon, she found him watching *Gone with the Wind*. 'Something to help me sleep,' he explained.

'Trouble sleeping?' When he nodded, she said, 'Me too.'

'Also, it's your mother's favourite film.'

'It is?' Claire looked at the screen with interest.

'I took her to see it on our first date. It was a small cinema playing old films. I imagined holding hands, feeding each other popcorn, that sort of thing. But your mother would have none of it. She was completely under Scarlet O'Hara's spell. For four hours she sat still like a mouse and only had eyes for Scarlet. Not once did she even glance in my direction. And afterwards all she wanted to talk about was the movie. I had nothing to say because I wasn't paying any attention. I only had eyes for her. Since then, she must have seen the movie a hundred times.'

'That sounds so romantic. We should watch it together sometime.' Claire wanted to feel closer to her mother. She wanted to know everything about her, to read the books she liked, to watch the movies she enjoyed. It occurred to her that she hadn't heard from Angela in a while.

'Maybe when your mother comes back, we can all watch it together. Something tells me she won't say no.'

'You are so lucky to have each other. It's so rare, to find someone you trust so completely, to feel so in love after all those years. Not many people have that.'

Suddenly, she felt close to tears. Tony sensed that. He had a knack for seeing through the mask. 'Is everything okay, darling?'

She shrugged. 'Paul and I are like strangers. And I don't think my memory loss has anything to do with it.'

'Marriage is like a dip in the sea in winter. It could be good for you. It could be great, invigorating. Or you could get a cramp and drown. Problem is, you don't know until you try.'

'I think our marriage got a cramp and we're drowning.'

'The key is to work at it. There's an old Georgian saying.'

'Georgia as in America?'

'Georgia as in the former Soviet Republic. Your mother and I went there on our honeymoon. Hidden away in the mountains of Caucasus, it is the most exotic place I've ever been to. Anyway, an old wise man from Georgia told me once that no matter what happens, through highs and lows, through sun and hail, a married couple must always sleep on one pillow. That's the trick to a happy marriage. To sleep on one pillow.'

'Paul and I don't even share a bedroom, let alone a pillow.'

'I think what it means is working together as a team, sharing the core values in life. And never going to bed angry. No matter how much we argue, your mother and I always make sure we work it out, even if it means staying up all night talking. In my opinion, silence is the number one enemy of a relationship. When arguments stop and the silence begins, then you know you're in trouble.'

'That's our problem right there. The silence. The small talk.'

'But sometimes, you owe it to yourself to acknowledge that the relationship is over and to move on with your life. If being with someone doesn't bring you joy, maybe it's time to let go. Does being with Paul bring you joy?'

'I don't know him well enough to answer your question. Sometimes he scares me, Dad.'

Tony nodded. It was as if he was agreeing with her, as if he knew she had reasons to be scared.

'Has Paul ever done anything?' she whispered. 'Has he ever hurt me?'

Tony took her hand and squeezed it. Her eyes filled with tears at this simple gesture of sympathy and support. With a kind smile on his face, he said, 'I don't know, darling. You never confided in me about things like that. Why don't you ask your mother?'

* * *

Gaby dropped in at noon, bringing tickets to *Swan Lake*. It was Claire's ballet company's production, once upon a time performed by Claire herself. She gasped in excitement when she saw the tickets.

'But . . .' She hesitated. 'Will Paul let me go?'

'What do you mean?' exclaimed Gaby. 'Why wouldn't he let

you go? He's not your keeper.' How Claire wished that was true but it did feel like he was her keeper and she was his prisoner.

Gaby announced she was whisking Claire and Molokai away. 'Enough moping around the house. We'll have a day out.' She took them to the park, where they found a perfect spot underneath a giant of an oak tree that was surrounded by birches and chestnuts like a king by his vassals. Its branches reached for the ground in a majestic canopy, capable of sheltering a dozen people, giving the tree a magical appearance, as if it didn't belong in Central London but in a forest in Narnia.

Molokai ran in circles around the small pond, chasing ducks, while Gaby opened her backpack and revealed a perfectly folded picnic blanket, spreading it on the grass. A carton of orange juice followed, half a dozen sandwiches and two slices of cake. There were grapes, strawberries and even a mango. As Claire watched, astonished, Gaby poured the juice and unpacked the sandwiches, looking pleased with herself.

'You prepared a picnic for us?' Claire exclaimed, before starting to cry.

'That's not the reaction I was hoping for.'

'I've just been so emotional lately.'

'You know you can tell me anything.' Gaby handed her a glass of orange juice. 'What's on your mind?'

'What was I like before the accident?' asked Claire, absent-mindedly sipping her juice, watching the swans floating on the water surface.

'You were the heart and soul of every party. Lively and fun and always up to mischief.'

Claire wanted to know what kind of mischief but didn't dare ask. She couldn't imagine being the heart and soul of anything. She definitely didn't feel lively or fun. 'It doesn't sound like me at all.'

'You threw the best parties. Everyone was invited. We would dance, drink, play truth or dare. Your partner Jason would play the guitar.'

'My partner?'

'Dance partner. I always suspected something was going on between you two but never knew for sure.' Gaby glanced at Claire as if expecting her to deny or confirm it.

'What made you think that?'

'I once asked you if he was seeing anyone. I wanted to ask him out. He's gorgeous and I thought, why not. But you got so upset. You tried to hide it but I could tell. And then you told me he was gay.'

'Maybe he is.'

'I was quite drunk that night, so I asked him directly. He said he's not gay but he's dating someone special. And yet, I've never seen him with a girlfriend.'

'Do you have a photo of him?'

'I don't but you do. Just check your Facebook.'

Gaby pointed out a photo of a gorgeous dancer wearing a tight leotard. The camera had captured him mid-pirouette, showing off his athletic body, black hair, black eyelashes and dark eyes, the type that made women go weak in the knees. But there was something odd about him. As if his hair was too glossy, his teeth too white, his lips too smiley, like he didn't just play the part of a fairy-tale prince but fancied himself one in real life.

'Do you remember him?' asked Gaby.

'I feel like I've never seen him before in my life.' Claire waited until her friend looked happy and relaxed, like a cat on a sunny roof, before she asked, 'Has Paul always been controlling? Is that what you meant when you said we had issues? Was he . . .' She hesitated. 'Abusive towards me?'

Gaby became visibly less relaxed. She took a few sips of her wine. 'Why do you ask?'

'I keep having this nightmare. Like someone is threatening me.'

'It's just a dream. You've been through a lot.'

'It feels like more than just a dream. You are the only one I can ask. The only one who will tell me the truth.'

Gaby turned away from Claire, as if she could avoid this conversation by looking the other way. She didn't say anything.

'Please, Gaby. What is Paul really like? I need to know. I live under the same roof with him and don't know what to expect. Am I in danger? Should I be afraid of him?'

'I don't want to be the one to tell you,' Gaby said finally.

'There's no one else I can ask,' repeated Claire.

'When Paul gets angry, he can't control himself. For years he refused to see a counsellor.'

'What makes him angry?'

'Anything, really. The most innocent things. If you forgot to tell Nina not to put fabric softener in his laundry. Or left your clothes lying around the living room. Or said something in public he didn't like. It happened in front of me once. One minute he was the most pleasant host, the next he turned into a monster.'

'Why? What happened?'

'You said he had fallen asleep during a ballet performance. You were teasing, of course. But he took it as a criticism. I left quickly. I didn't want to interfere in your argument. But then you came to my house in tears. It was the look on your face that scared me. You looked so afraid, and at the same time embarrassed, like it was you who had done something wrong. I told you to leave him immediately.'

'Why didn't I?'

'You always made excuses for him. Blamed yourself. I think until the last moment you were hoping things would get better. But they only got worse. Men like Paul don't change.'

'When was that?'

'A couple of months ago.'

'Just before I filed for divorce.' She wished she could curl up in bed and sleep for a thousand years. And maybe when she woke up, she wouldn't have to deal with the disaster of her marriage.

'I'm so sorry, darling. I didn't want to be the one to tell you.'

'It's okay. You didn't tell me anything I didn't already know.'

That night, Claire tried to imagine her old self, trapped in an abusive marriage, hoping each incident would be the last and having her heart and her trust broken time and time again. She imagined walking on eggshells every day of her life, of trying to please him, of watching her every word from fear of provoking him. Of wondering if what was happening was her fault.

The old Claire might have lived like this for years, making excuses for an angry man who enjoyed hurting her, but the new Claire couldn't stay with him another day. She couldn't sit across the dining table from her husband and smile as if nothing was wrong. Every time her nightmare returned, she would know that the person she was so afraid of was only a thin wall away. If she cried out, he would come. He would put his arms around her, like he had done the first time she had had the dream, and he would hold her and tell her he would protect her from anything. And she would have to pretend that she believed him, when in reality he would have to protect her from himself. What if she upset him one day? Now that her father was here, she wasn't alone in the house with Paul. But Tony was bedridden and couldn't come to her rescue. If anything happened, it would be just Claire, frightened and alone, against Paul's terrifying anger.

She said to her father that evening, 'We have to leave. I can't stay here another day.'

'We don't have to leave. This is your house. Your mother bought it for you. But you can ask *him* to leave.'

* * *

Claire expected to feel devastated by her friend's revelations but the truth was, all she felt was fear, not heartbreak, perhaps because Paul was like a stranger to her, who hadn't been particularly kind to her or loving. Their relationship was a sham and now she knew why. Besides, she had already suspected the truth. Ever since her first nightmare, she had a feeling something terrible had

105

happened to her. There was an ominous presence in her dreams, a threat from someone close to her. What Gaby had told her didn't come as a surprise.

In the car on the way to see her doctor one morning, Claire fought nausea and unease at finding herself in such close proximity to her husband. Paul looked relaxed but he didn't fool her now that she knew what he was.

The cars spilled out of the hospital's carpark, stretching down the road like a livid snake, horns hooting. Claire wondered what Paul would do. Whether he would lose his temper, swear under his breath or open his window and shout abuse at someone. But he didn't do any of that. He waited, his hands motionless on the steering wheel, his face betraying no sign of impatience. Even when a woman in a four-wheel drive cut him off, stealing the parking spot he'd been waiting for, he remained calm, as if he didn't have a care in the world.

This zen serenity went against everything Claire believed about Paul. In her imagination, he was a raving maniac who couldn't control himself, someone who derived great pleasure from other people's fear. If Paul and the shadow from her nightmare were one and the same, it wouldn't take much to provoke him. Suddenly, that was all she wanted to do. She needed him to reveal his true face. If he got angry, surely he wouldn't hurt her too much, not here, in a public place? And even if he did, so what? He couldn't possibly make her feel any worse than she already did. What did she have to lose?

'Don't tell the doctor but I've decided not to take my meds anymore,' she said slowly.

'What are you talking about?' Paul took his eyes off the cars in front of him and squinted at Claire. His eyes fixed on her, he looked sinister and unkind.

'They make me feel like a zombie wading through life. I will never get better if I'm medicated out of my mind. I need to think clearly. I need to feel human.'

'Maybe you should discuss it with your doctor first.' Paul turned back towards the road.

This wasn't the reaction Claire was hoping for. 'What do the doctors know?' she exclaimed, her voice trembling. 'They give me pills to make themselves feel better. To pretend they are doing something when they aren't. Am I making any progress?'

'I will not allow—'

'What are you going to do?' She squared her shoulders like a boxer in the ring, prepared to take a punch but also willing to hit as hard as she could. 'Force the pills down my throat?'

'I just don't want you to go against your doctor's orders.'

'I don't care about my doctor's orders. And I don't care what you want. It's not about you.'

Paul didn't look angry. He looked concerned. 'What's gotten into you? I don't understand. I've never seen you like this before.'

'I'm just sick of everyone telling me how to live my life. Tomorrow I'm going to the ballet studio. I want to get back to work. How can I remember who I am if I don't dance?'

'So dance at home. Your doctor . . .'

'Stop telling me about the stupid doctor. I can make my own decisions. I am not a prisoner you can lock up in the house. I will call the police. I will complain.'

'You are not a prisoner. You can go anywhere you like. I just don't think you are ready to go to work, that's all.'

'It's not up to you!' Claire screamed, the volume of her voice startling her and, by the look on his face, taking Paul by surprise.

'It is clear to me that you are not in the best state of mind to make decisions for yourself. Look at yourself. You're hysterical.'

'I'm not hysterical!' she shouted, punching the glove compartment in front of her. It felt good to express her anger, to not care what he thought or did. It chipped away at her despair a little bit. Suddenly she felt more in control. Her car window was open and she could sense strangers' eyes on her. An elderly couple stopped pushing their overloaded trolley and stared straight at her, their mouths open. A woman holding a toddler's hand was adjusting her glasses, as if in anticipation of the latest episode of *EastEnders*. A teenage girl walking a bulldog paused in the middle of the pathway, oblivious to the dog's attempts to pull her towards the nearest bush. Claire felt the colour rush to her cheeks. 'I am not hysterical,' she repeated quieter. 'You have no right to keep me in the house. I'm my own person. I will go to the studio whenever I want to. I will go tonight, just as soon as I *don't* take my meds.'

'Fine. Go to the studio. If you can remember where it is.'

Not a muscle moved on his face, while she was shaking with rage. Maybe it wasn't him who had a problem with anger at all. Maybe it was her. Or maybe he was a good actor. She wanted to hurt him, to dig her nails into his flesh and draw blood, to hit him over the head with a blunt object. Instead, she sat quietly while he parked the car, while on the inside she was screaming.

* * *

In the hospital, Paul insisted on staying in the room with Claire while the doctor checked her progress, making her uncomfortable and tongue-tied. The drive back was just as awkward. Neither of them said more than two words to each other. Back home, she hid first in her father's room and then in her studio. She couldn't bear the thought of running into Paul.

As she stood at the barre and practised pirouettes to take her mind of everything that had happened, she thought she heard a doorbell but didn't come out to see who it was. She needed to be alone.

The more Claire thought about it, the less she understood it. It was hard to imagine anyone living with violence for ten years and not doing anything about it. She felt angry at her husband for putting her through it. But most of all, she felt angry at herself for allowing it to happen. Why hadn't she packed her things the first time he hurt her? Gaby was right, violent men never changed. Everyone knew that. So why did she stay for more? And why didn't her mother sit her down and talk some sense into her? Why didn't she protect her, take her by the hand and force her to leave?

Nina had said Angela didn't like Paul. Now Claire knew why. What kind of mother would be okay with someone hurting her little girl?

The ballet moves, so natural to her, brought the relief she craved, transporting her to another place and another time, the time she couldn't remember but could experience anew. Losing herself in the movement, she didn't hear her phone ringing. Only when it rang the second time, she rushed to answer, her heart beating at the sight of the familiar overseas number.

As soon as she heard her mother's voice, she asked the question that had been keeping her awake all those nights since she had learnt about Paul

'Claire, my darling girl, I'm so sorry you had to find out this way,' exclaimed Angela with tears in her voice. 'I didn't want you to know, so I didn't say anything.'

'You should have told me.'

'It breaks my heart that you would stay with a man like that. So many times I tried to persuade you to leave. I cried, I shouted, I begged. You wouldn't hear of it.'

'But why? I don't understand.'

'Love works in mysterious ways, darling. It makes us blind. It forgives the unforgiveable. You refused to hear what anyone had to say. You said you couldn't live without him.'

Claire found it hard to reconcile the passionate picture of love her mother was painting with her cold and unemotional marriage. 'But I did come to my senses eventually. I found divorce papers in my drawer. Clearly, I wanted a divorce and Paul didn't. When I asked him, he pretended we were happy.'

'Of course he did. Violent men can't live without their victim nearby. They feed off fear and heartbreak. But don't worry. I'm coming home soon. I already booked my ticket. And when I'm back, I will take care of you. You can come and stay with me and Daddy. You can forget all about Paul.'

Claire burst into tears. For a moment she couldn't speak.

'Darling, are you there? Are you okay? Why are you crying?'

'I'm here, Mum. I'm just so happy.'

They spoke about all the things they would do when Claire's mother was home. Angela told her about a shop and a little café at Piccadilly Circus where they used to meet every Sunday for tea. It was a tradition they'd had for many years. 'Their ice cream is to die for. Even the queen shops there. We'll have all the time in the world to catch up. You can tell me everything.'

'No, Mum. *You* can tell me everything. When are you coming back?'

'Next week.'

Claire was trembling when she hung up but this time from excitement. One more week and she would see her mother. Even though she couldn't remember anything about her, in her heart she knew Angela would be her best friend and confidante, just like Tony. Now that she was coming back, nothing else mattered. Not her missing memories, not her nightmares and not even her abusive husband. Her mother was the light that would guide her to safety. When she was back, her family would be complete.

Chapter 10

Claire rushed to her father's room, eager to give him the news, no longer caring if she ran into Paul. She couldn't wait to see Tony's reaction when he heard Angela was coming home. She knew how much he'd missed her. He often had a faraway expression on his face, as if he was a million miles away. Helpless and bedridden, he had found it difficult to adjust. Sometimes it took all of Claire's imagination to conjure a smile on his face, if only for a moment. But now everything would be different. Angela would take care of him. She would take care of both of them and make everything alright.

The door to her father's room was firmly shut, which wasn't unusual. He often asked Claire to close the door if he wanted to sleep or read or be alone. But Claire could hear muffled voices. And something else too, the pitiful sound a cat might make when it was in pain. Had something happened to Tony? Fear like ice paralysed her and it took her a few moments to push the door open.

What seemed like a crowd of people gathered around Tony. Claire saw Paul, Nina, the familiar police officers and a woman in a business suit she didn't recognise. They were all talking at once but fell quiet immediately when Claire walked through the door. Now only the soft whimpering could be heard. With trepidation she realised it was her father sobbing quietly in his bed. His eyes stared into space and his face looked grey. He didn't seem to notice her.

Paul jumped to her side and put his arm around her as if to support her. It was so unexpected that Claire sprung away from him and hit the wall with her elbow, yelping in pain. 'Is everything okay?' she asked.

'You'd better sit down,' said Paul.

'I'm okay, I don't need to sit down,' she said but her legs gave out and she sank into the armchair. 'Will somebody please tell me what's going on?'

The woman in a business suit stepped forward and raised her hand, as if she was at school and needed permission to talk. 'Hi Claire. My name is Kelly. I'm a social worker assigned to your case.'

'My case?' Claire repeated, feeling like she was trapped in one of her nightmares and unable to wake up.

'I'm afraid we have some bad news.'

Claire didn't like the idea of bad news delivered by perfect strangers. Nothing good had ever come from it. She waited but Kelly stopped talking. It was PC Kamenski who told her what had happened. *Your mother . . . body . . . stabbed . . .* Disjointed words that made no sense reached her through the buzzing in her head. It felt surreal, like a bad movie. 'Sorry, what?' she asked dumbly, her mind refusing to understand.

'It's your mother. We have found a body we believe could be her,' Kelly said. The two police officers withered into the background like chastised children, as if this was all their fault.

'No,' whispered Claire. 'No, no, no,' she repeated. Paul put his arms around her and this time she didn't move away. She barely noticed.

'You are in shock. That's understandable. I can recommend a doctor. A psychologist.' Kelly sounded like she was reciting a poem she knew by heart. How many times a week did she deliver the same speech to different families, Claire wondered.

'I'm not in shock. What you've found . . . It's not my mother.' She thought of her mother's upbeat voice on the phone, of excitement of only a moment ago. 'It must be some mistake. I just spoke to her. She said she was coming home. She's going to be here next week.'

The visitors were watching her in silence. Paul squeezed her shoulder. 'My wife has been through a lot. Her memory is affected. Sometimes she gets confused.'

'I'm not confused,' cried Claire but by the look on their faces she knew they were not taking her seriously.

'Did Angela have any enemies? Did anyone hate her enough to . . .' PC Stanley stammered, glanced at Claire, shaking in Paul's arms, at Tony, crying on his bed, and stopped talking.

'She was the sweetest person in the world. Who could hate her? Who would do this?' Tony sounded like a wounded animal, barely able to produce croaky sounds through his constricted throat.

'It could be a stranger. An intruder. There was no sign of forced entry in the house but maybe she opened the door to someone.'

'You found her in the house?' asked Claire, her heart in her throat, thinking of her recent trip to her parents' place when she had peered through the curtains, trying to catch a glimpse of what was inside.

'My Angela, my love. My beautiful angel,' cried Tony.

'We need someone to identify the body,' PC Kamenski said uncertainly.

'I can do it,' said Paul. Claire watched him carefully for any sign of emotion but his face remained expressionless.

'No, it should be me,' said Tony. 'I'm her husband.' He broke down again, collapsing on the pillows.

'I want to be there too,' said Claire.

'Absolutely not,' exclaimed Paul and Tony together.

'I know it's not her,' said Claire. 'It can't be her.'

But no one was listening to her. When the police officers finally left and it was just Claire and Tony in the room, he took her hand and lay still and silent, his eyes unfocused.

'Dad, it's not her. It can't be her. I just spoke to her,' said Claire, squeezing his fingers hard to make sure he was listening.

He didn't seem to hear her. 'I remember the day we met. It was the happiest day of my life.' As if in a trance, Tony kept talking. When he met Angela, he was reversing in his truck without looking. He was in a rush and distracted, as always running late, and suddenly he heard a soft whimper. Did he just hit someone? Someone's pet perhaps? Shaking, he jumped out of the truck and came face to face with a young girl, small like a bird, with the most beautiful face he'd ever seen. Her eyes like saucers, she was standing in the middle of the road. Dressed in a yellow dress, her hair in pigtails, she made him think of sunflower fields and bright summer days. She looked about 15. Thankfully, he hadn't run her over but he had come close and she was scared. He felt like the most despicable human being. Suddenly he wanted to take her in his arms and cover her breathtaking face with kisses. And never ever hurt her again.

When he dropped her off at her parents' place, he didn't want to say goodbye. He wanted to take her out for dinner, to make up for what had happened, wanted to hold her and make her smile. She reminded him of his mother – delicate, blonde, blue eyes wide and vulnerable.

She'd never reproached him for almost running her over. In all the years they'd been married, she'd never reproached him for anything. She loved him just like his mother had loved him – unconditionally.

They started dating and Tony treated his girl like a queen. He couldn't afford expensive presents but he gave her all his time, which was enough for her. Before they had Claire, while still in the spring of their love, Angela and Tony took up ballroom dancing. They weren't particularly good at it. Nor were they serious about it. But it was something they had enjoyed, something they had shared as a couple. Every Friday evening they would head to the local church hall dressed in their dancing best. Tony could still see her, he said to Claire, twirling in front of him, laughing and giddy, her skirt like a parachute around her small hips, her hair wild and eyes happy. He loved the feel of her in his arms, the way she fit in his embrace, like she was meant just for him, like he was meant just for her. They learnt the foxtrot and waltz and the elaborate tango. The samba was designed to torture him as he tried hard not to step on her feet, but what a sensual dance it was! It was the happiest time of his life. If only he had known it then, he would have cherished every moment, every embrace and every smile.

Faster and faster Tony spoke, like he was struggling with a particularly challenging tongue twister, eager to share his happiest moments with Claire. His face was pale, his lips trembling. He would have looked unemotional if it wasn't for the tears streaming down his cheeks. These silent tears affected Claire more than sobbing and lamenting would have done. There was a raw desperation in them, a quiet despair.

She could swear she had forgotten how to breathe as she listened to her father. Perched on the edge of his bed, she was quiet like a mouse, too afraid to move in case he stopped talking. Wiping her own tears away, she reached for his hand and squeezed hard, letting him know she was there for him.

'Don't worry, Dad. The woman the police have found . . . it's not her. I know that for a fact.'

'They said she was stabbed. That she let someone into the house and this person stabbed her . . .' His voice broke. 'And now she's gone. My poor love. My darling Angela. How scared she must have been. If only I'd been there. It's all my fault. I should have been there.'

'Dad, listen to me.'

Gently Claire shook his hand until he looked at her. He fell quiet, and for a moment she didn't speak. She held him like she would hold an innocent child she loved more than anything in the world, rocking him and herself, lulling them both away from the fear, towards the light. But he saw no light, she knew it by the way his face was twisted in pain. 'It can't possibly be her,' said Claire emphatically, trying to convince herself as much as him.

'Who then?'

'I don't know. I don't understand what's happening. But I just spoke to Mum. She's coming home. She already booked her ticket.'

'She did?' He blinked, his eyes glistening.

'She'll be here next week.'

'She called you? When?'

'A moment ago. Aunt Judy is better. Mum is on her way.'

'Thank God,' whispered Tony. 'It's a miracle. It's a God's miracle.' He cried in her arms, his lips moving in silent prayer. 'I will do anything. Anything at all to hold her in my arms again. I don't care if I never walk again, as long as she's with us.'

'This time next week, she will be.'

Claire thought of her mother and felt for her, trying to imagine her as a young girl, carefree and in love. In her mind, she saw her twirling in her yellow summer dress with flowers in her hair, her arms around the man she loved. How beautiful she was and how alive. Soon they would be reunited and this nightmare would be behind them.

* * *

When Tony and Paul were whisked away in a police car to view the body, Claire sat by the window, waiting for them to return, hoping for good news but fearing the bad. Who was this woman found stabbed at her parents' house? A friend, perhaps, or a relative. Someone who happened to be in the wrong place at the wrong time. Claire felt terrible for her and her loved ones. The crime in London was out of control. No one was safe anymore. But she wasn't going to think about it now. All she could think about was Angela.

Her mother was alive. It wasn't her the police had found at the house and that was all that mattered. When she was back, Claire would find all the answers she so desperately searched for. All the jigsaw puzzle pieces of her life would finally fall into place. And who knew, maybe seeing Angela was exactly what she needed to start healing. The doctor said it would take a powerful trigger to unlock her hidden memories. What could be more powerful than finally seeing the woman who gave birth to her?

Claire couldn't wait to lay her eyes on Angela. In her mind she constructed conversations and experiences the two of them would share, meals they would have together, shops and museums they would visit. She couldn't wait.

And then she saw the car pull up. Paul helped her father out and into his wheelchair. Claire tried to read the expression on their faces but couldn't quite see. She ran downstairs and flung the door open.

'How did it . . .' she started saying and stopped. The look on her father's face shocked her into silence.

Tony was slumped in his wheelchair, lifeless and glum. Only his lips were moving. 'It's her. It's her,' he repeated again and again like an incantation. Paul stood behind him, looking years older with his shoulders stooped and his eyes dark.

Claire would never forget her father's face as he whispered to himself like a man possessed. She would never forget how the light fell on his withered frame, how his fingers trembled. But if someone asked her how she had spent the next twenty-four hours, she wouldn't be able to say. She waded through darkness, without aim and without hope. She walked from room to room . . . looking for what? She didn't know. She sat with her father, who couldn't talk or sleep or eat. She knew how he felt. She couldn't do any of those things either. All she could do was hold him and weep.

'He's in shock. The police told us it happened on the same day as the accident. Your father blames himself for not being there when it happened. For not being there to protect her,' said Paul, administering a strong sedative. Finally, Tony slept.

'Can I have some of that?' asked Claire. She wanted not to feel, not to think, not to long for the impossible.

'She's gone,' cried Tony when he woke up. 'She's gone.'

How was it that she couldn't live without someone she couldn't even remember? And yet, Claire felt like all the sunshine in her life was forever gone. Only the clouds remained. She would never know Angela. She would never meet her, hold her in her arms, touch her forehead with her lips. Never, what a cruel word it was. What an unforgiving, unfathomable word.

Through waves of grief, Claire wondered who had been calling her all this time pretending to be her mother if Angela was gone. Was it someone's idea of a sick joke? Or was it her imagination, giving her what she wanted? Did she imagine her phone ringing, her mother's soothing voice talking to her? Was it nothing but a hallucination, her mind playing tricks on her?

Hurting and afraid, Claire didn't want to be alone. She could no longer talk to Tony, who didn't seem to notice anything around him and spent his days staring into space. Two days after the terrible news, Gaby came to see Claire, bringing a single white rose. 'White, for hope,' she said.

'Hope for what?' muttered Claire but took the rose and placed it next to her bed, so it would be the first thing she saw in the morning and the last thing at night.

The good friend that she was, in the days that followed Gaby sat through countless reruns of *Gone With the Wind*, holding Claire's hand as she sobbed. Then one day, a week after – that was how her life was divided now, before and after she thought she had a mother – Gaby was busy and Claire found herself alone. She hid in a small study at the back of the house, photos of her mother in her lap. But she couldn't look at Angela's face. Every glimpse was like a knife in her heart. So she watched as a pale sliver of light illuminated the wall and the grey flowers came to life, forever in bloom on the old wallpaper that was frayed and torn in places. This room was at odds with the rest of the house and looked out of date and old-fashioned. Loose strips of wallpaper drooped from the ceiling like spooky Halloween decorations. Seventy-eight flowers from left to right, and forty-seven from top to bottom, Claire counted.

Hours passed, the sun faded, and still Claire played loves-me-loves-me-not with the ghost paper garden on the wall, when she realised her phone was ringing. The overseas number she knew by heart appeared on the screen.

'Hello,' said Claire in a voice she didn't recognise.

'Darling Claire, it's Mum.'

Claire threw the phone down so hard, it bounced off the floor and landed in the corner. Petrified, she stared at it. 'Claire, are you there? I can't hear you.' And that was when Claire screamed. Her screams drowned out the soft voice coming from her phone. But when she paused to take a breath, she could still hear it. 'Darling, is everything okay?'

Groaning, Claire covered the phone with a cushion and when that wasn't enough and the phone continued talking, she picked it up and hurled it hard out the window. The sound of the broken glass was like an explosion in the room, so loud, Claire thought her head was going to explode. She wrapped her arms around her stomach, bent over as if in great pain, and howled.

Nina rushed into the room, followed by Paul. Their voices were piercing, invading her senses like thoughtless knives. Somewhere on the other side of the house her father was calling out in alarm. All she wanted was silence but they wouldn't give it to her. She wanted peace but they grabbed her hands and shook her. She fought against them. As hard as she could she struggled but she wasn't strong enough. Together, they managed to lift her and carry her to bed. Through her screams she heard snippets of conversation. 'A strong sedative . . . A psychotic episode . . . Needs rest.'

Then she felt an injection, like a bee sting in her arm. Finally, everything went quiet.

Chapter 11

Claire didn't know how long she had spent in a heavily sedated mist. It could have been an hour or a week or a month. Day after miserable day she felt herself falling into a dreamless hole from which there was no escape. And then one night, her nightmare was back, hovering over her like a terrifying ghost. The minute she closed her eyes, the dream was there, ready to pounce. She didn't feel safe anymore, not under her blankets, not at night, not during the day. She was pursued, hunted, under siege. In her dream, she would see herself running away from an unknown danger, her heart thumping. Then a sudden fall, crashing through the air, branches hitting her face. She would wake up abruptly, gasping for air. When she was awake, she would scream. A piercing scream of hopelessness, stifled by a pillow.

When she felt strong enough to walk, Claire forced herself to get dressed and made her way downstairs. Nina was there, not so much cleaning as guarding the front door, judging by the speed with which she blocked Claire's way. 'You can't leave, Miss Claire.'

'And why not?'

'Mr Paul say you are too weak. You have psychotic episode. You stay in bed.'

'Mr Paul is not my jailer, Nina. He can't keep me here against my will.'

'He tell me not to let you out of sight.'

'That's fine. You can come with me if you like. But I'm not staying here.'

Claire stepped outside into the world that went on as before, as if nothing had happened, as if life hadn't been turned upside down once and for all. The cars still moved past and the traffic lights changed. Just like always. As if her mother getting killed wasn't enough to alter the universe like it had altered Claire's whole existence.

As she walked down the deserted street, she looked at the cobalt of the skies and tried to make sense of her life. There wasn't a soul around because a storm was coming. The gale began, the dust twirling in a desperate tango, the first drops of rain appeared, and suddenly Claire felt a little better. It wasn't just her – the skies themselves were about to open up in floods of tears. A dark cloud hung over London and over Claire as she walked hunched over in the rain. It was appropriate, really – as if the whole world was mourning Angela. There was nothing but the noise of the wind and the noise of thoughts rustling through her head.

Under the beating rain she ran, exposed and defenceless. She wished she had remembered to take an umbrella. With Nina in pursuit, Claire walked into Matilda's practice and rang the bell. When there was no answer, she rang again and again, finally hurling the bell to the floor and shouting, 'Please, help! Is anybody here? I need help!'

Matilda appeared, wide-eyed. 'Claire! Is everything okay?'

'I need to talk to you.'

'Do we have an appointment today?'

'It's an emergency.'

'I am with another patient right now. Would you mind waiting?'

'No, please. You don't understand . . .'

121

There must have been something wild in her face because Matilda nodded and said, 'Give me a minute. Please, take a seat.'

When she was gone, Claire didn't take a seat but paced like a caged lion, back and forth and back again around the spacious waiting room, past Nina, who was relaxing with a magazine in her hands. Claire wanted to scream. She wanted to grab Nina's magazine and tear it to pieces. How long had it been? According to the clock above her head, only a few minutes but that was impossible. The clock was lying like everyone in her life was lying.

Finally, Matilda emerged and motioned for her to come in. Nina got up, ready to follow. 'Please, excuse us,' said Matilda to Nina. 'This is a therapist's office. Only patients past this point.'

By Nina's face Claire could see she was about to argue but Matilda's voice didn't allow for arguments. Claire felt relieved and grateful to the therapist. The last thing she needed was Paul's spy in the room with her when she bared her heart and soul.

In the comforting familiarity of Matilda's room, Claire collapsed into a chair. She clasped her hands to stop them from shaking but it didn't help. All of her was shaking, not just her hands. Silent tears ran down her face.

It took a while for her to compose herself enough to speak. In that time, Matilda handed her a tissue, made a cup of tea and held her hand.

'I can't,' repeated Claire. 'I can't! I don't know what to do. I can't do this anymore.'

'Take a deep breath and tell me what happened.'

'I think it's my meds. They make me crazy. I'm hallucinating. Hearing voices. I need to stop taking them.' Her words made no sense even to herself.

'You are hearing voices?'

'I'm getting phone calls from someone I can't possibly be getting phone calls from. I had a breakdown. Paul calls it a psychotic episode.'

'Paul is not a psychiatrist, or is he?'

'No, he's not. But he controls my meds. He's the one who gave me my new prescription. Is he doing this to me?'

'Why don't you start from the beginning?'

Incoherently at first, getting lost in words and emotions, breaking into sobs, Claire did her best to tell her therapist everything. Matilda listened patiently. She sat very still, as if Claire was a bird that could be frightened by a sudden movement. Her eyes were kind and compassionate.

'My mother was killed on the same day as the accident. The police told us.' Was it a coincidence? Or were the two seemingly unrelated events connected somehow? 'We are both dead in a way, my mum and I,' Claire concluded. 'I am still here but I wouldn't call this living. I feel so empty inside. Hollow. I can't function. I feel overwhelmed and lost.'

'But you *do* feel something. That makes you alive. Feeling is living.'

'I don't sleep. I'm scared that the minute I close my eyes, the nightmare will come back. And it usually does. I'm scared that the minute I open my eyes, my phone will ring and my mother will speak to me, as if everything that happened wasn't real but a figment of my imagination. Am I imagining the phone calls? If it's a hallucination, then why does it feel so real? Or is it normal, for the person hallucinating to think what they are seeing or hearing is real?'

'I don't believe you can hallucinate a phone call. That's not how hallucinations work.'

'I don't trust myself anymore. How do I know you are real? How do I know I'm here and not locked in an institution somewhere?'

'Believe me, I'm real.'

'I feel like I'm living someone else's life. I don't even know what my life should be. Any moment I expect to wake up, like this, too, is a nightmare. I don't know who I am.'

'Not many people do, not really. The hardest thing in life is to know yourself. To see yourself for what you are. Not who you are. What you are. Can you see the difference?'

'I don't.'

'You might know who you are. You are Paul's wife. Tony and Angela's daughter. A successful ballerina. But what makes you *you*? That's what you need to find out.'

'How do I do that?'

'Answer one question for me. What do you believe in?'

For a moment Claire thought about it. 'I believe in my father. He's always been there for me. I believe I had a life before the accident. I believe I was happy once. I'd like to be happy again.'

'That's a good start.'

'I feel like I'm a vase that's been dropped on the floor and shattered into a thousand little pieces. Can a broken vase ever be put together?'

'You need to rebuild your life, Claire. With time, bit by bit, you need to rebuild yourself.'

'How do I do that?'

'Only you can answer this question.'

'What is happening to me? Am I losing my mind?'

Matilda sat up straight, her eyes boring into Claire. 'I don't think you are losing your mind. I don't think you are hallucinating or hearing voices. But it seems someone is deliberately trying to make you believe that you are.'

Part II

Chapter 12

Claire spent her days in bed, not sleeping but not quite awake either. On the rare occasions she managed to get up, she felt like she was wading through water, her brain hazy and unresponsive, even though she had stopped taking her medication. Every evening she would place the little pills in her mouth while Paul was watching, as ever the zealous jailer, but as soon as his back was turned, she would rush to the bathroom and spit the pills out into the sink. And yet, she wasn't feeling any better. What if Paul knew what she was doing and had found a different way to drug her? It would be so easy. All he had to do was ask Nina to add something to Claire's food.

Or was she being paranoid? Was it just her grief and lack of sleep that made her unable to concentrate on anything other than the dark thoughts swirling around her head? Day after miserable day, she would hover around her bedroom like a ghost, not knowing where to turn. If only she could talk to someone. She craved her mother's voice over the phone. Logically she understood it couldn't have been Angela calling her all this time. But in her heart she wanted to believe differently, and did. She desperately needed something to remind her of her mother, to paint a picture of who she was and what she was like. More than anything she wanted to feel close to her, so she spent her sleepless nights turning the house upside down, looking for something that had once belonged to Angela.

And then she found it. Her mother's Bible was sitting on the bookshelf next to *Gone With the Wind* and *War and Peace*, hiding in plain sight. For the first time that she could remember, she felt a glimmer of joy. Her fingertips trembling, she opened the holy book as if it contained a piece of her mother's soul.

The Bible was old and heavy, all brown leather and golden writing. Claire wanted to press her face to the cover, to feel its smooth surface with her lips, to kiss it like she would kiss her mother's forehead. Something undecipherable was scribbled on the cover page. She had never seen her mother's handwriting before. It took her a good ten minutes to make sense of the note, letter by letter, word by word.

You have heard that it was said, An eye for an eye and a tooth for a tooth. But I say to you, Do not resist the one who is evil. But if anyone slaps you on the right cheek, turn to him the other also.

Claire wondered what her mother was trying to tell her by choosing these particular words from Matthew for the cover page of her Bible.

Claire closed her eyes and repeated the words, like a prayer, except she wasn't praying for her soul or guidance. She was praying to forget.

Suddenly, while her eyes were closed, her fingers felt something hidden between the pages. The edges felt rough to the touch and the paper was thick and glossy. It contrasted sharply with the wafer-thin pages of the Bible and this contrast jolted Claire out of her reverie and into reality. She opened her eyes to find herself holding a folded photograph. Moving closer to the circle of light from her bedside table, she stared at her mother's face, decades younger, perhaps Claire's age. Angela's hair was like straw, yellow and free and hippy-long. Her face was in profile and her arms were around someone, hugging them close. Claire unfolded the photograph, expecting to see her father. But it wasn't him. Another Angela looked back at her, smiling.

Claire blinked once, twice. Was she imagining it? No, it was right there, as real as the buses driving past or the dogs barking outside – the image of two women, two identical Angelas. *Tegan and Angela 1987,* she read on the back of the photograph. Feeling faint, sick to her stomach with a dark foreboding of some kind, Claire hid the photo in the back pocket of her trousers. At dinner, she wanted to ask her father about the mysterious Tegan. But he seemed so sad, his eyes shrouded in tears, so she didn't say anything. When she kissed him good-night, she gave him her mother's Bible and his face lit up with a rare smile.

The next morning, as she walked in with an omelette and an orange juice, he was sitting up in bed, his reading glasses on. It was a surprising change from the last few weeks when he did nothing but stare into space.

'What are you reading?' asked Claire, placing the tray on the table next to his bed.

He nodded in the direction of two books in his lap. 'Voltaire and the Bible. You might think they contradict each other. But it's not quite the case.'

She had no idea what he was talking about but it was nice to see him showing an interest in something. 'What do you mean?' she asked, getting comfortable in her armchair.

'Many people believe Voltaire was anti-God but that's not exactly true. Voltaire was a deist. He preached the natural religion and believed God has built the universe and then distanced Himself, giving man free will to do as he pleases. It is up to man to observe the moral laws, and in due course God will reward the good deeds and punish the bad.'

'You are right. That doesn't sound like someone who didn't believe in God. Why do people think otherwise?'

'Voltaire didn't believe in Christianity. He believed God was the Father of all men, not just Christians. Therefore, Christianity was not the true religion. He saw it as full of superstition and blasphemy. Almost everything that goes beyond the adoration of the Supreme Being and of submitting one's heart to His external orders is superstition according to Voltaire.'

'Like going to church?'

'Exactly.'

She picked up the book and looked through the table of contents. 'There are other philosophers here too. Didier . . .'

Tony wrinkled his nose in disapproval. 'Now, Didier does believe there is no God.'

'How can there be no God? Look at all the beauty around you.'

Tony shrugged. 'Some might find Didier's view convenient. If there is no God, imagine how liberating that would be? No God means no sin, no conscience, no punishment and no judgement. And most importantly, no remorse. But I don't agree with him,' he said, his hand on the Bible. 'As human beings, we always feel remorse. That's our greatest weakness. Dostoevsky was right. The true punishment is not what society imposes on you. It's not the prison or community service or even the death sentence. The true punishment is what's inside us. The remorse we feel. It's always there. It never goes away. There is no escape from it.'

'If God does exist . . .' She hesitated. 'How can He allow such horrible things to happen?' Her chest thumped with pain at the thought of her mother, stabbed in her own house, gone before her time. The wounds were still so fresh. Would there be a time when she could go a minute without her heart breaking over Angela?

'God doesn't make horrible things happen. People make horrible things happen. Free will, remember?'

He tucked into his omelette and she sat still, while her hand was in her pocket folding and unfolding the photograph she had found inside the Bible.

'Why does it seem like you are a million miles away? What's on your mind, Teddy Bear?' asked Tony.

She might as well go ahead and ask the question that was tormenting her. 'Did Mum have a sister?'

'No.' His answer came out brisk and abrupt, like an axe falling on a piece of wood. What was that expression on his face? He didn't ask why she was bringing it up, nor did he comment any further. His *no* was like a full-stop at the end of a conversation.

Claire didn't say a word as she handed him the photograph and he didn't say a word as he took it. In silence she studied him, while he studied the women in the picture, his face white as if he was seeing ghosts. Finally, he placed the photograph on the bed and pushed it as far away from him as possible until it fell on the floor and remained there, face down. Only then did he say, 'Where did you find that?'

Claire didn't want his questions. What she needed was answers. 'Who's Tegan, Dad?'

There was a pause that lasted a long time. Finally, he said, 'Tegan is your mother's twin sister.'

'But I just asked you if she had a sister. You said no.' She watched him through narrowed eyes.

'Tegan has always been jealous of your mother and me. We haven't spoken to her in ten years.'

'So you lied to me?'

'For your own good. I don't want you to go looking for her.' His eyes filled with loathing. For Tegan? Claire hadn't seen this side of her father before. She hadn't seen anything from him but kindness and affection. It took her by surprise, how unnatural it felt. 'Your mother's sister betrayed us,' he added. 'She tried to break up our family. I don't want you to mention her again.'

He looked like a different man, bitter and angry. This man was a stranger. She didn't know him. 'What did she do?'

'That's between your mother and Tegan. It's nothing to do with us.'

'You mean, with me? You mean, it's nothing to do with me?' When he didn't reply, his face impassive and cold, she asked, 'Where does she live?'

'Does it matter?'

'I'd like to talk to her. I didn't know I had family other than you and Mum.' She fell quiet as she remembered that her mum was gone and all she had now was him.

'Didn't I just tell you to stay away from her?'

'I'm not ten, Dad. I can make my own decisions.'

'I don't want her poisoning you with her lies. Besides, I don't know where she lives. She's moved. We've lost touch. It's probably for the best.'

There were so many questions she wanted to ask. But she knew he wouldn't tell her anything, by the way he turned his head away, by the way his eyes wouldn't meet hers. Suddenly he seemed closed off like a book long read and forgotten about.

Chapter 13

Night after sleepless night, Claire lay in her bed and longed for Angela and wondered about Tegan. One thought above others tormented her. Her mother didn't die of natural causes. What happened was not an accident. It was an act of evil that deprived Claire of her mother. Because of it, she would never know her and would never be able to rebuild the relationship they had once had.

There was only one person in her life who was capable of evil.

Nina had told Claire she had often seen Paul and Angela arguing. What if one day he'd had enough? What if Angela had threatened him and paid with her life? Paul couldn't control his temper. Had he lost it with Angela, with fatal consequences?

One night, when everyone was in bed, Claire locked herself in the bathroom and searched through her text messages. Thank God her phone had been salvaged after its fall through the window and into the flower bed. Scrolling to the date of the murder, which according to the police also happened to be the date of the accident, she read her frantic messages to Paul.

Where are you? Why aren't you picking up?

And even more desperate:

Please answer your phone. Something happened. I need help.

And one more:

Please call me back before it's too late.

'Before it's too late'. What did that mean? Bewildered, Claire checked her call history. There were ten unanswered calls to Paul that day.

According to Gaby, Paul and Claire's relationship had been cold and distant. Before the accident, they were barely talking. The divorce papers Claire had found in her room confirmed that. And yet, here she was, calling her husband not once but ten times and bombarding him with panicked messages. Claire looked at other dates in her phone and there were hardly any calls or messages to Paul. What had happened on the day of the accident to make her turn to her soon-to-be-ex-husband for help? It had to be something big to make her forget their differences. Something bigger than an imminent divorce and their growing animosity.

And even more importantly, where was Paul on the day her mother had been murdered? Why wasn't he picking up his phone?

As soon as Paul left for work, Claire shared her suspicions with her father.

'You have to tell the police,' Tony said. Although his face looked grim, his eyes burned with a passion she had never seen before.

As she sat on the terrace, watching the rain pounding the trees outside, she followed the progress of a lone passer-by whose umbrella had been wrestled from him by the wind, barely noticing that she, too, was soaked through and shaking from the cold. She tried to summon the courage to call the police. What if she was wrong? Paul was controlling, with a history of abuse, but it didn't mean he was capable of murder. What if he got arrested for a crime he didn't commit? If Paul was punished for something he didn't do, Claire would have to live with it for the rest of her life, while the real murderer walked free.

Finally, she decided the police had to have all the facts. It was their job to make sense of them and draw their own conclusions. If she didn't tell them the truth, how would they catch the killer? In her handbag she found the card PC Kamenski had given her at the hospital. As she was about to call, the doorbell rang.

Through a narrow gap in the door she could see the sombre faces of PC Kamenski and PC Stanley. They looked like they had come to deliver more terrible news. Claire blinked, stunned. She glanced at the card in her hand, wondering if she had summoned the officers by merely thinking about them. After a few seconds of silence she opened the door wider and invited them inside.

When they were seated on the couch, PC Stanley said, 'We have a few questions to ask you if you don't mind.'

Claire fidgeted with the card in her hand. 'I was just about to call you. I have something to tell you.'

'You go first.' PC Kamenski took out her notepad. Claire wondered how many of those she went through every month. She glanced at the clock, hoping Paul wouldn't come home from work and surprise her as she was about to give him up to the police. But it was barely four o'clock. She had plenty of time.

She told them about her suspicions and showed them the messages. As she was talking, she expected their eyes to light up with a sudden realisation. Instead, they listened to Claire mutely.

When she finished, PC Stanley said, 'Thank you for sharing this with us. It couldn't have been easy. But I assure you, your husband didn't kill your mother.'

That was not the reaction Claire had been expecting. 'How do you know? He wasn't answering his phone. And they hated each other. My housekeeper told me they were always arguing.' Her voice quivered as she tried to make them understand. But judging by their faces, they were not taking her seriously.

'Do you *want* your husband to be the killer?' asked PC Kamenski and her eyes narrowed with curiosity. Suddenly Claire felt like she was under a microscope.

'Of course not. But I want the truth to come out. Whoever did it . . . I want him to be punished.'

'Your husband has an alibi for the day of the murder,' said PC Stanley.

'Alibis can be faked.'

'We don't have any reason to believe that could be the case.'

'Can you tell me what his alibi is?'

'We are not at liberty to disclose that,' said PC Stanley. Was it her imagination or were the officers looking at her with pity?

'But if he didn't kill my mother, who did?'

'That's what we are trying to establish.' PC Kamenski looked inside her notebook. 'Does the name Nathaniel mean anything to you?'

Nathaniel. Claire pondered it, searching her mind for the name she felt she had never heard before. 'I don't think so,' she said finally.

'You've never heard of your brother, Nate Wright?'

Claire thought she misheard. Did the woman just say, her *brother*? 'That's impossible. I'm an only child.'

'I'm afraid that's not entirely correct. You had a brother.'

'Had? What happened to him?' When they didn't reply, she asked, 'Where is my brother now?' The police officers exchanged a silent glance. 'Please, tell me,' Claire begged. As always, she was praying for answers and not getting any.

PC Kamenski coughed, as if there was a fish bone stuck in her throat. 'Can you tell us anything about your years in Windsor?'

'My years in Windsor?'

'You don't remember the place where you grew up?' asked PC Stanley.

'I grew up in London.'

'You lived in Windsor until you were 16 and then you moved abruptly. Any idea why?'

Claire shook her head.

'The next question is very important and we need you to answer truthfully. Where were you on the day your mother was murdered?'

'I was in the car. You told me so yourself.'

'Where were you prior to the accident?'

'I don't remember.' Claire felt tears perilously close and clasped her fists to fight them off.

'A neighbour saw you arrive at your parents' house around the time the murder took place,' said PC Stanley. Both of them were watching her closely as if searching her face for clues.

Clues or guilt? She shuddered. 'That can't be true.'

'If it's not true, can you please tell us where you were? Is there someone who can confirm your whereabouts?'

Claire felt like screaming at the top of her lungs. Instead, she whispered, barely audible, 'I don't know. I can't remember.'

'Are you familiar with the terms of your mother's will? Did you stand to inherit any part of her fortune?'

'I don't know. I don't remember.'

'Your memory loss is very convenient,' remarked PC Kamenski, narrowing her eyes on Claire. 'Perhaps you could try harder?'

Claire grabbed the sofa to steady herself. 'Am I a suspect?'

'We are not at liberty to discuss that,' said PC Stanley. But from the look in his eyes she knew that the answer was yes. 'Can we speak to your father, please?'

'He's sleeping right now.' Claire said, hoping they would go away. Her father needed his rest. He didn't need the police poking their noses into his business, asking pointless questions. Didn't they have real criminals to catch? 'He hasn't been well lately.'

If PC Kamenski understood what Claire was hinting at, she didn't let on. 'It's important that we speak to him. We won't take too much of his time. Would you mind waking him up for us?'

Claire wanted to tell them that she would in fact mind, that her father was a sick old man who didn't want to be disturbed. But she knew there was no point. They had a determined look about them. She took them to Tony's room and left them alone with him. More than anything she wanted to know what they were going to talk about. But the door shut firmly behind them and she didn't want Nina to catch her eavesdropping.

Claire made herself a strong cup of tea and sat at the dining table, watching it go cold. In the kitchen, Nina was banging pots. Claire could smell cakes baking in the oven.

A possibility occurred to her, a terrifying possibility she had never considered. What if it *was* her? It seemed impossible and yet . . . how well did she know herself? What did she know about her relationship with her mother? All she had were questions that no one could answer – not her husband, who tried to avoid her as much as possible, not Angela, who was gone, and not her father, who tried to protect her from everything and everyone around. She had no one to turn to, no one to tell her what she was thinking was ludicrous.

But what if it wasn't ludicrous?

And if by some cruel twist of fate she did have something to do with her mother's murder, what did the phone calls mean? Did someone know what she'd done and tried to manipulate her in this sick way? Was it an attempt at blackmail or intimidation? Then why were there no demands, no accusations? Why pretend to be her mother?

She sat trembling and staring until the police officers finally left half an hour later.

'What did they say?' she asked her father. 'Did they ask about me?'

Tony's hands were on Angela's Bible. His eyes were on Claire. 'No, darling. They asked many questions about Paul and his relationship with your mother. You did the right thing telling them the truth.'

'But they didn't believe me. They said he's no longer a suspect. That he has an alibi.'

'You misunderstood. They still suspect him.' He took her hand in his, pulling it to his chest. 'Have you thought any more about asking him to leave?'

'For the last few weeks I've thought of nothing else.'

'What are you waiting for? Once he's gone, we can be the perfect family. Just you and I.'

But not Mum, Claire thought with sadness.

She wanted to ask him other things, about Nate and Windsor and what the police meant when they said she *had* a brother. But Tony looked tired and gaunt, like he had aged ten years in one day. She didn't want to burden him with more questions.

Chapter 14

Claire stood in front of the mirror, studying herself as if she didn't know who she was, like she had once done at the hospital. Was it her imagination or was there something sinister and unkind in the way she pursed her lips, in the way her eyes stared? She knew for a fact she was capable of misleading those close to her. After all, she had never told anyone about her mysterious brother. She had lied about growing up in London. What other dark secrets was she hiding? Were the police right to suspect her?

They said she had been at her parents' house at the time of the murder. Even if she hadn't been involved, she must have seen the person who was. Had she witnessed what happened to her mother? The thought filled her with black, blinding terror. Was that what her brain was trying to protect her from by leaving her mind blank and bare of pain but also of memories?

She needed to learn what happened that day and soon, before the police arrested her for her mother's murder. No matter how traumatic the memory, she wanted it back. Nothing could be worse than this debilitating uncertainty.

Among thousands of photographs in her albums, Claire searched for the other Angela, the mysterious woman who looked identical to her mother. Would Claire even be able to tell them apart? How did she know which sister she was looking at? She spent hours staring at her mother's face, going through snapshots taken at birthdays, weddings, barbecues and family vacations. Soon, her eyes were aching and she couldn't stop crying. The photographs became a blur and she could no longer see.

As she was drifting off to sleep that night, a sudden thought made her sit up in bed. What if it had been Tegan all along? What if she had been calling Claire, pretending to be Angela? Tony had told her Tegan had held a grudge against Angela for many years. But why would she do something like that? What did she hope to gain? Claire felt like she was missing a piece of the puzzle.

If she had indeed grown up in Windsor, was it possible her aunt had lived there too? Was she still living there?

'Nina, how far is Windsor?' she asked over breakfast one day.

'I don't know, Miss Claire.'

'I don't think it's far. Would you mind driving me?'

'You want me to go to Windsor, Miss? But these tiles won't clean themselves and the fridge is a mess.'

Claire glanced at the spotless house. Not a thing was out of place. Everything sparkled as if a thousand elves had stayed up all night scrubbing and polishing. 'The tiles are clean enough. And the fridge can wait.'

'Wait for what, Miss Claire?'

'Come on, it's too beautiful outside to stay in. We'll have a picnic. Just the two of us. And why don't you call me Claire?'

'You don't pay me for picnics,' grumbled Nina as she prepared a basket of fruit for the two of them to share.

The picnic was the last thing on Claire's mind as she glanced out the car window at the English countryside – the emerald hills, the topaz skies, pure and unblemished, and all she could think of was Nathaniel and Angela's twin sister. 'Let's not tell Paul about this,' she said. 'It will be our secret. You know how he worries.' Claire shuddered at the thought of Paul finding out about their trip. What if he lost his temper? What if he locked her in the house and refused to let her out?

'Too many secrets from Mr Paul, Miss. No good for relationship,' said Nina, her eyes steady on the road ahead as she coasted towards their destination ten miles below the speed limit.

The green digits on the dashboard showed midday. At this rate, Paul would come home before them and find Claire gone. 'Does your car go any faster? Or we won't get there till tomorrow.'

'But we'll get there in one piece,' replied Nina, slowing down further. 'And that's all that matters.'

Claire tried to still her trembling hands, drumming the seconds away on her knees. But her breath came out in puffs and her throat felt tight, as if her childhood memories were waiting behind the next bend of the road and she was too afraid to face them.

'Nina, have I ever mentioned anyone called Nate?'

'No, Miss Claire.'

'Have I ever said anything about my brother?'

'You have a brother?'

'Did I ever talk about my childhood?'

'The only thing I heard you say on phone once was how lucky you were to live so close to one of the best schools in London growing up.'

She hadn't just lied to Paul. She had lied to everyone. But why? 'Have you ever seen Paul and I argue?'

If Nina was surprised by the barrage of questions unleashed on her, she didn't show it. 'Never, Miss Claire. At first, you were most loved up couple I ever see. Then little by little you stop talking.'

'Stopped talking? What do you mean?'

'I think you drift apart.'

'So you've never seen Paul be violent or angry towards me?'

'Mr Paul! Of course not. He most gentle person in the world. He not hurt a fly.'

Claire wondered how much Paul was paying Nina. Clearly

enough to not only spy but cover for him too. Her temples aching, Claire remained silent until they reached a turnoff for Windsor.

'Where are you from, Nina?' she asked. 'Moscow?'

'Novosibirsk,' Nina said the word slowly, and Claire repeated the difficult syllables but they came out all wrong. Nina laughed. 'Is town in Siberia. Very cold.'

'How cold?'

'Minus forty in winter. Snow everywhere. There's nothing much to do but hide inside and drink vodka.'

'Is it a small town?'

'Not so small.'

'As big as London?'

'Nothing is as big. London is monster. Beautiful monster.'

'I wish I could visit Russia one day.'

'Oh, you went once,' said Nina, taking her eyes off the road for a moment as if surprised Claire couldn't remember. 'With your dance company. You spent weeks telling me how much you hated it.'

'Did I go in winter? I'm not much for vodka.' Claire smiled sadly. 'Do you go back often?'

'Every year. Good to see family but also to see familiar places. Everywhere are memories. You know what I mean?'

'I wish I did.'

'You walk down street and suddenly you go back in time. You are 10 years old when you fell off bicycle in that park. Or 15 having first kiss in that cinema.'

'You miss home,' said Claire. She wondered if her old self felt the same way. And if she did, why keep it a secret from everyone? Why pretend she had grown up somewhere else?

Before Claire knew it, they were driving around the castle that presided over the lively town. She could see a string of shop windows, dull and unappealing, and a smattering of pubs advertising meat pies and traditional Sunday roast. *Is this where I lived for the first sixteen years of my life?* she wondered. It didn't

143

seem possible. She felt she had never set eyes on the place before. Then again, she felt that way about her house in London and her parents' house. What did she expect, her childhood memories to come flooding back the moment she stepped out of the car?

They turned around the corner. The houses were squeezed close together, vying for space, their walls touching like teeth of a giant animal. With trepidation Claire stared inside each window. Most were closed, with their curtains tightly drawn, but a few were open, welcoming the rare sunshine. She saw a young girl reading on the sofa and a middle-aged man playing with a dog in his living room. She wondered if perhaps one of these houses had once belonged to her family, whether as a child she had walked down this street, holding her mother's hand. She liked Windsor. It was quiet and peaceful. No hustle and bustle of the big city. The air smelt fresh.

When they finally found a place to park, Claire emerged cautiously, giant sunglasses like a shield over her face. What if someone recognised her, cried out to her from across the street? A childhood friend, perhaps, or a teacher from her old school? But wasn't that what she had come here for, to find answers? She pushed the sunglasses to the top of her head.

'Where to now, Miss Claire? You like to have our picnic?' asked Nina, her face mournful, as if she would rather be at home scrubbing tiles than out meandering aimlessly through the streets of a town she had never visited before.

Claire didn't have a plan. She assumed she would know what to do once they got here. With no particular direction in mind, they ambled down the street past residents and visitors sipping their lattes and chocolate milkshakes. Claire thought they looked relaxed and happy under the big café umbrellas, like they didn't have a care in the world. Wondering if once she'd been one of these relaxed and happy people, she felt a longing – to remember, to belong, to understand. She stared at every coffee drinker and shop-goer, hoping to spot one familiar face in the sea of strangers.

They walked past a Waitrose and behind it, tucked away in

a narrow side street, she spotted a ballet studio. A dozen little girls in white tutus like a flock of exotic birds chattered excitedly nearby. Claire wondered if once she had been one of these girls, whether this was where she had first learnt to dance. If so, this place had a tremendous significance for her. It must have shaped her career and her entire life. She closed her eyes and touched the door handle, waiting for memories to seep through her fingertips.

She heard Nina's voice. 'Miss Claire, you okay?'

'I'm fine, thank you, Nina. Wait here for me, please.' Opening the door, Claire walked up the stairs to a brightly lit studio. It was deserted, and she crossed the wide hall to the window, placing her hands on the barre, her feet moving into the ballet position. In the mirror, she could see a tired young woman, her eyes bleak from lack of sleep. She needed to look past her, to the little girl she had once been, practising twirls and pirouettes in this room.

'Can I help you?' The stern voice made Claire jump. Spinning around quickly, she removed her hands from the barre, as if touching anything without permission was a misdemeanour she would be punished for. A tall woman was watching her from the doorway. She wore a summer dress and a pair of high-heeled sandals. The way she moved, the way she held her shoulders betrayed a ballerina.

'Yes,' Claire stammered. 'I was just wondering . . . do you know me?'

'Am I supposed to?'

'I might have been a student here many years ago.'

'Might have?' There was the familiar look of pity and curiosity on the woman's face. And then something shifted in her eyes and she squinted at Claire in surprise. 'I do recognise you.'

'You do?' Claire's breathing quickened. She had come here looking for someone who would remember her, and now someone did. The woman looked similar age to Claire. Perhaps they had attended this school together, even been friends once. Claire grabbed the barre, steadying herself.

'Of course. You're Claire Wright.' It wasn't a question but

Claire nodded anyway. The woman continued, 'We all went to London to see you dance in Cinderella a few months ago. You were magnificent.'

'Oh.' Claire felt her shoulders stoop with disappointment. 'Thank you.'

Her feet in third position, her face lit up in admiration, the ballet teacher devoured Claire with her eyes, as if wishing to commit her face to memory. 'If you were a student here once, I'm sure I'd know. Fancy someone like you starting out in our little studio.'

'How long have you been teaching here?'

'Not long at all. Miss Alison, the previous teacher, passed away four months ago. I took over from her.'

Claire wanted to ask if they kept photographs of former students here. Would she even recognise herself as a little girl?

'Our classes are over for the day but you must come back tomorrow. The girls would be ecstatic if you could teach a lesson. I can imagine their faces—'

'I'm sorry, I can't.'

'Of course, you must be so busy. How about a photograph for our wall, of you and me together?'

'I have to go, I'm sorry.'

'Are you sure—'

But Claire was already halfway down the dark staircase. Her headache was back, a thousand daggers furiously piercing her temples. She found Nina where she'd left her. The tiny ballerinas had long disappeared and in their place were three old ladies talking animatedly as they made their way towards their favourite café. When Claire got her breath back, she saw Nina looking at her with concern. It was important to maintain the illusion of a carefree excursion, otherwise Nina might tell Paul about their trip. Claire faked a smile and said, 'I wonder how big Windsor is.'

Nina, who was busy eating a croissant, held up two fingers. Her face visibly relaxed.

'Two thousand people?' When Nina shook her head, laughing,

Claire added, 'Twenty thousand?' That sounded about right. The town seemed tiny. Blink and you would miss it.

'Two hundred thousand,' said Nina. 'I just looked it up.'

Claire wondered if she could stop two hundred thousand people, if she could ask the same question two hundred thousand times. *Do you know me? Do I look familiar?* Could she knock on every door, hoping for a spark of recognition inside her brain that was like an old car engine with its battery long dead? What was she even thinking, coming here? There were no answers here, only more questions.

'What would you like to see now, Miss Claire? Museum? There is library here, too. And what about our picnic?'

'Take me to the library,' said Claire.

The library was a square white building next to the church. Claire imagined coming here as a young girl, to meet friends and read her favourite books. Telling Nina to wait in one of the cafés, she walked through the glass doors. Inside, the air was pleasantly cool. The library was almost empty. Understandably so – it was too nice a day to be cooped up indoors. But it wasn't completely empty. A teenage couple in the corridor were glued to each other, half a dozen books by their feet. An elderly lady was using a computer. Claire found a desk as far away from them as possible.

At the counter, she asked if they kept old copies of the local newspaper. The librarian looked her up and down and in a bored voice requested, 'What date, love?' Her purple hair was caught in a knot at the top of her head and she was vigorously chewing a gum, as if determined to give her jaw a workout.

Claire's breath caught in her throat. It took her a few seconds to reply. '2009.' In 2009 she was 16. According to the police, this was when her family had suddenly packed up and moved to London. Claire didn't know what she was hoping to find. Whatever had happened ten years ago had probably been a private matter that didn't make the papers. But what if it did?

Without a word the librarian turned on her heels and walked

through a set of double doors. She was gone a while, so long, in fact, that Claire contemplated leaving. Some things were better left in the past where they belonged. Even if they could shed light on who she was.

But she couldn't leave. She had come this far.

The librarian reappeared, carrying a pile of old newspapers. 'Here is all we have for 2009,' she said, blowing a pink bubble with her gum.

Claire thanked the girl and took the newspapers back to her desk. She arranged the newspapers in chronological order, starting with the date of her sixteenth birthday. Painstakingly she read about a local poet winning a national competition, the town's oldest resident, and the talent performing at Windsor Festival. Nothing seemed important to her until she reached the last newspaper – December 2009.

An article on the front page caught her eye right away. She repeated the headline twice to herself: 'North Street Fire Tragedy.' A sudden chill ran through her, a strange premonition that this was what she had come here to find. There was a photograph of a spacious family home, not unlike her parents' house in North London. The house was engulfed in flames and the firefighters were struggling to control it.

A fire broke out at 11 p.m. on a quiet street of Windsor. Nathaniel Wright, an engineering student at the Royal Holloway University, died in the blaze. He is survived by his sister, Claire Wright and his parents, Tony and Angela Wright.

Nathaniel Wright, she whispered to herself. Nate Wright. The brother no one knew she had – not even Paul – had died in a fire ten years ago.

On shaking legs she stumbled out of the library. While she'd been inside, it had grown cold and the sky turned ominously grey. Like a drunk she staggered down the street, turning the corner and walking blindly – where, she didn't know. She had a brother and now he was gone. There was an acute pain in her chest, an ache that had been there ever since she found out her mother was dead. But now her heart was hurting not only for Angela but for her brother, too. She walked quickly past the shops and the cafés and the houses. Soon it was dark but she didn't care. Her phone rang but she ignored it. When she glanced at it, she saw missed calls from Nina and Paul. It didn't matter. Only when she saw Nina running towards her with her hands outstretched, her face frantic, did she realise that she had come full circle. She was back at the library, where her world as she knew it had turned upside down once again.

* * *

It was a long and silent journey back, and when they finally pulled up outside the house, Claire followed Nina blindly, climbing the stairs to the front door slowly, mechanically. Gaby's car was in the driveway. Claire barely noticed it. She could feel a start of another migraine, like a drill boring its way through her skull.

She could hear soft music coming from the living room. Freddie Mercury wanted to live forever and Steven Tyler didn't want to miss a thing. Without pausing to take off her shoes, she locked herself in the study and searched through every photo album that contained her childhood photographs, yearning to see her brother. Out of all the things she had forgotten, she wished she'd remembered him the most. She wanted to know the colour of his eyes, his favourite food, his favourite books. But most of all she wanted to know what it felt like to have an older brother, someone to look up to, someone to turn to when she needed it the most. There were thousands of photographs of Claire as a child but none at all of a little boy slightly older than herself. It was as if Nate had never existed. Why would she tell everyone she was an only child? Why keep her brother a secret? She didn't know what hurt more, that Nate was dead or that he seemed forgotten, all memories of him gone without a trace. Didn't he deserve better?

Lost in thought, she didn't notice the key turn in the lock and the door open. Suddenly, Paul was standing over her. Her heart in her throat at the sight of him, she jumped up, spilling the photographs all over the floor. If only Nina had driven a little faster, if only Claire hadn't walked aimlessly around Windsor but returned to the car immediately, Paul wouldn't have known she'd been out and wouldn't be looking at her with anger. To her surprise, she realised she didn't care anymore. She was beyond caring.

'Where have you been? I've been worried sick.' Paul didn't raise his voice but Claire could see his mouth twitching.

Without saying a word, she pulled her shoes off. She left them by the desk and, without a backwards glance, set off for her bedroom.

'Claire!'

Still she didn't turn around. She needed to get away from him, so she could be alone to think about her brother.

In three giant strides he caught up to her and grabbed her hand. 'Where do you think you are going? I asked you a question.'

She sighed wearily. 'I was out. I needed some air. Please, let go of my hand. You are hurting me.'

'You were out this late in the evening?' He didn't let go.

'I'm not a child. I can take care of myself.'

'So when Nina calls me at work, interrupting an important surgery, and tells me you are missing and she doesn't know what to do . . .' His voice was trembling. In anger? She felt herself trembling, too. If he didn't let go of her hand immediately, she would have a breakdown right here, in front of him. Was that what he wanted? Did he want to see her broken and upset? She pulled away and this time he didn't try to stop her. 'Where have you been?' he repeated.

'Why don't you ask your spy?'

'Nina is not my spy. She was worried and, frankly, so was I. You shouldn't have—'

Gaby appeared in the doorway, as always clutching a glass of wine as if her life depended on it. 'Leave the poor girl alone. She told you she needed some air. It must be terrible being stuck in this house all day.'

'I understand,' said Paul quietly, stepping away from Claire. 'But next time please don't disappear without letting us know first.'

Relieved, Claire smiled at her friend. 'Gaby! What are you doing here?' She had never been more pleased to see her. She knew Paul was unlikely to lose his temper in front of Gaby.

'Just stopped by to see how you're doing . . .' Gaby looked like she was on her way to a nightclub. She had on a short miniskirt, a skin-tight top under a Chanel jacket, jewellery in excess and Jimmy Choo sandals. Her raven hair was curled to perfection and framed her face impeccably, her lips were ruby and her eyelashes charcoal.

'Why don't you tell us where you've been?' asked Paul, his eyes boring into Claire.

'Stop questioning her!' Gaby's hand went on Paul's arm as if trying to restrain him. 'She hasn't done anything wrong.'

'It's okay,' said Claire. 'I went to Windsor.'

'The castle is beautiful.' Gaby nodded her approval. 'I always feel transported to another world when I visit.'

'I didn't see the castle. The police came around asking questions about my years in Windsor as a child. And about my brother.'

'You have a brother?' asked Gaby.

'She doesn't,' said Paul. 'Did you take your meds today?'

Claire wanted to put her hands over her ears and scream. What an effort it was, to stand in front of them and answer their questions, while they talked about her like she wasn't even there. All she wanted was to be alone so she could say her brother's name out loud in the hope it would trigger something inside her, a memory or a feeling that was long gone. 'I'm sorry. I'm not feeling well. I'd better take myself to bed. It was nice to see you, Gaby.' She stumbled to her room, where she lay fully clothed on her bed. 'Nate,' she whispered to herself. But even though her eyes were swimming in tears, her mind was blank. Once again, she was mourning someone she remembered nothing about.

Chapter 15

A knock on her bedroom door reached her as if from a great distance. Claire realised she had been asleep. After hours of tossing and turning, she must have finally drifted off. It couldn't have been for long. Her eyelids felt heavy. Groggily she rubbed them. Was it early? It was dark but that didn't mean anything. Her room was always dark, curtains drawn, keeping the world at bay. Her gaze fell on the clock on her bedside table. Eight in the morning. Claire rolled to her side and pulled the blankets over her head.

But whoever was at the door was insistent. Through the haze of sleep she heard another knock, and another. What if something had happened? The thought propelled her out of bed, making her throw off her blanket and walk to the door. Outside stood Helga. In her accented voice she informed Claire that Tony was asking for her.

As soon as he saw her, he sat up in bed and grinned. He always had the kindest smile waiting for her. 'Hey, Teddy Bear.'

'Hey, Dad.' She felt the familiar warmth spreading through her at the sight of him, at the sound of his voice. Tony was watching her with such tenderness. The ice block of heartache she had carried inside for the past few weeks seemed to melt a little when she was with him.

'I heard shouting yesterday. Is everything alright? Why do you look so sad?'

The mask she was trying to put on didn't fool him. He was so tuned in to her feelings, he instantly knew something was wrong. How did she tell him about Windsor and about Nate? He'd been through so much, how did she bring up what was possibly the most painful period of his life? She shrugged and shook her head. 'Tell me a memory. Something to cheer us both up.'

'I know just the thing.' He reached for her hand and squeezed it. 'One day, your mother came home with a bucketful of kittens.'

'A *bucketful* of kittens?'

'She found seven of them by the side of the road. Someone must have dumped them. She didn't want them to get scared in the car, so she placed them in a bucket and walked two kilometres home, while they meowed and tried to escape. They scratched her all over but I'd never seen her so happy.'

'What happened to them?'

'We kept them.'

'All seven?'

'All seven. Your mother and you couldn't resist their pretty little faces. And I could never say no to you.'

'What did we call them?'

'Pluto.'

'What about the other six?'

'You named them all Pluto. You were obsessed with the cartoon. You said the name suited them. We tried to point out they were cats and not dogs. But you thought they were playful and fun, just like your favourite character. So they all became Pluto.'

'That's a wonderful memory,' she whispered.

'We were so happy then, the three of us.'

'How old was I?'

'Eight or nine.'

He turned his own brave face to her but just like him, she could see right through it. 'The four of us, you mean?' He looked up in surprise but didn't say a word. She added, 'I know about Nate.'

Something seemed to shut down in his eyes at the mention of her brother. Claire could no longer read him. 'Did you remember something?' he asked.

'The police mentioned him the last time they were here. Why haven't you told me about him?'

'Your brother died in a fire ten years ago when you were 16. I didn't want to tell you and break your heart all over again, when there is so much already on your mind.'

She shuddered, not so much at his words as the expression of doubt and sheer heartbreak on his face. 'All this time I thought I was an only child.' She had lost a brother. She didn't even want to imagine what that must have been like. But her father had lost a son. She took his hand, brought it to her face and kissed his rough skin. 'Were we close?'

'He loved you with all his heart. And you loved him.' There were tears in his eyes. She moved her chair closer, moved herself closer, so she could hold him and make it all better. 'It was a tragic accident. Your mother and I were away on a romantic weekend. Only half an hour away, and yet, we didn't know what happened until we got back. That's what kills me. That we went hours without knowing. We were still happy and he was already gone.'

'What happened?'

'Our house caught fire while Nate was asleep inside. Faulty wiring. I pray it was quick. I pray he didn't suffer. Every day of my life I thank God you were at a friend's house that night.'

Claire wished she could inject herself with memories, so she wouldn't feel so empty and confused. 'What was he like?'

'He was very much your mother's son.'

'I'm so sorry, Dad. How do you live with something like this? How do you get over it?'

'You don't, not really. It stays with you forever. Like your mother's death will stay with us forever. But as long as there is love in your life, it's worth living. And my life is filled with love because I still have you.'

'Poor Mum,' she whispered. 'Poor you. I'm so sorry, Dad.' She sobbed in his arms and he stroked her shoulders, gentle touches that made her feel like she wasn't alone.

'Our family has been through a lot. But we've always been there for each other. We've always been close. And now there's only you and me. Just the two of us left.'

'Yes,' said Claire. 'Just the two of us.' At that moment, as he rocked her gently like an infant, she knew she would do anything for him. He was the only one she loved and the only one she trusted. She had no one else but him.

Chapter 16

On the first truly warm day, Claire wanted to take her father to the park in his wheelchair but he refused, as if even a glimmer of joy would be a betrayal of his beloved Angela. He looked especially gloomy and the only thing that seemed to cheer him up was Angela's Bible. Claire read to him until her eyes were weary and her throat dry. And then she closed the Bible and asked, 'What were your parents like? My grandparents?'

'My mother was a saint, with a heart of gold. When I think of her, I remember her kindness and tenderness and her singing a quiet lullaby as I drifted off to sleep.'

'She sounds wonderful. Have I ever met her?'

'She died shortly before you were born. I loved my mother more than anything. And then I met Angela. She reminded me of Mum. She was just as kind, just as beautiful and always knew the right thing to say to brighten up your day.' Tony gritted his teeth as if fighting back tears.

'What about your father?'

He was about to say something when they heard Paul's voice. 'Claire, can I talk to you?' A second later his head appeared in the doorway. 'Alone?'

'Anything you want to say, you can say in front of Daddy.'

Claire didn't want to be alone with Paul. She wanted to stay with her father.

'Very well. I found this in the kitchen sink.' He held up something small and with horror Claire recognised one of her pills. Paul didn't say another word but seemed to wait for her to explain. When she didn't, he added, 'How long have you been doing this?'

'What I do is up to me. It's none of your business.'

'You are my wife, which makes it my business. I only want the best for you. I'm sorry if you can't see that. Now you are lying to me, pretending to take your meds—'

Tony lifted himself up on one elbow. 'Who are you to talk about lies?'

Claire could see the colour rising in Paul's face. Suddenly he looked angry enough to strike her father. But he didn't. His voice remained calm when he said, 'This is a family matter. Please, stay out of it.'

'I *am* family,' said Tony. 'The only family she has.'

Paul turned away from Tony and faced Claire. 'I'm making an appointment with your doctor tomorrow. You can explain to him how long you've been doing this and why.' With that he walked out, closing the door quietly behind him.

When they were alone, Claire asked, 'What did you mean, Daddy? When you talked about lies? What is Paul lying about?'

It was as if Tony was waiting for her question. He took her hand and said, 'I didn't want to be the one to tell you. But Paul and your friend Gaby . . .' He seemed to hesitate. 'They are having an affair.'

At first she thought he was joking. She waited for him to laugh and say, 'Got you.' But his face remained serious. 'That's impossible,' she said. 'Gaby is my friend. I trust her.'

'Maybe you shouldn't trust her quite so much. Helga left me in my wheelchair one day and went to the shops. I got so bored sitting by the window watching the traffic, I decided to wheel myself to the kitchen. And that's when I heard Paul on the phone to her. He told her he loved her, that he couldn't wait to see her. I'm so sorry, darling. I hate to upset you. I just thought you had the right to know.'

Forcing a smile, Claire said, 'You didn't upset me. Paul is like a stranger to me. He can do as he pleases.'

Tony spoke quickly, his hands trembling. 'Let's go away. We can go somewhere no one will find us and start a new life together. You won't have to worry about anything. I will take care of you.'

'I'd like that,' she whispered, knowing full well that she would be the one taking care of him, wanting to take care of him, and at the same time, feeling suddenly alone and afraid.

* * *

It was dark in Claire's bedroom, like she was trapped underwater, desperately gasping for air. Curled up in her bed with her clothes still on, she felt a wave of nausea that wouldn't pass. She hadn't eaten anything, she realised. Not that she could force anything down. She blinked, chasing away the vision of Gaby and Paul together. Unsurprisingly, it wasn't Paul's betrayal that hurt the most. She had meant what she said to her father. Her husband was a stranger to her. As far as she was concerned, he owed her nothing. But Gaby was a different matter altogether. Other than Tony, she was the only person Claire could turn to. Claire had trusted her with everything. She'd told her everything. And all this time Gaby was shamelessly pretending to be her best friend, while planning a future with her husband. The irony of it, the pain of her betrayal. Claire felt she was going to be sick.

How they must have laughed behind her back. Poor ridiculous Claire, who couldn't remember her own name and couldn't see what was happening right under her nose. Well, she saw it all now. And she wasn't going to let Gaby get away with it.

Over and over she called her friend but there was no answer. She left three frantic messages but was secretly relieved when by midday Gaby hadn't called her back. It was easy to lie over the phone. But would Gaby be able to do that to her face? Claire wanted to look in her friend's eye when she confronted her.

After lunch when she watched her father eat and touched nothing, she asked Nina to drive her to Gaby's house, which was only ten minutes away but felt like a world apart. It was in a suburb of London that didn't look like it belonged in the city at all. There were no busy roads nearby, no dwellings joined together in an endless urban harmonica, only trees and flowers, a small forest embracing the tiny house that was nothing more than a cabin, drowning in the sea of pink, red and purple. Bright and flamboyant like its owner, it suited Gaby perfectly.

Hesitating only for a moment, Claire rang the bell. When there was no answer, she rang again and knocked on the window, peering through the curtains for any sign of movement. It was dark inside and she couldn't see anything. Impatiently she called out Gaby's name and rattled the door.

When she was about to leave, she thought she heard a soft rustle behind the wooden door. A curtain trembled. 'Gaby, is that you?'

'Who is it? What's all this banging?' Gaby sounded croaky, like she was recovering from a cold. 'I have a headache, go away!'

'Gaby, it's me,' cried Claire, knocking one more time. There was a moment of silence, long enough to make Claire doubt Gaby was ever going to open the door. 'Is everything okay?'

'Claire, what are you doing here? I'm not feeling well today. Must be the virus that's been going around. I wouldn't want to pass it to you. Please, can I call you later? I want to lie down.' Gaby's words were slurred and suddenly Claire realised there was nothing wrong with her friend's health. She was drunk.

'Have you been drinking?'

'So what if I have?'

Claire could swear Gaby's footsteps were moving away. 'I need to talk to you.'

The footsteps paused for a second, then Claire heard Gaby walk back and fiddle with the chain. A ghost of the Gaby she knew greeted Claire. There was nothing flamboyant about the woman in front of her. She clearly hadn't showered or brushed her hair. There were red circles under her eyes as if she had been crying. Even more perplexing, Claire's glamorous friend was wearing tattered pyjamas that were coming apart at the elbows. There was no usual layer of makeup to shield Gaby from the world. Despite her height, she looked vulnerable and small.

Gaby didn't say a word but blocked the doorway, deliberately stopping Claire from entering. Even without her high-heeled shoes she was looking down at Claire. 'What did you want to talk about?'

'Can I come in?' When Gaby didn't move, Claire added, 'Why didn't you return my calls?'

'I'm sorry. I didn't even look at my phone today,' said Gaby, finally shuffling out of the way.

Gaby's living room was a reflection of Gaby herself – a mess. On the floor, there were ice cream wrappers, dirty laundry and plates. There was only one glass on the coffee table but Claire could see two empty bottles of wine. 'Were you drinking all by yourself?'

Gaby looked like an animal backed into a corner. 'I told you this wasn't a good time. I don't want you to see me like this.'

To Claire's dismay, Gaby slid into an armchair, covered her face with her hands and began to cry. Instantly she forgot all her anger and suspicions. Her friend had always been there for her. Now Gaby needed her. She perched next to Gaby and put her arms around her. 'Is everything alright? Why don't you tell me what's wrong?'

For a few minutes nothing could be heard but Gaby's sobbing and Claire's quiet and affectionate 'sh-sh-sh'. Finally, Gaby said, 'Everything is such a mess. I feel like my life is falling apart. I just lost the only man I ever loved. He said . . .' She sniffled and blew her nose. 'He said after all these years he no longer wants me. He is going to give his marriage another chance. Have you ever heard anything more ridiculous? Such a cliché. I love him so much, Claire. I love him with all my heart. And still it's not enough.'

'Things don't always work out the way we want them to,' said Claire carefully. 'Did you say years? How long?'

'Three years.' Shocked, Claire withdrew her arm and sat next to her friend in silence. Gaby continued, 'His wife is a wonderful person but she doesn't love him. Never has. He's blind if he can't see that.'

'It sounds like he might still have feelings for her.' Was Gaby really talking about the cold, unemotional husband Claire had come to loathe so much?

'Come on, say it. Tell me I get what I deserve for falling in love with a married man. But things are never black and white. We can't help who we fall in love with. We made plans. They were getting a divorce. Now suddenly he wants to go back to her. And she doesn't even want him.'

'Are you sure about that?'

'She told me she's afraid of him. That she can't stand being in the same house with him.'

Claire moved away from Gaby until no part of her was touching any part of her friend. 'But Gaby,' she said slowly, a sudden realisation making her hands tremble. 'I told you I was afraid of him because you convinced me he was violent. All I had was your word. I don't have any memories of our time together. You told me Paul had anger issues and I believed you. Did you say that just so you could have him all to yourself?'

'You know about me and Paul?' As if by magic Gaby's tears were gone. Her eyes were on Claire, large and unblinking.

'It's pretty obvious. And the more I think about it, the more obvious it becomes. You had the key to our house. You were always trying to convince me we had issues. You did your best to poison me against him. I thought you were my friend, but all this time you were lying to me.'

'I *am* your friend.'

'You tried to take my husband away from me.'

'We can't help who we fall in love with,' repeated Gaby. She looked inside her glass as if hoping to see red liquid miraculously appear out of nowhere. 'Remember our last high school dance?' The smile was wide on Gaby's face. But it wasn't a kind smile. 'Of course you don't. Paul invited you to be his date and you agreed but then cancelled at the last moment. He hired a limo and you blew him off for some stupid dancing commitment. He took me instead. I thought it was my chance to get closer to him. But all he did was stay in the corner all night. Didn't speak to anyone, didn't dance, no matter how many times I asked.'

'Why are you telling me this?'

'Because I was in that corner, too, refusing to dance with anyone. Hoping if I waited long enough, he would notice me. Hoping he would realise he didn't need you. But he didn't see me because all he wanted was you. It was like a spell you'd cast and suddenly he was blind to everything around him. He loved you unconditionally and for what? So you would betray him and break his heart?' Gaby laughed but there was no warmth in her laughter. It scared Claire, made her go weak in the knees.

'Betray him?'

'You don't know anything, do you?'

'What do you mean, betray him?'

'You've been unfaithful to him for years. That's how I know you didn't love him.'

'I had an affair?' Claire whispered, stunned.

'Everyone knew about it except Paul. And when he finally found out, it almost broke him. He loved you so much and that's how you treated him. What does that say about you?'

Claire knew for a fact she couldn't trust Gaby. Her friend had lied to her too many times before, pretending to be something she wasn't, gaining Claire's trust so she could mislead her time and time again. Would she invent an affair to prove that she deserved

Paul's love more than Claire did? Yes, decided Claire. That was exactly the type of thing Gaby would do. But if by some miracle she was telling the truth, if Claire indeed had been unfaithful and broke Paul's heart, then everything would make sense – the divorce papers in her drawer, separate bedrooms, Paul's cold detachment and aloof indifference. 'Don't you see what you've done? You told me Paul was violent and all this time I thought he'd killed my mother.'

'If you believe that, you really are more stupid than you look. Paul is the kindest man I know. He wouldn't hurt a fly.'

'My mother knew about your affair. That's why they were arguing.' The thought made Claire tremble with pain and affection. Her mother was trying to protect her. How much she must have loved her.

'She confronted me too. She told me I should be ashamed of myself. And I was ashamed. But you know what they say. All is fair in love and war. I love him. That's all that really mattered to me.' Gaby started to cry again but this time Claire didn't feel like comforting her. 'We could have been so happy. If it wasn't for your accident, the two of you would be divorced and we would be together.'

Seeing her friend in tears of despair, Claire felt a sudden pang of guilt. Gaby was the one having an affair with her husband, and yet it was her, Claire, who felt sorry for coming between them and hurting Gaby's feelings. She didn't know what to say, how to make it all better. She wished she knew how her old self would react to the news of their betrayal. Would she feel devastated? Or relieved because now she was free to go on with her life without him? Was Gaby right? Had she never loved Paul? But why would she marry someone she didn't love? And if Paul felt nothing for her, surely he would have stayed with Gaby.

'You said you hated him,' exclaimed Gaby, crying softly.

'I only said that because I don't remember.'

'You said you hated him even before the accident.'

'See, Gaby, you've told so many lies, I don't know if I believe you anymore.'

Suddenly, all Claire wanted was to go back home. She couldn't believe she thought of the house she shared with Paul as home. But it was the only place where she could be alone with her thoughts, where she could leave the alien world behind. She couldn't stand Gaby's tears, her accusing eyes on Claire as if she expected her to step aside and let her have her husband for her own.

On the way back, Claire no longer thought of Gaby. She thought of Paul. As she watched the unfamiliar streets roll slowly by, she imagined his face when he had met her at the hospital for the first time, his eyes on her as he made sure she took her medication every night, his voice as he had offered to bring her father home. Was he hiding his true feelings for her underneath his cold exterior? What she mistook for a controlling nature could be genuine concern for her.

If Gaby was telling the truth, all this time Claire had been wrong about Paul. He wasn't the terrifying shadow from her nightmare. But who was?

* * *

The door to Paul's bedroom was open and Claire could hear him whistling a popular tune to himself. On the bed were two large suitcases. Molokai was curled up in one of them like a giant yellow python, taking up all the space, only his tail and nose sticking out. The other suitcase was overflowing with clothes. Paul was standing in the middle of the room, a business suit in his hands, a puzzled expression on his face. With his hair messy and glasses askew, he looked like a lost little boy. For the first time Claire saw him as a human being, not the violent monster she had imagined him to be. Conjured by Gaby's lies, the monster wasn't real.

Claire pointed at the suitcase. 'It won't close. You've put too many clothes in there.'

'That's why I have two.'

'You mean you aren't packing the dog?' she asked, for the first time noticing what a nice smile he had. It transformed his face, made it appear kind, more open. 'Are you going on holiday?' A few hours ago, seeing Paul packing his bags would have made Claire exhale with relief. Now she didn't know how she felt about it.

'A business trip for a couple of weeks.'

'Molokai seems to think he's coming with you.' The dog was asleep inside the suitcase. He was snoring.

'Is everything okay? Did you want something?'

Claire took a deep breath. 'I spoke to Gaby. I know about the two of you. It's probably none of my business and I'm not accusing you of anything. But now that I know the truth, you don't have to hide anymore. We can get a divorce. You can be with her.'

Paul put the suit down and turned to Claire. 'There is nothing going on between us.'

'She said there was. Are you saying she made it all up?' But she knew the answer to that question. *All is fair in love and war*, Gaby had said to her.

'She didn't make all of it up.'

Claire could tell by the look on his face this conversation was difficult for Paul. But she felt no sympathy for him. This conversation was difficult for her, too.

'We did have an affair. But I broke it off.'

'Why?'

'Why was I having an affair?'

'Well, yes, but . . . why did you break it off?'

'Because Gaby is not the one for me. When you came home from hospital, you seemed so lost and vulnerable. All I wanted was to take care of you. I felt like the old Claire was back, the woman I fell in love with all those years ago. I was lying to myself, pretending I could be happy with someone else. But I can't.'

'Tell me what happened. Why were we getting a divorce?'

'We drifted apart, I suppose. With our schedules, we hardly saw each other. Before we knew it, we were living separate lives.'

'And that's why you had an affair? Drifted apart – isn't that the excuse all married men make when they cheat on their wives?'

He looked away from her, staring into his hands. His face twisted as if he'd just taken a gulp of something sour and unpleasant. Finally, he said, 'I wasn't the one who cheated first. You were.'

His words confirmed what Gaby had told her but Claire didn't want to believe it. Was she really cable of betraying someone who loved her, smiling to his face and breaking his heart behind his back? Claire watched Paul closely. Was he lying to her? But he didn't look like he was lying. The pain in his eyes was real.

'You met someone. Another dancer. When I found out . . . I felt like you were slipping away from me and I didn't know what to do. I fought for our marriage but you completely shut me out. Gaby was there for me when I needed her. I didn't want to be alone. But it wasn't her I wanted.'

'I had an affair with another dancer?' She remembered the photographs Gaby had shown her in the park one day and felt sick to her stomach. If it was true and she did have a relationship with this man behind her husband's back, then she didn't know herself at all. Everything she had imagined herself to be was an illusion. The reality was very different. The reality was that she was an adulteress, lying, scheming and cold-hearted. Someone she didn't even like. What else was she capable of? She thought of the police visit and their suspicions and shuddered. 'Is that why you didn't want me to go back to the studio?'

'I was afraid that the minute you saw him, your feelings would come back. I knew your relationship was over. But I didn't want to risk it. Your accident, as terrible as it sounds, seemed like a second chance to me, a clean slate. If only I kept you all to myself and took care of you, I thought I could win you back. Gaby . . . I was weak and I regret it.' She pressed his hand to say, *You don't need to explain anything, I know.* He continued anyway, 'If I'd still had you, there would have been no Gaby.'

His eyes were pleading with her to believe him. And she wanted to, more than anything. 'On the day my mother was killed, on the day of the accident, you were with Gaby? That's why you never answered my calls?'

He lowered his head as if he was ashamed. 'I'm sorry. I understand if you don't want me around anymore. I can leave. This is your house and you can have it.'

'I don't want you to leave. But I feel like everyone around me is lying.' Suddenly she was crying and Paul had his arms around her. 'I don't know how I feel about any of it. I don't remember our relationship or my feelings for you. Before I can make sense of it all, I need to find out who I am.'

'Do you want me to cancel my business trip?'

Trying to compose herself, smiling through her tears, she nodded. 'You'd better unpack the dog.'

Chapter 17

Claire didn't tell Tony about her conversation with Gaby and Paul. She didn't know why but she wanted to keep it to herself until she knew how she felt about it. While Tony was listlessly chewing on a pancake she had made, she asked if she could have the key to his house. 'I want to see where I lived when I was younger. I want to see my old room. It might trigger something, a memory or a feeling.'

'I don't think it's a good idea. Your mother . . . That was where they'd found her. I couldn't go back there. Are you sure you are strong enough?'

'I know I'm not. But it's something I need to do.'

Claire could see hesitation in his face, as if he was searching for a way to talk her out of it. Finally, he gave in and she asked Paul to drive her to her parents' house. The revelation about their marriage had been a good thing in a way, she thought. It encouraged them to talk and helped her see him for who he truly was, and not someone she had invented. She was grateful he would be with her when she visited her parents' house because she didn't think she could handle it alone.

Just like her father, Paul didn't think it was a good idea.

'I want you to stop trying to protect me from my past,' she said to him. 'I need you to help me find it.'

When they pulled up outside the familiar house in North London, it took Claire a moment to muster the courage to get out of the car. Motionlessly, she stared at the large brick structure where she had once lived. With trepidation she pushed the gate, walked on the brown carpet of withered grass and stood with her hand on the front door, listening. She wondered what it would feel like had things been different. Had her mother been home waiting for her, with cookies baking in the oven perhaps and a pot of tea brewing on the dining table. The fantasy was so heart-warming, she almost turned around and fled. She couldn't bear seeing the house empty. But she had to face her past in order to discover who she was in the present.

Once again, the letterbox was stuffed to the brim with letters. Fresh newspapers littered the front yard. The neighbour was in her garden, pruning. She had on the same apron, the same pair of trousers and shirt. Her dog was sleeping in the shade of an apple tree. It was a Boston terrier, smooth and bug-eyed. After a moment's hesitation, Claire peeked over the fence, said hello and waved. Her voice woke the dog and it barked indignantly at this disrespectful invasion in the middle of a peaceful afternoon. Thankfully, Old Sue didn't seem to hear. Claire wasn't up for small talk.

Coughing to clear her dry throat, she followed Paul inside the house, which was even more imposing on the inside than it seemed from the outside. Everywhere she looked were expensive paintings and old-fashioned furniture. The ceiling was so high, the living room so spacious, if she spoke, Claire was sure her voice would ricochet off the walls in a loud echo. She could sense ghosts in the house, their eyes following her every move, but everything was silent. There were no whispers from the past, only the din of traffic outside.

Claire asked Paul to lock the door. She wasn't sure what she was expecting to find here but she knew she didn't want to be disturbed when she found it.

This is where I lived with my mother and father, she thought, shuddering. *This is home.*

The house smelt like a hospital – of bleach and sanitiser. It must have been professionally cleaned after the forensic team was done with it. Everything was spotless, except for a piece of furniture here and there that looked out of place, as if pushed out of the way and forgotten. The sofa was in the corner instead of directly opposite the TV. The umbrella stand wasn't by the front door but abandoned in the middle of the room. In the gaps between floorboards she could still see traces of white powder the police had left behind. 'They use it for fingerprints,' explained Paul, watching her carefully.

Not knowing where to start, Claire walked around the perimeter of the walls, tracing the flowery pattern of the wallpaper with her fingertips. Finally, she paused next to the coffee table and touched its smooth surface. She could imagine Angela on the sofa, her hands in her lap as she watched TV, relaxing after a long day. Claire listened to the silence and thought of her younger self running through these rooms, of her mother's voice calling her for supper. Inside these walls, she had a life once, even if she knew nothing about it.

Her parents' mail didn't contain anything of interest. Utility bills, a greeting card from someone called Olivia, a credit card application form. Claire made her way into the dining room. It seemed like the safest place to start. If there were secrets waiting for her inside these walls, she doubted she would find them here. Although she longed to learn who she was, she was desperately afraid of her past.

'What is it you are looking for?' asked Paul.

'Clues,' replied Claire. Clues to who she was. Clues to what happened to her mother. The missing pieces of the puzzle.

The dining room contained an old round table covered with a flowery tablecloth and eight chairs like knights crowding around it. Just as Claire suspected, no devastating secrets here.

The kitchen was nothing like their high-tech kitchen at home – yellow cupboards and yellow tiles, some of them cracked, an old-fashioned cooker and a kettle that whistled. It seemed her mother collected tea towels from around the world. Claire could see towels from Barcelona, Tenerife, Paris. Even one with a koala on top of the Sydney Harbour Bridge. Taking it off its hook, her hands trembling, she wondered if she had brought it for Angela as a present when she had toured Australia with her ballet company. She opened cupboard after cupboard, examining containers filled with tea and sugar. An empty fridge and a fully stocked freezer that seemed to have everything, from frozen pies to cartons of ice cream. And then she spotted the knives and her legs gave out. Petrified, she sunk to the floor.

Instantly Paul was by her side. 'Are you okay? Do you need anything? A glass of water?'

'I don't think I can do this.'

'You can do this. I'm right here.'

Seeing the look of concern on his face, feeling his strong arms around her, she knew he meant it. And she felt better. 'Where did they find her?' she muttered. Paul didn't seem to hear. Maybe he chose not to hear. Could she blame him, when it was the last thing she wanted to talk about? But she needed to know. 'Where did they find my mother?' she repeated louder, words getting caught in her throat, threatening to choke her.

'Right here, in the kitchen. That's what the police told us.'

Claire closed her eyes and searched for a memory, imagining herself walking through the door on the day her mother was murdered and seeing . . . what? Her mind was blank.

Suddenly, she felt faint and short of breath. Shaking, afraid she would collapse, she leaned on Paul's shoulder when something shiny caught her eye in the corner. It was a silver charm – a dove carrying an olive branch. It must have belonged to her mother. Eagerly Claire reached for it and held it up for a few seconds, studying it with reverence. And then she saw a tiny brown spot on the dove's head, like an old tomato ketchup stain. Claire knew instantly what it was – her mother's blood. She threw the charm on the floor and fled from the kitchen. She never wanted to set foot in here again. As she was about to step into the dark corridor, she glanced behind her one more time and saw Paul bend over, pick up the charm and place it in his pocket.

It took her a few minutes to get her breath back, to be able to think straight. Blinded by terror, she walked up the stairs. Not a thing was out of place in her parents' bedroom. Family photographs adorned every wall, as if her mother wanted to be reminded of the people she loved everywhere she looked. There was a younger Angela, impeccable in her bridal beige, and Tony, tall, good-looking and smiling from ear to ear. There were pictures of her mother and father holding hands on a beach and kissing in front of the Statue of Liberty. And pictures of Claire as a baby, a toddler, a young girl, riding a bicycle, holding a puppy, posing on stage in a white tutu.

There were no pictures of Nate.

On the bedside table she found a small bottle of perfume. Her doctor had told her scents were particularly good at bringing back memories. She undid the cap and closed her eyes, trying to concentrate. Did it smell familiar? A hint of jasmine and vanilla, and something else, something she couldn't quite place. The fragrance was light, almost girly. She sprayed some perfume on the inside of her wrist because she wanted to smell like her mother.

In the wardrobe, there was a little bit of everything – clothes, shoes, books and magazines. Timeless and elegant dresses, all straight lines and understated colours, mature and grown-up, something a schoolteacher or perhaps a librarian might choose. Absentmindedly Claire touched the fabrics, imagining a tall elegant woman wearing this suit or that skirt or that pair of trousers, with an aura of jasmine and vanilla about her.

'Oh, Mum,' she whispered, wrapping her arms around a cardigan, burying her face in it, trying to catch her mother's scent and to feel her mother's presence, all the while struggling not to cry.

Painstakingly she opened every drawer of the bedside table and went through gardening magazines and old newspaper clippings on the mantelpiece. They were mostly about Claire and her ballet, with an occasional ad for a holiday resort. A caravan park in Cornwall, a cabin in the South of France.

The room next door was slightly bigger. Even before she stepped inside, Claire knew it had once belonged to her. There was a ballerina cover on the bed and a ballet poster on the wall. Suddenly, she wanted to hide from the world under her childhood blanket until her mother came home and held her in her arms, telling her everything would be alright.

On either side of the bed, she could see two bedside tables, both empty. The rest of the furniture consisted of a tall mirror, an old wardrobe, bare bookshelves and an ancient piano. Claire ran her fingers over the piano keys. It hadn't been tuned and sounded like a church organ, eerie and disturbing.

As she meticulously searched the room, she wished she knew what she was looking for – then perhaps she would know where to find it. If she were a young girl, where would she hide something she didn't want anyone to see? A diary perhaps? Old love letters? There was nothing under the mattress and nothing under the bed.

Behind the piano, a dozen boxes were haphazardly stacked on top of each other, held together with tape that was old and dry and peeled away easily. As fast as she could, Claire searched inside every box. They seemed to contain her whole teenage life – clothes, books, pointe shoes, magazines, posters and greeting cards. She imagined her younger self wearing the tutus, what it had felt like, what she had looked like. She glanced through the ballet magazines that had once inspired her to dance the best she could, to work hard and reach for the stars. Looking at her pre-adolescent dreams all there in front of her – in every poster and carefully preserved newspaper article, she felt proud of herself. Proud of the old Claire, whom she couldn't remember but who had strived and achieved.

But the clothes, the books, the magazines felt as if they had belonged to a stranger. It couldn't have been her, reading *National Geographic* and making notes in her school notebook. The clothes – short skirts and tight tops, something a teenager might wear when she wanted to impress a boy – still fit perfectly. And then there were the books with her own notes in them, a few words here and there, a random thought or a witty comment. *This made me cry. I don't agree with this. This is funny. Must read this again.*

Finally, at the bottom of the last box, under an anthology of poetry, she came across a small notebook. A diary. She could feel her heart racing. Was this what she had come here to find? Her hands trembling, she read the first entry – it was about ballet, what she had learnt and how much she had improved. There were drawings on every page – of ballet positions, butterflies and flowers. In the corner of the room she found a small box and placed the notebook inside. Then she returned to her parents' bedroom, opened the bedside table and added some gardening magazines and newspaper clippings to her box, so she could go through them at home and see what her mother had been reading.

'I think we are done here,' she said to Paul.

'You don't want to see the rest of the house?'

'I found an old diary. I want to go home and read it.'

But the truth was, she couldn't stay in her parents' house another minute. Her head was spinning and her throat was aching as if she was coming down with a bad cold. Every old photograph, book and magazine, every piece of furniture and clothing seemed to taunt her with the images of a life that was forever gone. *You don't remember us*, they seemed to shout to her at the top of their voices, *but we remember you. We remember you as a carefree little girl, rushing home to tell your mother all about your day. We remember you when you were happy. And look at you now.*

* * *

Nina had whipped up an elaborate three-course meal for them that evening but Claire felt queasy just looking at the food. Telling Paul she had a headache, she locked herself in her room and opened the notebook. In the dim light, the pages looked dog-eared and worn. At first glance they contained everything you would expect to find in a young girl's diary. Transfixed, she read through detailed descriptions of arguments with her friends, movies she had seen, books she had borrowed and clothes she had bought.

Quicker and quicker she turned the pages, hoping for a glimpse into her life that would shed the light on who she was, a mention of her brother, perhaps, or a passage about her mother. After fifteen minutes she was halfway through the notebook and her eyes were tired. She almost closed her diary and went to bed, but something caught her attention. She had to go back a few pages and there it was – a dot in the corner, as if the page had been accidentally smeared by a red marker pen. She would have ignored it if, a few pages later, there wasn't another dot. By the time she reached the end of the diary, she counted a dozen similar marks.

The red dots were not an accident. They meant something.

She bookmarked every page where the dot appeared by bending the corner slightly, and then returned to the first one. The letters were smaller here and the writing was difficult to decipher, as if the author was in a hurry to commit her thoughts to paper. Claire read the entry three times but the words made no sense. It was as if her brain refused to understand.

I wish I was deaf, so I wouldn't have to hear him. I put a pillow over my head but it doesn't help. I hate him!

The last sentence was crossed out, as if the person writing didn't want anyone to read it. But behind the veil of black ink the letters were still visible.

What did it all mean? Who was the young Claire talking about? Chilled by a sudden fear, she found the second red dot.

*Why does he have to be so angry all the time? I hate him
so much.*

And this time there was no attempt to hide the 'I hate him'. It
was right there, in bold letters, for the world to see.

Claire looked at the dates. There was a red dot every few
weeks. And in the meantime, as if nothing was happening, there
were school assignments, sleepovers and trips to the seaside with
friends. Just a normal life of a typical teenager.

And then the final red dot, dated December 2009:

*This time he's gone too far. And one day he will pay. He will
pay for everything. I will never forgive him for this. I hate him!*

The writing changed on that page. It became uneven, disturbed.
As if the hand holding the pen was shaking. Claire was shaking
herself as she read the words one more time.

After December 2009, there were no more entries.

Chapter 18

As hard as she tried, Claire could find no mention of her brother in her diary. Like any teenage girl, Claire rarely wrote about her family. Instead, she talked about her friends, hobbies and dancing. But every now and then, there would be a few words about her mother that would take her breath away and she would read them aloud to herself until she could recite them in her sleep, longing for a picture of Angela that wasn't too far removed from reality.

From the lines of her diary, a kind and warm woman came to life, a little absentminded perhaps, but one who adored Claire. When Claire was 14, her mother had made her a new tutu for a ballet performance. She had stayed up all night finishing it and then watched proudly as her daughter danced her heart out on stage. She had cooked oatmeal for breakfast every morning, was overprotective and constantly worried about her daughter.

When Claire turned 15, Angela had taken her to see a film about ballet. There were two pages describing the movie, when all Claire wanted were a few sentences describing her mother. She had so many questions. She wondered if Angela had enjoyed the film, if they had shared a box of popcorn, if they had gone out for a bite to eat afterwards. She wanted to know what they had

177

talked about, whether they had laughed together, whether they'd enjoyed each other's company.

The thought of the unconditional love her mother had for her, of the love she still felt for her mother, even though she couldn't remember her, filled Claire with an unbearable longing she didn't know how to control. At moments like that, she thought the police suspecting her of murdering her own mother was laughable. How could she ever hurt someone she adored? Would PC Kamenski see her feelings as proof of her innocence? Why did Claire doubt that? And then Claire read an entry that made her heart beat faster.

Today we helped Aunt Tegan move to her new house. She bought an old terrace behind the library.

White-faced and shaking, Claire reached for her phone and loaded the map. There was a small street behind the Windsor library that wound its way towards the station. Meticulously she studied every house on the street, wondering which one had once belonged to her aunt and if she still lived there after all these years.

The next morning, Claire persuaded Paul to take a day off and drive her to Windsor. In the car, she told him everything she had learnt about Nate. 'In ten years that I've known you, you've never mentioned a brother. I always assumed you were an only child, like me,' Paul said.

'Don't you find it strange that I had a brother and never told anyone? Why would I hide something like that from you?'

'Maybe you weren't hiding it from me as much as from yourself? Some things are too painful to talk about.'

'Perhaps you're right.' Claire thought of her father, whose face twisted in pain every time she mentioned her brother. She thought of his silence on the subject until she brought it up herself.

Paul pressed her hand reassuringly, while his eyes remained on the road. 'No matter what happens, I want you to know you are not alone. I'm here for you.'

Claire asked Paul to wait in a nearby café. If she found her aunt, she wanted to talk to her alone. Something told her Tegan wouldn't open up in front of a stranger. But as she walked alone past a row of houses on the small street immediately behind the library, she felt a strange sensation in the pit of her stomach, like she didn't belong. Afraid of what she might discover, she wanted to run. She wished Paul was with her, so she wouldn't feel so alone.

Nervously clasping her purse to her chest, Claire approached the first house, which was also the largest.

She stood with her finger on the buzzer, too afraid to press it. Finally, she rang.

When there was no answer, she turned around and walked away. But a hundred meters down the road, she returned, found a pen and a piece of paper in her handbag and wrote a note to her aunt asking, if she did indeed live there, to call her. With trepidation she slipped the note under the front door, then wrote another note and another, leaving them at every house on the street.

* * *

Matilda's office was quiet and dim as Claire reclined on the couch and closed her eyes. This was the only place where she didn't feel afraid, hidden away from the world, like a small island lost in the ocean, alone and undisturbed, with nothing around but calm waters and blue skies. And that was what she longed for as she shared her deepest fears with the therapist – this illusion of safety, of being secluded from all things threatening and dark.

'I thought the violence I experienced in my dreams was something to do with my husband. But now I'm convinced it's connected to my childhood.'

'It wouldn't surprise me. Childhood experiences often stay with us for life, haunting us even when we don't remember them,' said Matilda.

'In my dream, I'm about to face the person threatening me. But I always wake up before I can see their face. If only I could stay asleep longer.'

'Your mind is trying to protect you from something. We need to let your mind know you are strong enough to deal with it.'

'Is my mind trying to protect me from my past or from what happened on the day my mother was murdered, the day of the accident? The police say I was there. A neighbour saw me at the time of the murder.' Claire hesitated. She had never shared her fear of being involved in her mother's murder with anyone. She didn't want to acknowledge it was real by putting it into words. 'I think they suspect me. They asked questions about my mother's will, trying to establish a motive.'

'Just because you benefitted from her will doesn't make you a suspect. Does it seem like you needed your mother's money?'

'I don't think so. We seem to have plenty. But what if there was a conflict between the two of us I know nothing about?' Her hand on her heart, she paused, trying to get her breath back. 'What if it *was* me? I can't bear the thought of it. I wish I could remember what happened that day. No matter how terrible it is, I'd rather know for sure.'

'You don't strike me as someone capable of murder. You are not the type to lash out or lose your temper.'

'If I was there, I would have seen who did it. I must have known . . .' The thought made her tremble in terror. 'Please, help me remember. I need to know what happened or I will go insane.'

'I don't know if I can help you remember. But I can try helping you calm down and get your thoughts straight. Why don't you lie down and close your eyes?'

Matilda's voice was like a lullaby, soothing and calm, and Claire felt herself drifting till she was on the verge of sleep. She no longer feared her nightmare, so accustomed she had become to it. But she was afraid of what the nightmare represented.

'Find yourself in your dream,' said Matilda. 'Experience it fully. Without fear or concern, see it in your mind as if it was happening right now.'

But as hard as Claire tried, the nightmare wouldn't come. She couldn't conjure the terror, nor see the disturbing images. What she experienced instead was something completely different. An image came to her, of happiness and joy and laughter. Was it a dream or a memory? It was impossible to tell.

The little girl was squealing in excitement, happy and safe in her father's arms. 'Faster, faster, Daddy!' Her father was lifting her up in the air, twirling-twirling-twirling, until everything became a blur – the horses, the riders, the blue skies and the green hills. Even though she was getting more than a little dizzy, she didn't want him to stop and he didn't, spinning her faster and faster. Finally, he placed her on the ground gently and gave her a peck on the cheek. 'You made your old man proud today, Teddy Bear. Did you enjoy your lesson?'

'Of course, Daddy. I loved it.' The truth was, she had been afraid of the horse, who seemed as tall as a mountain and as unpredictable as her dance teacher Miss Plum, who would often shout and storm off without the slightest provocation. But the girl couldn't tell her father that because she didn't want to disappoint him.

'I have a surprise for you. Close your eyes and follow me. No peeking,' said the man, taking her hand.

'Can I open my eyes now?' she asked impatiently after they had barely walked ten paces. Even though she couldn't see where they were going, she could tell he was taking her back to the stables.

'Not yet.'

'Tell me what it is.'

'If I tell you, it will no longer be a surprise.'

Another hundred paces. It felt strange walking with her eyes shut, like she was moving through a dark tunnel. But she knew she could trust her father. 'Will I like it?'

'You tell me. You can open your eyes now!'

She did as she was told and found herself face to face with the tallest horse she'd ever seen. She hoped she wouldn't have to ride him during her next lesson, which was only a week away. Her favourite horse at the stables was Dolly. She was old and docile and moved no faster than a snail, which suited Claire perfectly. But this horse looked young and energetic. He would be fast and she wouldn't like that. Fast was dangerous, especially when it came to horses.

'What do you think of Xander?' asked the man.

'He's beautiful.' It wasn't a lie. The horse was magnificent. White like fresh snow, he was all muscle and nervous energy. The girl wanted to pat him on the nose but didn't dare.

'I'm glad you like him. He's yours. Your birthday present!' The man beamed, pleased with himself.

Since she was little, the girl had dreamed of having a dog, a Golden Retriever she would call Poppy. In her imagination, Poppy and her were inseparable, going on long bicycle rides and learning how to steer a canal boat together. In the evenings, Poppy would curl up in the girl's lap and give her an occasional lick on the hand, while they read and watched films. Could she share adventures with a horse? Xander definitely wouldn't fit in her lap and would look out of place walking around town.

Her father was watching her expectantly, an excited twinkle in his eyes. For his sake, she had to fake excitement to match his. 'My own horse! I can't believe it. Thank you so much, Daddy. Where will Xander live?' She knew the horse couldn't live inside the house but was their garden big enough?

'We'll keep him in the stables for now. You can visit and ride him any time you like.'

'Wait till I tell my friends. I'll be the envy of everyone at school.'

'You can invite all your friends here if you like. But let's not tell Nate about Xander just yet. You know how he gets.'

* * *

A week after she found out about her husband's affair, Claire woke on the sofa, where she must have fallen asleep reading. When she opened her eyes, she saw Gaby sitting next to her. Only half-awake and confused, Claire watched her friend in silence. She had been dreaming of a dark-haired boy, his face distorted in anger – or was it fear? – his arms flailing. He was trying to tell her something but what? She could see his face clearly but couldn't hear the words. And she desperately wanted to hear the words. Was he screaming at her? Or was he warning her? Was the boy Nate? Was she remembering him or was it another nightmare her tired brain had conjured? She wished she knew what her brother had looked like, so that she could tell her memories apart from her dreams.

This dream scared Claire more than her old nightmares ever had.

'I hope you don't mind. I let myself in. I knocked but no one answered,' said Gaby, smiling at Claire with affection, as if their last conversation had never happened. 'I brought you something.' She pointed at a basket by her feet. It was filled with muffins and cakes. It seemed the old Gaby was back, with her hair brushed to perfection and her makeup carefully applied. Claire could almost believe she had imagined the matted hair and tattered pyjamas of a week ago. But she could see through Gaby's attempt to fake normality. There were dark circles under her eyes and her face looked thinner.

Did Gaby think pastries would make up for an affair with Claire's husband and for the web of lies she had woven? Because of her, Claire had thought her husband was a murderer. She was scared for her life living under the same roof with him. 'I think you should leave,' she said, pulling herself up on the couch, so she wouldn't have to look up at Gaby.

'I'll understand if you never want to talk to me again. To be honest, I wasn't expecting you to.'

'If you weren't expecting me to, then why are you here?'

'I joined AA. Two days sober and proud of it.'

'Good for you, Gaby. Why are you telling me this?'

'The first step to recovery is taking responsibility for my actions and making amends. Or so my sponsor says. I'm here to apologise.'

Claire didn't know what to say, so she said nothing.

Gaby continued, 'I don't know if I can ever stop loving Paul. But he chose you and I respect that. The thing is, you and I have been friends for most of my adult life. I don't want to lose that.'

Gaby looked so sad, sitting awkwardly on the edge of the couch, tall and thin like an exotic bird and just as beautiful. Claire felt a pang of something resembling pity. But only for a moment. 'I don't remember the friendship you are talking about. But I do remember trusting you with all my heart and having that trust broken. I don't think I can ever get over that.'

Gaby's eyes filled with tears and she looked pleadingly at Claire. 'Every time something happens, I want to tell you about it. I reach for my phone to call you and then remember and . . . I miss you, Claire. I hope you can forgive me one day. Even if things are never the same between us, I still want you in my life.'

Claire wanted to ask Gaby how it was possible that she truly cared about her friend and still plotted to turn her life upside down. How could she exploit a vulnerable situation Claire had found herself in for her own good? Gaby had sat in her living room, looked her in the eye and lied. And Claire, lost and confused and not knowing who she was, believed every word. 'I don't understand,' she started to say and stopped. There was no point. If Gaby's conscience had been asleep until now, nothing Claire could say could awaken it.

Gaby didn't seem to notice what was so apparent on Claire's face. 'That's not all I wanted to tell you. After you left that day, I remembered something. It's about your brother.'

Suddenly, Claire forgot all about the affair and the lies. She gripped her seat so tightly, her fingers turned white.

'A couple of years ago, you said something when you had a

few too many drinks. I was drunk too, so I can't be sure exactly what it was. But you said something like, my brother should have minded his own business. Everything would have been okay if only he minded his own business. And you cried, a lot. I remember wondering what you meant. But then I thought I must have misunderstood. Easy to do after a bottle of wine and half a dozen tequila shots. When I questioned you the next morning, you said you didn't know what I was talking about.'

Claire couldn't see straight from the pounding in her head. 'I think my nightmares might have something to do with Nate. In my diary I wrote repeatedly that I hate someone. What if this someone was Nate?'

'Why would you hate your own brother?'

'I don't know. I wish I did. I wish I knew what he'd done.'

* * *

Claire didn't want to be alone. Like a ghost she hovered over Nina, following her every move as the housekeeper mopped, polished and dusted. And when everything was spotless, Claire watched while Nina made spaghetti Bolognese, Tony's favourite. The sauce simmered cheerfully on the stove, the little blue flame twirling and drawing Claire's gaze. So small, and yet, so deadly. Capable of the greatest destruction, of burning houses and killing brothers.

In the evening, she played cards with Tony, losing game after game because all she could think of was her vision and the face she had seen in Matilda's office, her father's young face smiling up at her as he threw her in the air. She told herself it was just another dream. She must have fallen asleep on her therapist's couch and didn't realise. What she thought was a memory was in fact a figment of her imagination. 'Daddy, who is Xander?'

'You remember Xander?' Tony beamed. 'You spent all your free time at the stables, looking after him. The adventures the two of you had shared! You had an unbreakable bond.'

'Did you give him to me on my birthday?'

'Your twelfth birthday. You looked uncertain at first, like you were afraid of him. But as you got to know him, you fell in love. It was hard not to. Xander was loyal and affectionate and when he loved someone, he gave his heart fully.'

'I remember him.' She was crying, tears of fear and relief, grateful for the darkness in the room because she didn't want her father to see. 'I can see him now. Snow-white and tall. Intimidating.'

'Let me tell you, you weren't intimidated for long. Once he let you pat him and accepted a carrot, the two of you became the best of friends.'

It hadn't been a dream after all. It was her first memory. She no longer felt like a blank canvas. Now that she remembered a part of her childhood, however small, other memories might follow. She could sense them at the edge of her mind, teasing her. Why did it fill her with dread instead of joy? 'Something in my memory didn't make sense. You asked me not to tell Nate about Xander. "You know how he gets," you said to me. What did you mean by that?'

Her father watched her in silence, as if wondering what answer he could give her. Whether she was ready to hear it. When he finally spoke, he seemed to weigh his every word. 'Nate was a little overprotective. He hated the idea of you riding. He said it was too dangerous. Besides, for once I wanted you to have something to yourself. All your life you had to share everything with Nate.'

Was it the truth? Half-truth or whole truth? Tony didn't meet her gaze. Was he hiding something from her? 'Did we tell him eventually?'

'Of course we did. He wanted to know where you disappeared to every day after school.'

'And did he approve?'

'Once he saw how happy you were, he did.'

Claire asked Tony to tell her everything he could remember

about Nate. She wanted to know what he was like and what he enjoyed, what books he read and what sports he loved. Most of all, she wanted to hear stories that would make her brother seem real. But before her father had a chance to reply, her phone rang. It was a number she didn't recognise. Was it the call she had been waiting for? Turning away from Tony, wishing she was alone, she answered.

'Hello?'

'My name is Tegan. I found your note.'

Claire's hand flew up to her mouth as she glanced at her father. 'I'm happy to hear from you,' she said quietly into the phone.

'Claire, is that really you? On the news I saw about Angela . . .' The voice on the other side trembled. It was a few moments before the woman continued talking. 'I've been going out of my mind but didn't know how to contact you. Then I found your note . . . When can you come to see me?'

Tegan sounded desperate to see her niece, and since Claire was desperate to see her aunt, she said, 'I'll be there first thing tomorrow. If that's okay.'

Tegan assured her that it was more than okay, that seeing her would make her the happiest person in the world.

'Who was that?' asked Tony when she hung up.

'Just an old friend,' she replied quickly. She hated lying to her father and yet, she had a feeling telling him the truth would be a mistake.

Chapter 19

Claire and Paul were in the car, about to drive to Windsor to meet Claire's aunt, when a police van appeared out of nowhere and turned into the driveway, blocking their way. PC Kamenski stepped out of the driver's seat, looking dishevelled, a forced smile plastered on her face. PC Stanley wasn't with her.

'I won't take up too much of your time,' she said to Claire when they were seated in the living room. 'Someone saw you argue with your mother outside her house a week before her murder. Can you tell me anything about it?' She consulted her notes, went back a few pages as if to double-check something and finally fixed her expectant gaze on Claire, who wondered what other evidence against her was hiding inside the little notebook.

'I don't know,' she stammered, gripping the strap of her handbag so hard, her knuckles turned white. She felt her cheeks redden as if she had something to hide. The problem was, even if she did have anything to hide, she couldn't remember.

As if reading her thoughts, PC Kamenski said, 'You need to start remembering, and soon. You are not doing yourself any favours.'

'If arguing with one's mother was a crime, you'd have to arrest just about everyone.'

'Not every mother is found stabbed in her own house.'

'You think it was me, don't you? You think I had something to do with it? That I picked up a knife and stabbed the woman who gave birth to me, who held me and nursed me, who cooked chicken soup for me when I was sick and helped me with my homework.' Claire didn't know if any of it was true. But the police officer looked embarrassed enough to shrug apologetically and glance away. Encouraged, Claire continued, 'Do you have a mother? Let me guess, the two of you never had an argument?'

'Just doing my job. I didn't mean to alarm you.'

'I'm not alarmed and you know why? Because I didn't do anything wrong. So, if there's nothing else, I have to go.'

'There's nothing else,' said PC Kamenski, pursing her lips as if she wanted to add, *yet. There's nothing else, yet.*

While Paul drove in silence, Claire tried to remain calm – and failed – by watching the cars speeding down the M4. Two things were bothering her. Firstly, the police still suspected her. And secondly, they might actually have a reason to. That meant she could have had something to do with her mother's murder. And that was the worst part – the *could have*. The not knowing for certain.

Tegan's house looked weathered and old, its walls hidden behind an onslaught of Boston ivy. The brick, where it was visible, looked like it had been bleached by the sun. The front yard was drowning in dahlias and there was a hint of lavender in the air. Claire had a sudden feeling this house and this garden and these walls and these flowers held the key to her childhood.

With trepidation she stood on the porch, wishing once again that Paul was with her instead of in a nearby café getting breakfast and his fix of daily news. Windsor looked different in the rain, grey and sombre, all the colours smudged together, but she liked the freshness in the air and the crispy feel to it. The castle, like a grim giant, lurked in the background, its outline barely visible in the mist. She was about to ring the bell when the door flew open and a small woman appeared. Claire couldn't quite read the expression on her face. There was anxiety and surprise, as if she couldn't believe her eyes, and there was joy, too.

It was as if her mother's photograph had come to life. Her aunt had the same graceful build, the same blonde hair and grey eyes. Claire studied her, searching for little clues to what Angela had been like, taking in her bright smile and kindly face. Her mind was playing tricks on her, and she almost opened her mouth and said, 'Mum.'

After a moment of quiet observation, Tegan threw her hands up to her face and said, 'Please, forgive me for staring like this. I haven't seen you in so long. Come in, come in.'

Claire followed her aunt down a narrow corridor into the living room. Once there, Tegan turned around sharply and hugged Claire, taking her by surprise. She had expected small talk, a polite conversation one might share with a stranger. What she hadn't expected was the warmth of her aunt's reception. It felt unsettling and she didn't know how to respond. Despite what her father had told her, Tegan seemed kind and genuinely happy to see Claire.

'Thank you for inviting me, Ms Moore.'

'What is this Ms Moore nonsense? You've always called me Aunt Tegan.'

'Aunt Tegan.' Claire repeated the words, tasting them like an exotic fruit she had never had before. Calling this woman her aunt made her feel happy and secure and a little less lonely.

'We must have tea!' exclaimed Tegan, her face flushed. 'Is Earl Grey still your favourite?' Without waiting for an answer she rushed into the kitchen, adding, 'Since you turned 14, you refused to drink any other kind.'

'Earl Grey sounds perfect,' said Claire, even though she had no idea what it tasted like. But who was she to argue?

Unlike her parents' mansion in North London, this house was small and cosy, with quirky pillows on the sofa and candles on the coffee table. The walls were freshly painted and the furniture seemed new. Everywhere Claire looked, she could see old black-and-white photographs, faces frozen in happy smiles, moments of joy captured and framed. She longed to walk over and study them in detail, hoping to see her mother's face, herself as a child and, most importantly, her brother. But she didn't want to appear rude, so she remained on the sofa and waited for her aunt to come back.

Tegan returned with a tray. There were two steaming cups of tea, some strawberry jam, scones and biscuits. Claire wished she had thought of bringing something for her aunt and felt embarrassed.

'I only ever drink green tea myself,' said Tegan as she made herself comfortable next to Claire. 'Anything else is too strong for me. I'm sorry these are from the supermarket.' She pointed at the biscuits. 'Had I known earlier you were coming, I would have baked some myself.'

'These are perfect, Aunt Tegan, thank you,' said Claire, taking a biscuit and dunking it in her tea. 'You look so much like Mum. Not that I remember what she looked like. Only from photographs. Like I said in my note, I was in an accident. I lost my memory. I had no idea she had a sister until I found a photo in her Bible. Then Dad told me about you . . .' She was blabbering and couldn't help it.

The cup trembled in Tegan's hand and she placed it on the coffee table. Her eyes filled with tears. A wrinkled handkerchief appeared as if by magic in her hands and she blew her nose. 'I'm so sorry. Ever since I found out . . . I was watching the news one day and I saw . . . Angela, my darling sister! Since then, I've been such a mess.' She sighed and tried to dry her eyes with her handkerchief but the tears kept coming. 'I just can't get my head around it. Angela is my twin. Was . . .' She gasped as if in pain. 'She's always been by my side, even before we were born. If she's gone, how can I still be here? How am I alive without her?'

'I'm sorry, Aunt Tegan,' whispered Claire, herself on the brink of tears.

'Tell me what happened. Have they found the murderer? Who would do this? She was an angel. Who would wish her harm?'

'The police are investigating. They don't tell us much.' She wasn't about to admit to her aunt that she was a suspect. She could barely admit it to herself.

After Claire told her everything she knew about the accident and the murder, Tegan crossed herself and whispered, 'That's awful. I'm so sorry you had to go through that, Claire.'

'Thank you, Aunt Tegan. I'm trying to piece my life back together.'

'I haven't spoken to your mother in ten years. Last time I saw her, you were a 16-year-old girl.'

Tegan's face lit up as she spoke about the past. Enthralled, Claire listened about the day she was born, her first day at school and her first ballet lesson. All the firsts she longed to remember but couldn't. She learnt that she had a sweetheart when she was twelve and was convinced she was going to marry him. Her room had always been filled with flowers he gave her because his mum was a florist. She found out what food she had loved as a child and how much she had wanted a little sister. 'Instead, your mother gave you a doll. It was so realistic, it looked just like a real baby. You called your doll Barbara and never went anywhere without her.'

So many happy memories but Claire knew there were dark times in her past, shadows looming over her everywhere she looked. And that was what she wanted to hear about. She thought of the red dots marking the diary she had written at 16, like drops of blood announcing another battle lost. She thought of every entry in between, of a teenage girl trying her best to live a normal life, while something terrible was happening around her. She remembered the horror she experienced every time she had the nightmare.

'Did I have a good relationship with my mum? Did we ever argue?'

'You were as close as a mother and daughter could possibly be. You told your mother everything.'

Claire was silent for a moment, thinking about her mother, trying to picture her face. Then she realised – she didn't need to picture it, all she had to do was look at her aunt. As relieved as Claire was to hear Tegan's words, she realised that her aunt was

192

talking about her as a child. Everything could have changed since then. 'Aunt Tegan, I need to ask you about the fire.'

Tegan's face crumbled and for a few moments she couldn't speak. 'It was a terrible tragedy. Your brother . . . He was the sweetest boy. And I'm not just saying that because he was my nephew. He was the kindest boy . . . Look at me, you came all this way and all I do is burst into tears. I'm so sorry.'

Claire moved closer to her aunt and put her arm around her. Tegan's shoulders were shaking. 'My brother never got angry or violent?'

'Nate?' Tegan looked up at Claire, her eyes wide. 'That boy had a heart of gold. What made you think he was violent?'

'It's just this dream I keep having. Do you have any photos of him?' Claire was desperate to see her brother's face.

'Of course.'

In an antique chest of drawers by the window Tegan found an old album. It didn't take long – it seemed it had been placed on top of all the other knick-knacks, like a cherished book read over and over again. Claire put the leather-bound album in her lap and turned the pages slowly. Snaps of a happy family greeted her – nothing but beaming faces and wide smiles. Here was her mother, decades younger – or was it her aunt (it was impossible to tell) – posing outside a skating rink, skates around her neck, arms waving. And the two of them, Tegan and Angela, identical in every way, pushing a pram together. Just like the framed pictures on the walls, these photos were grey-scale, the silhouettes ghostlike.

'All these photos are black-and-white,' said Claire.

'When I was younger, I fancied myself somewhat of a photographer. I thought black-and-white was artistic. Now I wish they had some colour in them.'

And then there was a young boy, with his arm around young Claire, dressed in a school uniform.

'That's Nate,' whispered Claire. It wasn't a question. She knew her brother as soon as she saw him. With her heart beating violently she studied the face from her dream. Trembling, she touched the black-and-white image, wanting to get to know him, to absorb him through the skin of her fingers. Nate looked delicate, almost feminine. Even though he was taller than his sister, his shoulders wide, there was something about him that seemed fragile. Maybe because she knew that all too soon he would be taken away from her.

Claire looked at her younger self in the photograph, at her brother's smiling face. They seemed so full of joy, like they didn't have a care in the world. 'How old are we in this picture?'

'Nate had just turned 16. You were 14.'

No longer children but not yet adults, either. Their whole lives ahead of them. Except, Nate's life was about to come to an end. 'Can I keep this photo?'

'You can keep the entire album,' said Tegan.

Claire watched as once again tears ran down Tegan's cheeks. This album was the only link she had to her twin sister's family. It must have meant so much to her. Didn't twins share an unbreakable bond? What had to happen for that bond to turn into alienation, into nothingness? 'Aunt Tegan, do you have any children of your own?'

'You were the only family I had.'

Her heart thumping, Claire asked, 'Why did you and Mum stop talking?'

'I didn't approve of her choices, I suppose. And it hurt her feelings. I should have kept my opinion to myself.'

'When you say her choices . . .'

'I didn't think your father was the right man for Angela. She was too good for him. I never understood what she saw in him. But love is blind and she refused to listen.' Claire, who didn't think anyone was too good for her father, shook her head. Her aunt didn't seem to notice. 'The truth is, we fell out long before you moved to London. But being so close to you meant I could still see you. When you left, that was it. I never heard from my sister again.' Tegan dabbed her eyes with her handkerchief. 'Angela was engaged to a wonderful man when she was younger. If only she married him, everything would have turned out differently.'

'Who was he?'

'His name was David. He was kind and sweet, the type of man you would hope your daughter to meet one day. They were about to get married. The church was booked, the invitations went out.'

'What happened?'

'She was working in London and he was finishing his degree in Edinburgh, so they were apart for a few months. He came to see her one day and told her he had slept with someone else.' The handkerchief in Tegan's hands was knotted and twisted. There were tiny beads of perspiration on her forehead. She sat in silence for a long time, staring out the window, as if she would rather talk about anything else. 'People make mistakes. Nobody is perfect. He said it was a one-time thing and he felt terrible about it. That he loved Angela and regretted what happened straight away. That he wanted to be honest with her. He didn't want a relationship built on lies. He begged her to forgive him but she couldn't. She thought she could never trust him again. A week after they broke up, she found out she was pregnant. She met your father four months later.'

'Are you saying Dad is not Nate's biological father?'

Tegan nodded. 'Your parents never made a secret of it. Both you and your brother knew about it growing up and it didn't matter to you at all.' She took a sip of her tea and stared into space as if lost in thought. 'But it mattered to Tony. Between you and I, I don't think he ever loved your mother. He saw an opportunity and took it, exploiting a pregnant woman who'd found herself in a vulnerable position. What does that tell you about his character?'

'That's not true,' cried Claire. She knew her father. He loved her mother more than life itself.

'He's been unfaithful to Angela from day one. But your mother refused to believe it. Ironic, really. She didn't marry David, who would never have looked at another woman again in his life. Instead, she ended up with Tony.'

For a moment Claire couldn't speak. She was shocked into silence by her aunt's words. The only sound in the room was the ticking of the grandfather clock in the corner. Intricately carved, its hands moved heavily. The clock didn't show the correct time. It was two hours late. Tick-tock, heard Claire, as she thought of all the little white lies that defined her life. 'It doesn't sound like my father at all. He's been so kind to me. Mum's murder broke his heart. You should see him. He's not himself. That's not the man who didn't love his wife.'

Tegan reddened and her hand flew up to her mouth. 'I shouldn't have said anything. It must be such a shock for you to hear this after everything that's happened. I'm so sorry. I should have kept it to myself.'

'That's okay,' said Claire, even though it wasn't. She, too, wished Tegan had kept her accusations to herself.

'Before you go, I'd like to give you something.' Tegan left the room but soon returned, carrying a box filled with books, letters and notepads. 'Everything here belongs to you. You never know, it might help you remember. And I hope you'll visit me again soon. I have no family left other than you.'

Claire didn't reply. She stumbled out of her aunt's house with barely a hug and a kiss goodbye. It had taken her by surprise how profoundly unhappy it made her feel to hear someone speak ill of her father. Not that she believed a word of it. *Everyone is entitled to their opinion*, she whispered to herself in the car. It didn't mean that this opinion was correct.

* * *

In the box Tegan had given her, hidden among old magazines, photographs and books, Claire found another diary, dated a year before the fire. There were no red dots and no 'I hate hims' hidden inside the covers. But that wasn't what Claire was looking for. She devoured every word, searching for something, anything, about Nate, longing to fill the void in her mind where her brother should have been.

Nate starts uni next month. Mum's so proud of him, she's throwing him a party. Hope Kieran is there.

Nate came home from uni on the weekend. He wanted his football jersey back but I refused to give it to him.

Nate's friends are such dorks. Except Kieran. He's cute.

Mum said I should be more like Nate. His room is always tidy and mine never is. Not my fault he's such a clean freak. While he was gone, I made his room look more like mine. Wait till he gets home and sees it.

Nate bought a pizza. Sasha and I waited till he was in the bathroom and ate most of it.

Nate gave me a yearly subscription to the Ballet *magazine for my birthday. Best present ever!*

As Claire tried to read between the lines, she saw the camaraderie the two of them had shared, how much she had enjoyed teasing her brother and how he would let her because he loved her. How eagerly she had waited for Nate to visit once he'd moved out. And how he spoilt his little sister rotten. What she saw was love masqueraded as sibling rivalry.

That was when she knew – Nate hadn't been forgotten, for how could he be? Paul was right. He was hidden deep inside her heart, away from everyone she loved, because losing him was the worst thing that had ever happened to her.

And another thing she knew for sure – Nate had never been angry or violent to her in his life. He was not the shadow from her dream.

Unable to think of anything but Nate and Tegan, Claire found her father in his room having breakfast.

'Why didn't you tell me Nate was my half-brother?' asked Claire without hesitation. She was done with small talk.

'Who told you that?' Tony asked, looking up from his food.

Even though Tony was watching her with a kind smile on his face, Claire didn't want him to know she had spoken to Tegan. She didn't want him to know about her doubts. 'I found an old diary

I wrote as a child. There was something about me and Nate being so alike, even though we were only half-brother and sister.' She shrugged and looked away, hoping he wouldn't pursue it further. He didn't. 'Why didn't you tell me you weren't Nate's father?'

'Because as far as I am concerned, I *was* his father. I loved him like he was my own. I couldn't have loved a child more. You know what they say. It's not biology that makes you a father. It takes far more than that. It's the sleepless nights when they cry in your arms. It's the bedtime story you read over and over, evening after exhausted evening. It's the swimming classes you take them to first thing every Saturday morning when all you want is to sleep for another hour. It's the first smile, the first tooth, the first word, the first step, and all the tears in between. It's the first time you hear *Daddy*, the first time you teach them how to ride a bicycle, play football or drive a car. And that's why I didn't tell you Nate was your half-brother. Because he's always been my son. Just like you are my daughter. Nothing could ever change that.'

Wiping her tears away, Claire said, 'Do you know what else I found in my diary? Aunt Tegan's address. Do you still want me to stay away from her, even though Mum is gone?' As Claire said these words, she realised she was looking for his permission. If Tony told her she could visit her aunt, she wouldn't feel so guilty about having done so behind his back. She didn't like lying to her father. Of all the people in her life, she wanted their relationship to be based on honesty and trust.

There was that expression on his face again, as if something had shut down against her. 'Yes, I still want you to stay away from her.'

'But why? We don't have any other family. It would be nice—'

Tony interrupted her. 'Tegan always resented your mother. She's gone out of her way to make Angela's life hell. She's jealous and manipulative.'

'Why would she resent her own sister?'

'Because your mother was their father's favourite and he left all his money to her. Tegan was a wild child growing up.

Ran away from home, dropped out of high school. While your mother studied hard, Tegan partied and took drugs. She didn't see the point in education because she assumed she could fall back on her father's money. Your grandfather wanted to teach her a lesson. He wanted her to find her own way.'

'She . . .' Claire started saying and stopped, remembering just in time her father didn't know she had been to see her aunt. Tegan had seemed so different from the person her father was describing. But he was talking about Tegan when she was younger, Tegan of many years ago. Of course, she would have changed beyond recognition since then. 'Didn't Mum help her? Give her money?'

'She tried. But Tegan refused. She was bitter over her father's will and too proud to accept what she referred to as a hand-out when she believed half of it was rightfully hers. So she told lies. She would tell your mother she'd seen me with another woman. She would send anonymous letters to the house. Eventually, your mother couldn't take it anymore.'

'And that's why they stopped talking?'

'That's why they stopped talking.'

Everyone's truth was different. It was possible Aunt Tegan truly believed Tony was a womanising good-for-nothing. But Angela must have thought differently, or she wouldn't have stood by him all these years, shutting out all the voices that screamed otherwise. She chose to lose her twin sister rather than let doubt inside her heart. Her husband had her irrevocable trust. And that had been her truth.

My aunt is wrong, Claire whispered to herself as she lay in bed that evening. *She is mistaken. She doesn't know what she's talking about.* But deep inside, a tiny seed of doubt remained. What if Tegan wasn't wrong? How well did Claire actually know her father? He rarely spoke about the past and hadn't mentioned her brother until she asked. Was he trying to protect her? Or was he hiding something?

Chapter 20

Claire could believe her aunt but that would mean her relationship with Tony would never be the same again. It was easier for her to follow her mother's lead and trust her father. And every day she spent with Tony, he convinced her a little bit more that Tegan was lying. He made her smile and he made her forget. Every game of Scrabble, every lunch she cooked for him and every walk in the park she took with him melted the ice cube of doubt inside her a little bit more until it was almost gone. With Tony, she could be a child again. The child she couldn't remember but instinctively knew how to become.

At the top of the box Claire had brought from her parents' house, inside one of her mother's magazines, she found some old letters. Addressed to Angela, they looked frail with age, as if they belonged in a different lifetime. On the back of the envelope was Tony's name and a Cambridge address. Trying to steady her trembling hands, Claire took a deep breath and opened the first letter. Her father's clear handwriting was easy to read.

I must have done something right in my life to have someone like you love me. I have never been in love before. I didn't even believe it existed. And now, when I hold you in my arms, I

can't help thinking how naive I used to be. Sometimes I close
my eyes and wonder if you're real. I wonder if I deserve you.

Claire felt slightly embarrassed, like she was witnessing something special that wasn't meant for prying eyes, intimate like a diary entry of a stranger. Getting comfortable under her duvet, she read letter after letter, each as poetic as the first. Devouring every word, she tried to recreate her parents' incredible story, longing to imagine them young and happy and in love. More than anything she wished she could find someone who would love her *that* much.

At dinner one evening, Claire told Paul everything. He was a good listener. Just talking to him made Claire feel like the burden she was carrying was suddenly not as heavy. It wasn't completely gone but it was lighter. 'There are times when I trust my father implicitly,' she concluded. 'I look into his eyes and see nothing but affection. Then there are other times, when I can't seem to chase the doubts away. On days like that I wish I had never gone to visit my aunt. I don't know what to think or whom to believe.'

'Don't be silly. Of course you do. What your aunt told you doesn't sound like your father at all. Every time I saw him, he seemed besotted with Angela. He only had eyes for her.'

'Why would my aunt lie?'

'People lie for various reasons. Maybe she was jealous of Tony. Maybe she felt like he was trying to come between her and her twin. We all need one person we can turn to. Perhaps she felt Tony was trying to take hers away.'

In the absence of Gaby, Molokai had become Claire's best friend. He accompanied her everywhere as she walked the streets, trying to fill her head with sounds and images that had little to do with her life. In the park, she would often lie on her back in the grass and think of her parents and brother. She would shield her eyes from the sun, watching Molokai splash in the pond and creep up on birds.

One day, after she had been gone for a couple of hours, her phone rang.

'You need to come home right away,' said Paul. 'It's your father.' It wasn't her husband's words as much as the tone of his voice that made Claire's heart fall in a premonition of something terrible.

Paul refused to say any more on the phone. When she returned, he was waiting outside the house. 'What happened?' Claire exclaimed as soon as she was close enough.

'I found him in the bath. He wasn't breathing. Thank God I forgot my phone and had to come back. Another few minutes and it would have been too late.' Claire felt her legs trembling under her. Her face must have gone completely white, because Paul took her arm to steady her and said, 'He's okay now. Sedated and resting. We've been looking after him.'

'You saved his life,' she said quietly.

'It's lucky he'd left his bedroom door open. I heard the water running. I thought it was strange, without Helga there to help him. So I went in to check . . .' Paul shuddered.

'Was it an accident?'

Paul hesitated for a moment but when he spoke, his voice was firm. 'I don't think it was. And neither does his psychiatrist. They believe he's struggling to come to terms with what happened.'

'You think he tried to take his own life? I don't understand. I saw him this morning. He was fine. As fine as he's ever been.' But she did understand. She understood perfectly. Her father hadn't been fine in a long time. He had lost the love of his life, someone who had been by his side for most of his adult life. Judging by the letters Claire had read the night before, Angela was his only light. Now that she was gone, was it surprising he couldn't see his way out of the darkness?

The *what ifs* were swirling in her mind like a cloud of hungry mosquitoes as they made their way up the driveway. What if Paul hadn't been so forgetful? What if he came back a minute too late? What if he had rushed out the door without checking on Tony first? The more she thought about it, the more real the *what ifs* became. In her imagination, Paul hadn't been forgetful. He hadn't returned on time and hadn't checked on Tony. In her imagination, her father was gone. She felt this imaginary loss acutely, becoming painfully aware that, had it been real, she would have been all alone in the world, with no family to speak of. Icy cold fear gripped her as Paul led her through the front door and the ghost of a house greeted them. All the lights were out and it was so quiet, she could hear herself breathe.

When Claire peered into her father's room, she saw that he was still sleeping. Quietly she sat on the edge of his bed, watching him. He looked so peaceful, his chest rising and falling like waves rolling upon the shore. Claire took his left hand, her fingers circling the simple golden wedding band he was wearing.

An image rose to the surface, of his lifeless body submerged in the bath. She blinked, chasing it away. She could feel her whole body shaking. She had almost lost her father. If it wasn't for Paul, she would have received a very different phone call while out in the park with Molokai. 'I'm sorry Daddy,' she whispered, bending over him, her tears falling on his face. *I'm sorry I wasn't here for you when you needed me.*

He stirred. 'Ah. Look who's back.' He seemed pleased to see her. There was a smile on his face, as if nothing out of the ordinary had happened.

'How are you feeling?'

'Better now you're here.'

'What a fright you gave me. What were you thinking, Dad?'

He didn't try to pretend, didn't try to convince her he had fallen asleep in his bath while reading the Bible. She wished he would. Then she could believe him, accept it as a terrible accident and go on as before. 'Everything just seems so pointless. How do I live without your mother? For thirty years she'd been by my side. And now that she's gone, I don't know what to do. I'm just so lost without her, Claire.'

'I know, Dad. I feel the same and I don't even remember her. I can imagine how much harder it must be for you.'

He pulled himself up in bed. His smile was frozen on his face, as if someone had hit a pause button on a recording. His skin looked ashen. 'Sometimes I wake up in the middle of the night and I feel betrayed. Can you believe it? I feel angry at your mother for dying and leaving me alone. As if it was her fault. This is the absolute worst thing that's ever happened to me. How do I go on?'

'You better find a way. You have to promise me you'll never do anything like this again. Have you thought for one second what it would do to me?'

His voice hoarse, he said, 'I know you've been to Windsor. Did you find your aunt?'

Surprised at the change of topic and taken off guard, Claire wanted to lie, to pretend she didn't know what he was talking about. God knew this was not the time for this conversation. But he deserved better. There had been too many lies. To gain time, she asked, 'How did you know?'

'Nina told me.'

'I did find Tegan.'

'Did you speak to her?'

She nodded.

'What horrible things did she tell you about me?'

'Nothing,' whispered Claire. 'She told me nothing. You should get some rest. And I'll ask Nina to cook something special for dinner.' He nodded and closed his eyes. 'I love you, Dad,' she whispered so softly, she didn't think he would hear.

'I love you too, Teddy Bear. In all my life, I've loved you the most.'

She held his hand until he fell asleep again, afraid of letting go. How could she have doubted him? Tony could never hurt someone close to him. So distraught was he without Angela, he had tried to take his own life. He would never have betrayed her with another woman. After all, he was the kindest person Claire knew. He told her he loved her every day. He rescued stray animals, like seven cats named Pluto he had told her about, because he believed no one deserved to be scared and alone. And when she had been scared and alone, he came into her life and filled it with sunshine. Her aunt was a stranger to her. Why did Claire allow Tegan to poison her with lies, if only for a moment?

Chapter 21

One Saturday morning, Paul and Claire were in the car, having driven for over an hour, and Claire had no idea where they were going. *It's a surprise,* was all Paul would tell her. From the road signs she could tell they were in Oxford. All around as far as the eye could see were never-ending hills and forests that had just started to turn a deep shade of gold. It was so peaceful, she felt every muscle in her body relax. She could smell hay and manure, the scent of childhood, not that she could remember hers. But even to her it conjured carefree summer days of adventure, bike rides perhaps, canoeing down the river and camping in the woods.

'The countryside is so beautiful,' she said.

'You love it here. You always used to say the open space made you feel alive. You felt trapped in the city.'

'I can see why. Life seems to move at a different pace here.'

The landscape became increasingly more rural. When they turned off at a farm and Paul stopped the car behind a stable, it felt like London was not a couple of hours but a small universe away. Horses were grazing all around them, some nearby, others nothing but dark specs in the green and yellow of the fields. Claire's eyes lit up like a child's at Hamleys. She jumped out of the car and rushed to the horses, to offer them carrots Paul had packed, to put her arms around their large necks and her hands inside their manes. 'Is that the surprise? You took me to see horses?' she asked, touched. It was as if Paul had known about Xander.

'You love horses. I thought seeing them might trigger a memory.' Paul looked dishevelled that morning, as if he had just got out of bed. His hair was pointing in different directions, giving him an appearance of an untidy porcupine. There was stubble like a shadow on his face. Claire thought he looked adorable.

'I know I had a horse as a child but I find it hard to believe. I'm pretty sure I'm afraid of heights. And horses are so tall. Wait. You don't actually expect me to ride one of them, do you?' There was panic in her voice, and disbelief. Could Paul do that to her? Drive her all this way to force her to go on a horse?

'You are an expert rider. Trust me.'

'I might trust you but I wouldn't trust a horse. They look like they've got a mind of their own.'

Seemingly amused, Paul pressed her hand as if to reassure her. 'Don't worry. It's like riding a bicycle. It will come back to you in no time.'

'I don't think I know how to ride a bicycle.'

'It's like playing the piano or dancing. Your body will remember. It was you who taught me how to ride. And you did an excellent job. I only fell off twice.'

She could feel all colour drain from her face. 'Okay, we've seen the horses. Can we go now?'

'Don't worry. I didn't really fall off twice.'

'That's a relief.'

'Only once.'

'Paul!' By the expression on his face she could tell he was joking but she was afraid nonetheless. She glanced at a horse in front of her, a chestnut mare with its nostrils twitching. It didn't look like it would take orders from anyone, let alone her.

'Want to go home?' asked Paul.

Claire thought of the dark house they had left behind in London, of her father's misery as he stared at the walls of his bedroom, of all the secrets and the fears that lay in wait for her, ready to pounce as soon as she walked through the door. This trip to Oxford with Paul felt like a reprieve, albeit temporary. Although she knew it would end, she didn't want it to end too soon. 'And miss my chance to see you fall off your horse? I don't think so!' And then she saw a beautiful white stallion watching them warily from one of the stalls, his nostrils twitching. He reminded her of Xander. 'I choose him. That's the horse I want to ride.'

Paul was right. It *was* like riding a bicycle. Once the horses were saddled up, he only had to give her a tiny push and she flew up into the saddle. It was as if her body knew exactly what to do. Paul led the way down a narrow cobbled path towards the wilderness. When her horse started moving, slow and steady, as if he knew to take it easy on her, Claire shrieked.

'Look, you startled him,' exclaimed Paul. 'He's about to take off.' She froze, waiting for the horse to run off with her. Paul added, 'I'm only kidding. Let me show you how to control him.'

'Can you control him? Honestly? I don't think you drive the horse. The horse drives you.'

The horses took them off the beaten path. They didn't follow the main tourist track but made a turn at one of the smaller trails. The Xander lookalike she was on danced on the spot in excitement and for the first time that she could remember, she felt herself relax. There was something special about moving fast on a horse, the feeling of total freedom she found intoxicating. Her hair blowing in the wind, Claire pointed at everything she saw. A sparrow zooming through the skies, a magpie floating above their heads. A few times they spooked a crow and watched with a smile as it flew away, and once or twice they spotted a rabbit in the bushes and had to stop to take a closer look. It was so quiet and peaceful, as if it was just the two of them and not another soul for miles around. Claire almost forgot her worries.

Paul looked happy riding his old chestnut mare next to her, as if the aloof, monosyllabic man of the past few months was gone and in his place was someone who laughed a lot, teased her mercilessly and didn't take his eyes off her. 'Why are you looking at me like that?' she asked. What was that expression in his eyes? She could feel her heart beating fast.

'Like what?'

'Like you expect me to fall off my horse. Like you want to make sure you don't miss it when I do. Why don't you have your camera ready?'

'I don't want you to fall. I'm looking at you because I want to make sure you're okay.'

'But shouldn't you look where you're going? Otherwise we might end up . . . in the river!' she cried, pointing ahead. The river didn't look particularly wide, but Claire was worried. She didn't want their trip to be over just as she started enjoying it. 'Do we have to turn back?'

'Only if you want to.'

'I want to keep going. But how do we get across?'

'Horses can swim, you know.'

As if they understood English, the horses entered the water. Claire shrieked.

'Don't worry, it's not deep here,' said Paul.

The horses crossed the river and emerged on the other side, walking side by side like two old lovers.

'Why are you grinning?' he asked. 'Is it because we didn't drown?'

'It's just . . . There's no one here. It's so beautiful.' She marvelled at the river and the forest, at the trees hugging the water, their branches like arms reaching for the sky. She marvelled at Paul and how elegant he seemed in the saddle, how easy he made it look, as if he was born to ride, like a cowboy or a drover.

'I know.' He smiled like he was solely responsible for the natural beauty of the farm. As if he had built it with his own two hands.

'And there *is* someone here. There's a man fishing.' Paul pointed at the man wearing a camo jacket, crouching on the ground with a small fishing rod in his lap.

'Where did he come from?'

'There's a village nearby. We are not completely in the wild.'

'He looks like he's part of the forest. No wonder I didn't notice him.'

Side by side they rode through the trees. Only the birds could see them, and there were many birds – herons and crows that looked wise with years, and scarlet-chested robins like bright ribbons on the grass. 'I never had a chance to thank you for saving Dad. I don't know what I would do had something happened to him.'

'No thanks necessary. I'm glad I was in the right place at the right time. I knew he wasn't himself after the police had questioned him. He seemed upset and his eyes were red like he'd been crying.'

'I didn't know the police had questioned him that day.' In astonishment, Claire pulled on her reigns. The horse stopped.

Paul nodded. 'They looked like two bloodhounds following a scent. After they spoke to Tony, they wanted to see you. I told them to come back later.'

Suddenly, all the beauty around her vanished as if it had never existed and only the darkness remained. 'Dad never mentioned it to me. Why wouldn't he tell me?'

Her smile frozen on her face, she made small talk for the rest of the trip but her heart wasn't in it. When they got back to the stables, she could barely remember what they had talked about. What could the police have possibly told her father to make him try to take his own life? What was traumatic enough to drive him to do what he did? She could only think of one thing – they must have told him his daughter was responsible for his wife's murder. They must have proof of her guilt. And they would be coming for her.

Chapter 22

Claire expected to see the familiar police car parked by the house, waiting for her. But to her surprise, the driveway was empty. Before she did anything else, before she changed her clothes or had her dinner, she wanted to speak to her father. She needed to know what the police had said to him the day of his attempted suicide and why he hadn't said anything to her.

His room was quiet. The TV was off, the radio mute, his bed empty. She could hear the murmur of running water coming from the bathroom and Helga's muffled voice as she admonished Tony for not doing his exercises. Claire was about to leave when she saw an empty tray on Tony's bed. Reaching for the tray, she noticed his phone tucked under his pillow. Under normal circumstances, she would never dream of going through her father's phone. But something made her stop in her tracks and stare at it for a moment. The phone was playing a YouTube video. Tony must have forgotten to switch it off. She would do it for him, so it didn't drain the battery. That was the excuse Claire made as she picked up her father's phone, looking for answers that no one would give her.

Waiting a moment to make sure the water was still running and her father wasn't about to appear in front of her, she paused the video and quickly navigated to his messages. *What am I doing?* she thought, horrified at herself. She could see a few dozen messages from herself and some from Helga, asking what Tony wanted for dinner. Unable to stop, she scrolled down.

What she saw next made her freeze, her hand at her mouth, as if she'd been confronted by a ghost. Illuminated on the little screen were messages from the familiar overseas number. The number she had once believed belonged to her mother. Her hand on her heart, her face white, she opened the conversation.

You haven't paid me yet.
You will get paid in full. Please stop the phone calls to my daughter. I no longer require your services.
I want more.
More what?
More money.
Why?
You hired me to impersonate someone who's been murdered. I wonder, is it something the police would want to know? What about your daughter?
Call me.

Stupefied and unable to think straight, Claire threw the phone as far as she could and ran out of the door. What did the messages mean?

* * *

'They don't mean anything,' said Paul, who had rushed home from work when he heard Claire's trembling voice over the phone. She must have sounded like she was about to have a breakdown because he abandoned an important surgery and ran to her side. They were sitting opposite each other at the dining table, just like they did on Claire's first evening home, except now she was sobbing uncontrollably and Paul was struggling to make sense of what she was saying.

'He paid someone to call me and pretend to be my mother, long before the police told us about . . . about Mum. Why would he do that?'

'There must be a logical explanation.'

'How did he know my mother was gone? Even before the police told us about her murder, he knew but pretended he didn't.'

'Maybe he didn't know. Maybe he . . .'

'What?' asked Claire. Paul didn't reply. Just like her, he didn't seem to have any answers. Shaking, struggling to get the words out, she continued, 'There's more. Remember the silver charm we found in my parents' house where they discovered my mother . . .' For a moment she couldn't speak. Paul patted her on the arm. 'I think she was wearing it when she was murdered. And I've seen it before. The first time I met Dad in hospital, he dropped his wallet. All the contents spilled out and I saw a charm bracelet with charms just like the one we've found.' When she closed her eyes, she could still see it, curled up under the hospital bed like a small shiny lizard. She remembered the cold feeling in her hand when she picked it up. How could she not have thought of it before? 'Why would he have the bracelet my mum was wearing the day she was killed?' It occurred to Claire she had never asked her father where he was when her mother was killed. Never having doubted him before, she didn't have a reason to ask. She knew he had his car accident on the same day and assumed he wasn't with her mother. He was driving – where? Or from what? Grabbing the table, she tried to steady herself. Her head was spinning from all the questions swirling around in her head and she felt a cold chill running through her, even though the radiator was on and it was boiling in the house.

'Maybe she wasn't wearing it that day. Maybe the charm had always been there, in the corner. And your father kept the bracelet because he wanted to have something that belonged to your mum.'

'I saw you pick up the charm. Can I have it now?' When Paul returned, she snatched the little dove from him but her hand was shaking and her tears were blinding her. It took a few minutes for her to calm down enough to make out the dark stain on the silver surface. 'See here? It looks like blood. I'm pretty sure of it.'

Paul took the charm to the window to examine it under the bright light. 'You need to talk to him. He'll explain everything. Everything will make sense, as soon as you talk to him.'

'I can't. I just can't.' Her teeth chattered from the horror of it all. 'He always talks about leaving here, going away together. He's obsessed with getting rid of you, so we can be the perfect family. It was him who told me about you and Gaby.' Leaning on the table, she was all tears and red eyes and twisted limbs. She could hardly breathe, let alone talk.

'You can't face him like this. Let me give you a mild sedative,' said Paul.

'No, please. I want to be lucid. I don't want my mind to be clouded.'

'You are not lucid now. Look at you. What you need is a good night's sleep. Tomorrow everything will seem different. You'll see everything with fresh eyes.'

To sleep until morning, to not think about anything, how could she say no? She longed to forget, and not until tomorrow but forever because her sudden suspicion was so horrifying and unbearable, she couldn't live with it, couldn't think of it and couldn't put it into words, not even in her head, not even to herself in a tiny whisper.

* * *

Claire wished tomorrow would never come. But all too quickly it did come and she stood outside Tony's room, alone and afraid, like she was lost in the epicentre of an earthquake. The tectonic plates of her existence had shifted and continued to shift even

214

as she gaped in shock at the remnants of her life, at the Scrabble board abandoned on the table, at the books and the card games she had once shared with her father. Everything in her life had been a lie, like she was at a local fair, looking at herself through a mirror all distorted and wrong. She was a fly caught in a web of deceit. Was her father the spider? She didn't want to believe it.

Unable to get her head around the enormity of her fears, Claire spent the morning reading her father's letters to Angela. She hugged her pillow close and wept because every word was love. The greater the love, the greater the betrayal, she thought, shuddering.

Paul was right. She had to talk to Tony. But could she step inside his bedroom without stumbling, look him in the eye and not break down? Now that she suspected what he was, now that she saw right through him, could she hear his voice without crumbling into a sobbing mess?

She wanted him to lie. It would be so easy for him. God knew he was a skilful liar. She needed him to tell her she was wrong, that it was her imagination playing tricks on her overtired brain. More than anything she wanted to hear that black was white and white was black. And she would believe him. She would believe him irrevocably. Because she couldn't live in the world where the unthinkable was possible. She didn't want to be a part of the world where the person she had loved the most had no soul.

The door to his room was closed. That wasn't unusual. He often asked her to shut it behind her. So he could hide his true face from prying eyes? She turned the handle but it wouldn't give way. A cold fear numbed her, making her momentarily forget her doubts. He had already tried to take his life once. Would he do it again? The part of her that loved him unconditionally wanted to break the door down, to rush into his room and make sure he was okay. But there was another part of her, a voice inside her head that whispered, *If he did it, so what? What a perfect way out.* She didn't like that part of herself very much.

She stood with one hand on the door handle and another on her beating heart. Then she pushed the door harder and this time it opened. It was dark in the room. Tony always insisted on having his curtains tightly drawn. *I need rest*, he would say. But now she knew – monsters hid in the shadows. They didn't want anyone to see what they truly were.

The TV was on. The reflection of the screen played on his face. The images flickered red and blue, and his face looked distorted, like it wasn't a face of a human being at all. She didn't want to wake him, not yet, so she watched him sleep.

Tony stirred in bed. His movement triggered the sensors and the night light came on. Rubbing his eyes, he sat up straight. He didn't seem to notice her. She waited a few moments to see what he would do. He stretched and yawned and reached for a glass of water on his bedside table. When he took a few sips and placed the glass back, she said, 'Are you awake, Dad?'

He startled and his eyes widened. For a second, he looked afraid and she enjoyed seeing his discomfort. She wanted him afraid, squirming and remorseful. Unable to take her gaze off his face, she imagined herself in her mother's place. The fear, the disbelief, the sudden realisation when she had seen the knife in his hand. Claire felt the heat, the perspiration on her forehead, even though the heating was off and it was cold in the room. With horror in her heart she imagined the sudden pain, the life trickling out. She almost screamed.

'I didn't see you there. You scared me half to death. Is every-thing okay, darling? Why are you sitting in the dark?' He grabbed the remote and put the TV on mute. Now it was just the two of them. No other voices in the room, nothing to distract her from the train wreck of her life.

She couldn't ask him. As much as she needed to, she couldn't bring up her mother yet. She wanted to delay the inevitable, wanted a few more minutes of not knowing for certain. If her suspicions were correct, she wanted to know what had made him this way.

'Tell me about your father.'

Tony couldn't see the expression on her face. He couldn't see the terror, the distrust and the revulsion. As far as he was concerned, everything was fine between them. She was still the loving daughter and he was the doting father. Just like always. He started talking, uncertainly at first, then faster and faster.

* * *

Tony's first childhood memory was that of his father screaming. He couldn't remember what the screaming was all about, only that his dad sounded angry and the little Tony was afraid. There were other memories, too. Of his father pushing his mother, slapping her across the face, kicking her in the stomach, locking her in the bathroom and not letting her out till she lost her voice begging for mercy.

Tony's father was a respected police officer but no one at work knew who he really was. Never one to put himself in danger, stand up for the weak or say no to a bribe, his hobby was torturing those smaller than him. Every day at eight o'clock sharp he would get drunk and look for something to do. Since there wasn't much to do in their sleepy town, he would amuse himself by beating his only son. He didn't need an excuse or a provocation. All Tony had to do was be there.

Young Tony had the procedure down pat. Play dead while his dad drank himself into a stupor, walk past him quiet like a mouse, open the freezer, empty the ice tray into his mother's favourite kitchen towel and press it to the part of him that needed attention on that particular evening. Only once did he ask his dad why he hated him so much. He was twelve and nursing a black eye. 'Hate?' roared his father, who had just woken up with a massive hangover and nothing to take the edge off. 'Who cooks for you? Who brings you food when you can't go out? Ungrateful brat.' Tony wanted to point out he would be able to go out more often if he didn't 'walk into the door' quite so much. But he knew when to speak and when to stop talking. When it came to dealing with his father, silence was golden.

On his fifteenth birthday, Tony's dad had taken him water skiing to celebrate. At first Tony was excited at this unprecedented kindness. And then he realised his father's idea of fun was to drive his boat too fast, making young Tony beg for mercy, and then calling him a wimp. Up and down Tony went on his skis, gripping the handle tightly, until all feeling had left his fingers, while his old man laughed and revved the engine. Please, slow down, Tony pleaded silently. He didn't want to show how scared he was, didn't want to give his old man the satisfaction.

Faster and faster they went. A little more, and the boat would take off like an aeroplane. And then Tony was catapulted up, flying through the air for what seemed like forever. When he finally crashed, it felt like his head hit a concrete wall.

He was in hospital for days, drifting in and out of consciousness. Just how hard did he hit that water? He remembered waking up one morning and thinking, Mum would kill Dad for this. This time he'd crossed the line, and Tony couldn't wait to tell her all about it. They would sit with their arms around each other, like they used to when he was small, he would cry a little, while she gently rocked him back and forth, back and forth. Then they would pack a small suitcase. They wouldn't take much. Too many things would only slow them down. They would leave and never look back, travel across country on a train, and stay with a distant relative, somewhere Dad couldn't find them, somewhere they could start a new, happier chapter in their life.

And then he remembered. None of it was possible because his mother had left them months ago. He felt something deflate inside him, like a punctured tyre of a bicycle, leaving him feeling flat and empty. The last time he'd seen his mother, she had hugged him and said, 'Now be a good boy for your father.' Nothing had alerted him to the fact something wasn't right. Only her kiss goodbye lasted a few seconds too long. Only her eyes were moist with tears. But that was hardly unusual.

As he lay in his hospital bed, surrounded by machines, he wanted to curl into a ball and bawl his eyes out. But he couldn't do that. If his father came in and saw him like that, he'd call him names and laugh. He'd lean over with an intimidating sneer on his face and tell him real men didn't cry. Tony could almost smell his putrid, booze-laden breath. For his good-for-nothing alcoholic dad, he had to be strong.

On the day he returned home from the hospital, he took what money he could find and snuck out of his bedroom window, never looking back. He hadn't heard from his father since. Didn't know if he was dead or alive. Didn't give a damn. Living on the streets at 15 wasn't a walk in the park but it was paradise compared to the daily dose of fatherly love that manifested itself in bruises and broken bones.

The day he turned 18, he finally tracked his mother down. It had taken him a while to find her. It was clear she didn't want to be found. But it wasn't him she was hiding from, he knew. It was his dad.

She lived on a council estate, in a foul and filthy building with paint peeling and tattered underwear on the clotheslines outside. Tony couldn't imagine his mother in a place like this. Their house had always been immaculate and she had always been beautifully dressed. His heart threatened to jump out of his chest as he knocked on her door. He was about to see the only person in the world who had ever loved him.

A dishevelled man appeared from the flat next door. 'What's all this racket? People are trying to sleep.' It was eight in the morning and the man was already drunk. Or was he still drunk from the night before?

'I'm looking for my mother. Kate Wright.'

'She's not here.'

'Is she away?'

'She's dead.' The man slammed the door in Tony's face.

Tony knocked again, begging for details. What he found out was devastating. He was two weeks late. The cancer had got to her first. He wanted to ask her why she hadn't taken him with her, why she'd left him with that monster. After all, she had known what his dad was capable of. Was she afraid his father would never let her go if she took his only son away? Was 15-year-old Tony the sacrifice she was prepared to make for her freedom, for life without fear? And what a life it evidently had been from what he could see, three years in this hellhole. He hoped it had been worth it.

He had never blamed his mother, of course. He blamed his father. In his fantasies, his father was an old man broken by regret, who had lost everyone he loved and had nothing to live for. But in his heart Tony knew the bastard didn't give a damn. He had never loved a living thing in his life.

To this day, whenever he saw a police uniform, it reminded him of his father and he felt a nervous tremor in the tips of his fingers. Some things never changed, not even after forty years. His father had often told him the men of their family were no good. Criminals most of them, a few cops, all cut from the same cloth. Tony spent his life trying to break the mould. All he wanted was to be a good person, and so he went to church, St Andrew's every Sunday, in his best suit and with the most pious expression on his face. He was on the first name basis with the priest. He liked to think he was on the first name basis with God. Tony had always thought his greatest fear was his father's temper. But now he knew better. His greatest fear had always been growing up to be just like his old man.

* * *

Claire was crying, her heart breaking for him and for herself. Shaking, she jumped to her feet, not sure if she wanted to approach him or run out of the room screaming. She did neither and remained motionless in the corner, watching him. 'But you are just like him, aren't you? Worse than him.' Her father didn't reply but looked at her with surprise. 'Can I see your wallet, Dad?'

'What for, honey?'

'Don't ask questions. Just give it to me.'

Silently he handed it to her. She peered inside but couldn't see anything, so she felt with her fingers, searching for the silver chain. Her hands trembled too much and she dropped the wallet. Just like that first time in the hospital, the contents spilled out all over the floor and the bed. The bracelet fell on Tony's chest. In the eerie light of his night lamp she could see that it was a charm bracelet with three doves carrying an olive branch – identical to the one she and Paul had found in her parents' house. She didn't pick up the bracelet but reached inside her pocket. 'Here is the missing charm. Now you have them all. But this one has blood on it.'

Tony stared at her mutely. She whispered, 'I know, Dad. I know what you did.' It was like jumping in the water with your eyes closed, not knowing how deep it was. Not knowing whether there were rocks at the bottom. If you would drown or swim up.

He smiled. It was the smile she had grown to adore. It made her feel like she was the love of his life. He tried to take her hand but she moved away, jerked her body away from him. He wouldn't sweet-talk her, not this time. 'I know,' she repeated. She didn't think he heard her. She barely heard herself. 'I know everything,' she said, her voice breaking. What an effort, what torture it was to speak out loud of the one thing she couldn't bear thinking about. To acknowledge the nightmare was to make it real. And she didn't want it to be real. More than anything she wanted it to be a dream.

'What are you talking about?' But by the tense expression on his face, by the way his jaw tightened, by the flash of fear in his eyes, she knew that he knew. There was guilt and remorse and sorrow. It wasn't what she wanted to see.

'Don't try to deny it. I found the missing charm—' Her voice broke. She couldn't speak of the unspeakable, couldn't speak her mother's name without breaking. 'And I saw the messages in your phone,' she croaked. 'I was looking . . .' She fell quiet. Given what she had found, did it really matter what she had been looking for? 'Did you pay someone to pretend to be my mother?'

In the dim light Claire could see his face lose colour. He didn't deny it, nor did he confirm it. He didn't say anything at all. But his skin had gone white, as if there was no life left. As if her words had drained him of everything that made him human.

'What have you done, Dad?'

He looked like a trapped animal wishing to escape. For a long time he didn't speak, as if weighing his options, thinking of the right thing to say. Was there a right thing to say? She didn't think so.

'It was an accident,' he muttered finally. He didn't dare raise his eyes to her but looked down at the silver bracelet that was still resting on his chest.

'An accident? You accidentally picked up a knife and stabbed . . .?' Claire was suffocating and couldn't get the words out.

'We had an argument. You don't know what it's been like. Your mother hated me so much. Resented me for every time I got angry and . . . there was no forgive and forget with your mother.'

'So you killed her?'

'I didn't mean to.' His voice trembled. He sounded like a child. 'For a moment I went mad and lost my temper. Only for a moment, you see. I was in darkness, falling and unable to stop. It all happened so quickly. It was as if something possessed me, I don't even remember any of it. And when I saw the light, it was too late.'

Claire watched him, waiting for more. Was there more? Her legs trembled so much, she didn't think they could support her. Silently she sank back into her favourite chair. The same chair where she'd sat while they watched films together, played

Scrabble, laughed and read books. They did all that, even though Angela was gone. She was gone, and Claire didn't even know it. But Tony had known it, and not a tremor in his body had betrayed his guilt. That was the thing about monsters. They were good at concealing what was inside their black souls. They hid in plain sight and behaved like nothing was wrong. And maybe to him, nothing was. Maybe to him, the unthinkable had become the acceptable. Who was this man in front of her? She didn't recognise him.

He had told her he loved her mother, loved them both more than anything in the world. Told her Angela was the most wonderful woman he'd ever met. How blessed he was to have her in his life, how she'd healed him and saved him from himself. But Angela couldn't save herself from him. If he was blessed the day he'd met her, she was cursed. Had she happened to be walking somewhere else on that bright summer's day when young Tony was reversing in his truck, would she still be alive? Where would she be had their paths not crossed?

Where would Claire be? Would she prefer to not have been born so her mother could live, so her father wouldn't be a murderer?

But if he was guilty of a crime, he had to pay. Why did that thought hurt so much? Because she still loved him, she realised. His crime was an aberration that didn't affect the way she felt about him. The two were unrelated. They had nothing to do with one another, like dance and silence.

Tony was still talking. 'She said she couldn't take it anymore.'

'Couldn't take what?' When he didn't rely, she whispered, 'The diary entries were about you, weren't they? You are the angry man from my nightmares. You were the one hurting us.'

'Not you. Never you. I could never hurt you in my life.' He was trembling now, just like she was trembling. 'Your mother was going through Nate's things, finally, after all these years. She found some photographs of me with another woman.' He looked away, wouldn't face her. 'I had an affair. A long time ago. It was over, it didn't mean anything. It was nothing. But of course your mother didn't see it that way. She got angry.'

'I can't say I blame her.'

'I told her, "what are you doing? The thing you're so upset about happened ten years ago. Is it worth crying over? It was a different time, a different life. It's all in the past." But she wouldn't listen. She screamed about trust and loyalty and betrayal. She called me names, said I've been a bad husband. That she should have listened to her sister and left a long time ago. That she was sick of walking around on eggshells. That I was good for nothing. Told me she was leaving me, even though she knew I would never let her go because without her, I'm nothing.'

'So you reached for a knife?'

'I didn't mean to. I just couldn't let her leave.'

God had made him this way, Claire thought with horror. God had given venom to the snake and left it to bite. Was it the snake's fault if it did what God had intended it to do? 'You didn't mean to? Can't you see what you've done? You've deprived me of my mother. Not only that, but you've deprived me of all my memories of her. Now I'll never know who she was.' He was silent and only his lips were moving. Was he praying? Wasn't it too late for that? 'Wait,' she exclaimed. 'I was with you when you had your accident. I followed you to the car after . . .' She shuddered. 'I saw what happened, didn't I?'

A sudden memory flashed through her mind, a memory so terrifying, she put her hands over her head and groaned. All she wanted was to chase the horrific vision away, back to the bottomless void where it had been hiding all these months. But it was too late.

She could see herself, happy and carefree and whistling a tune under her breath as she knocked on the door of her parents' house. Excited at the prospect of taking her mother jogging in the park, she knocked once again but there was no answer, so she slid her key in the lock and let herself in. The house was filled with breakfast smells of burnt toast and pancakes, conjuring childhood memories of a lifetime ago. The birds were chirping and the spring sunshine was bright on Claire's face. 'Mum!' she called out. 'I'm here.' Her voice was lost in a loud scream. Claire recognised her father's voice, another – not so welcome – reminder of her childhood. *Not again,* she thought, rushing to the kitchen and stopping dead in her tracks. The first thing she saw was her mother's body. Angela was lying on her back, her dress white like fresh snow, like a pure canvas, except for a rosebud of blood that was spreading fast until there was a small red pool on the floor. Her hair was wild, like she hadn't had a chance to brush it yet. Her feet were bare. Claire forced herself not to cry out but her legs gave way and she collapsed on the floor. Thankfully, her father didn't hear. He was sobbing like a man possessed, a bloody knife in his hand.

Claire shook violently now, trying to chase the horror away, watching her father, his face twisted in pain, just like it had been that day. 'I saw what you did to Mum,' she repeated. 'I followed you and hid in the back of the car so you wouldn't get away with it.'

'I had no intention of getting away with it,' he said grimly.

From the look in his eyes and the tone of his voice, she knew: what happened that day in the car was not an accident. A chill ran through her. Did he drive the car into the motorway divider on purpose? Was it an admission of guilt, a confession, a cry for help? In his own perverse way, was he trying to set things right?

'I had no idea you were in the car,' he continued. 'Had I known that, I'd never have crashed it. I swear, Teddy Bear. I would never do anything to hurt you.' He looked like he was about to cry. He *was* crying! Was he looking for sympathy? Did he want her to feel sorry for him?

'You've done plenty to hurt me.'

'Everything I did was to protect you.'

'Protect me?' she whispered in disbelief, fighting a wave of nausea and not looking at her father. 'I remember now. I remember what Mum and I were arguing about. I wanted her to leave you. I told her she was foolish for not having done so years ago.'

A minute trickled by. A minute of him staring at the floor and not meeting her gaze. Finally, he said, 'Your mother should have known better. She shouldn't have provoked me. She knew how I could get.'

'I can't believe you can look me in the eye and blame her. What happened was not her fault.'

'She knew I have rages I can't control. They take over and I am not myself.'

'Just like your father.'

He recoiled as if from a slap. His eyes filled with pain. 'She should have been more careful. Instead, she humiliated me. I needed her to be forgiving and understanding. She owed me. Since the day we've met, I accepted her for what she was. Why couldn't she accept me for what I was?'

'What are you talking about? What did she owe you for?' Claire couldn't breathe. Her throat was so dry, she struggled to speak. 'Poor Mum,' she whispered.

'I married her when she was pregnant with someone else's child. I never blamed her. I loved her with all my heart. Everyone has a past. I accepted hers.'

Hearing him talk that way about her darling, sainted mother, dead before her time, murdered in cold blood, made Claire physically ill. Any moment now she would lose control of her body, break down and fall to her knees. She would become like him, unable to move, to run away. She would remain on the floor in a blubbering mess. What he was saying, the way he was saying it was almost sacrilegious. Blasphemous. 'Never blamed her for what? She's never lied to you, never betrayed you. And you did blame her. You spent your whole marriage punishing her. In return she loved you. She believed in you. She saw the best in you, despite everything. She took your side against her sister. And you isolated her from her family. You made her life living hell.'

226

Something resembling anger flashed through Tony's eyes. 'It was all Nate's fault. He was determined to destroy our family. He took those photos of me with someone else because he wanted Angela to leave me. I thought I had dealt with him. But no, ten years later, he was back to haunt me.'

Everything went dark as a terrible realisation blinded Claire. *Nate should have minded his own business,* was what Claire had said to Gaby many years ago. Suddenly it all made sense but she didn't want to believe it. Is that why she had written in her diary that she hated her father? Had she suspected what he'd done? Or had she known for a fact? 'The fire was not an accident.'

'Nate was the devil's spawn. He was conceived in sin and wicked through and through.'

'No one is wicked through and through.' *Except you,* she wanted to say but couldn't.

'He was horrible to everyone, petty and resentful. He despised me and hated you.'

'You are lying.' She knew that for a fact. She had read her diary. She had seen Nate's photographs. Her brother had the kindest smile.

'He resented you because your mother and I adored you.'

'Maybe if you'd showed him a little warmth and affection, he wouldn't have resented me quite so much.'

'It's hard to show warmth to someone whose sole mission in life is to defy you every step of the way. I couldn't say a word without him screaming that I wasn't his father and to leave him alone. Can't you see? I spent a lifetime trying to love him. I wanted to do the right thing, if not for Nate, then for your mother. But it was impossible. You can't love a serpent that bites you or a dog that takes a chunk out of your flesh every time you extend your hand to pat it. Nate was that serpent. He was that dog. He had never let me close.'

'Aunt Tegan was right about you.'

'I did what I had to do to protect our family. That's all I've ever cared about. Protecting our family.'

'Protecting us from Nate?'

'He wanted to take you and your mother away from me.' Tony's voice was impassive, his face indifferent. *He actually believes what he's saying*, thought Claire. *He believes what he did was for the best.*

'Who are you?' she whispered. 'I don't even know you anymore.'

'Nate tried to break us apart. He threatened us.'

'Nate didn't threaten our family. You did. Nate didn't betray us. You did.'

'No one needed to know about the affair. It wasn't a big deal. It meant nothing.'

'Would Mum think it wasn't a big deal? What would she have done? Would she have thrown you out? Left you penniless? Is that what you were afraid of?'

'I wasn't with your mother for her money. I was head over heels in love with her. I always found it difficult to share her with other people. Sometimes I couldn't control how I reacted. I lost my temper. But that's only because I loved her so much.'

'What happened to Nate wasn't your losing your temper. You planned it carefully. You thought of every detail. You made sure you had an alibi. You made it look like an accident.'

'Nate got what he deserved. An eye for an eye. Just like in the Bible.'

'The Bible teaches forgiveness. It teaches kindness and love. You believe in God and yet, you do something like this. How could God allow this to happen?' She was sobbing into her hands, her body twitching, feverish.

'God gave us free will so we could make our own mistakes. So we could pay for our mistakes. I guess I failed Him, like I failed everyone else. When I meet Him—'

'You won't meet Him. You think God will forgive you for what you've done? You'll be going straight to Hell where you belong.'

'I don't care if God forgives me. I want you to forgive me.'

'Forgive you?' she repeated like she didn't know what the word meant.

'All my life I've loved you the most. Please, don't turn away from me. Try to understand. All I want is for you to understand.'

'You want me to understand why you killed my mother and brother?' He was talking so casually about things so abhorrent. Suddenly she felt she was trapped in one of her nightmares and unable to wake up.

'Judge not, that you be not judged. For with the judgment you pronounce you will be judged, and with the measure you use it will be measured to you.'

Was he trying to justify his actions with a quote from Matthew? 'And the police? They don't suspect you? Why haven't they arrested you?'

'I know many important people. People who can vouch for me.'

'You faked your alibi,' she exclaimed, horrified. Why did she find that so surprising? He faked everything else, including being a devoted husband and father. 'But you won't fool them for long. That's why they were here on the day when . . .' She fell silent. Was that why he tried to take his life in the bath? Not because he was missing Angela but because the police were on his trail?

'Can't you see? I lost my temper and afterwards I couldn't fix it. She was gone. I couldn't live with what happened. I couldn't live without her. I got into the car and all I could see was darkness. I just wanted the pain to go away. That motorway divider was the only way out. But now I can see another way. We could be so happy, you and I. We can be the perfect family I always longed for. I want us to start over, like we did when you came to see me at the hospital.'

'I didn't know who you were then. I do now.' She was crying for her mother and her brother and for her shattered life. God help her, she was crying for her father.

'Please, Teddy Bear. I'm so sorry I've let you down. But if you forgive me, we can still be happy. Just the two of us.'

His eyes were swimming in tears. He looked at her like his life was in her hands. She couldn't stand seeing him the way she had always known him – kind, loving and gentle. She needed to see him the way he truly was – heartless and evil. Instead, he was a broken old man begging for forgiveness. She couldn't take it. As fast as she could she sprang to her feet, pushed her chair back and ran out of the room, away from him. Outside, she collapsed to the floor, leaning on the wall. She couldn't cry anymore. There were no tears left. Nothing was left. Only the emptiness remained.

* * *

There are monsters in this world. Most people never encounter them, never even think of them as they go about their daily lives. Others aren't so lucky. Monsters don't always come with a warning. Often they don't have distinguishing features – no horns, hooves or ugly snouts to set them apart from the general population. They look just like everybody else and they know how to blend in. You could walk past one on the street and not recognise it. You could let one into your life and into your heart, and not realise. When you meet them, they greet you with a smile and a kind word. They make you love them. And sometimes they love you back. Those are the most terrifying monsters of all.

As Claire sat inside a police station and watched people wander in and out, she had to remind herself monsters were not born. They were made by circumstances, by their inability to cope. Did Tony's terrible childhood break him and turn him into what he was? And did it matter? Could she forgive him if she understood him?

The station filled up and the queue grew. People approached a kindly female police officer behind the glass, and then some of them left, while others were ushered inside. There was an elderly man, hunched over as if by a thousand worries. A woman with a pram and a crying infant. A youth with long hair and high-strung, desperate eyes. Claire wondered if she looked just like that – high-strung and desperate. She wondered whether she, too, would be ushered inside the station if she told them why she was there.

She stared at the old man, the young mother and the strange youth, taking in every detail, trying to fill her mind with irrelevant thoughts and images. But it wasn't working.

Why had she stumbled into the police station, when what she needed was a church where she could pray? She wanted to ask God to make her forget. He had done it once before, he could do it again. Was it too much to ask when she couldn't live another day, another minute with the knowledge that everything in her life was a shamble? If Claire lost her mind, she wouldn't have to think of it. If she died, she wouldn't have to think of it. And that was what she was praying to God for as she sat in the police station, unsure what to do next – to take her sanity or her life. After what she had found out, how could she still be sane and breathing?

Claire didn't notice the officer approach her and jumped out of her skin when she heard her voice. 'Can I help you?'

After a long silence, during which the police officer looked more and more concerned, Claire muttered, 'No. No, thank you.' Then she got up and left.

He was still her father. She couldn't turn her back on him.

* * *

Claire watched him through the doorway, reluctant to walk in.

'Hey, Teddy Bear. I knew you'd come back.'

'How could you hurt her? How could you?'

'I told you, it was an accident—'

'Your entire marriage you were abusive to her. How could you do it? She loved you so much. She trusted you.'

'I loved her too. I just didn't love myself enough to get better, to seek help. I remember like it was yesterday the day it happened for the first time . . .'

* * *

His wife was everything to him. He knew he was the luckiest man in the world because he was married to the love of his life. She was his angel and his salvation, perfect in every way. If only he could learn to be perfect for her, too. Although he meant well, he could be demanding at times, and despite his marriage vows, he hadn't always been faithful to her. But it didn't mean anything. Boys will be boys and all that. What mattered was that he would gladly give his life for hers, and whatever happened, she would always forgive him.

And that was why, on the morning of his first wedding anniversary, Tony woke up with a smile on his face. Today was going to be the day she would never forget. He would make sure of that because she deserved nothing less. On any other Sunday they would enjoy a lie-in but not today. As soon as the sun was up, they were awake, ready and driving away in their little car. Excited about the day ahead, she was singing loudly to the radio. With one hand on her knee and the other on the steering wheel, he felt like singing too. They didn't have a destination in mind or any idea where they were going but that was what he enjoyed the most – the thrill of the unknown.

On the way, they explored Ardington House, a stunning Georgian residence built in the 1720s, and had a late Sunday roast lunch at a traditional English pub. A fire cracked cheerfully in the fireplace, even though it was summer, and a live band was playing, even though the place was empty. The Sinatra tribute act serenaded the two of them, telling them all about a bar in far Bombay and April in Paris with chestnuts in blossoms. Tony loved the pub, loved how cosy it felt. Then again, they could be in a field digging potatoes and he would have loved it, as long as he was with her.

In the nearby village they found a charming hotel. The building looked like it had been there since the time immemorial, like it had seen the Romans and the Vikings. It had a swimming pool, a sauna and a spa. But most importantly, it had rooms with windows overlooking fields where horses were grazing. Angela declared she was never going home. At least not until she had sampled every mud treatment and massage on the menu. Not until she had warmed her body in the Jacuzzi. 'Later,' Tony whispered in her ear as a smiling concierge handed them the key. 'We'll do it all later. Swim in the pool. Sit in the sauna. Dine at the restaurant. But right now, come upstairs with me.'

He didn't have to ask twice. Like a pair of teenagers intent on fooling around before their parents got home they dashed to their room, taking two steps at a time. And when they got there, he lifted her in his arms, carrying her over the threshold as if she was his bride and it was their wedding night.

'Look at you,' he whispered, unable to stop kissing her. 'Look how beautiful you are.'

'But you're not looking. Your eyes are closed.'

Afterwards, she lay in his arms, sleepy and content. More than anything he wanted to see a smile on her face, so he showered her with gifts – an amethyst necklace to adorn her beautiful neck, a pair of diamond earrings to make her eyes sparkle even more and the first edition of her favourite book. There was a knock on the door and a dishevelled man in grey delivered enough red roses to fill a bathtub.

'I love you,' she said, her eyes wide at the sight of them. He could see she was pleased and it made his heart flutter.

In turn, she presented him with a silver pen, so he could do his favourite crossword puzzles in style. And two slices of cake she had baked herself. The rest of the cake, she told him, was waiting for him at home and he could have it with his coffee every morning while he read his newspaper. Snuggled up to him under the duvet, she reached for the bigger slice.

'Look at you, taking the big slice, leaving me the small one,' he teased. With his thumb he rubbed the crumbs off her lips.

'Why? What would you have done?' she wanted to know, all innocence.

'I would leave you the bigger slice and take the smaller one.'

'But you have the smaller one. What are you complaining about?'

'Who's complaining?' He was laughing, tickling her and feeding her cake.

'Why aren't you eating?' she asked. 'Here, have some.'

But he wasn't thinking of the cake at all. Mesmerised by her, he was thinking that this was the happiest day of his life. He wanted to savour every moment and commit every detail to memory, so that when he was old and the best was behind him, he could travel back in time in his mind and see her like this, all slim limbs and long hair, naked in his arms.

The next morning, they got a late checkout and stayed in the room till midday. They never got a chance to visit the swimming pool or the spa, nor did they soak in the Jacuzzi or eat at the restaurant. Unable to keep their hands off each other, they barely had time to get out of bed and throw some clothes on before the cleaners arrived. On the way back home, they stopped at the same pub for lunch. In place of the Sinatra act was an Elvis impersonator who looked more like Boy George than the King of Rock'n'Roll. The fire in the fireplace was dancing to 'Jailhouse Rock'.

Her hand in his, she was teasing him and talking about the film they had seen a few days ago. He was hanging on her every word and didn't want the day to end. Who wanted to go back to their daily lives when they could have this? Without having had a drop of wine, he felt light-headed just sitting across the table from her. But then a waiter brought their food, a George Clooney lookalike with a Northern accent, and the spell was broken. She chatted with him for a minute, and as far as Tony was concerned, it was one minute too long. *Where are you from? Do you go back home often? Do you miss your family?* She laughed at his jokes and told him all about herself.

Tony felt the perspiration on his forehead, the sudden moisture under his armpits, the dryness in his throat. He closed his eyes, to avoid seeing the waiter's affectionate smile or her face that was turned to him with interest. *Interest! She's interested in him.* When Tony opened his eyes, all he could see was red. Something evil slithered inside him. The demons that lurked in the darkest corner of his soul stirred and arose, singing in his ear in irritating voices. *You are good for nothing. A failure. You will never be good enough for her. No wonder she's looking at another man, even on your wedding anniversary.*

Tony believed the demons and they knew it. Louder and louder they screamed until he could hear nothing else. He wished he could ignore them but the demons had acquired pointed arrows and skilfully aimed for his heart that was now bleeding and driving him mad with despair. *She can see right through you,* the demons murmured. *It's only a matter of time before she finds someone better. Be a man. Do something about it. Show her who's boss.*

Tony thought he would go insane. He wanted to put his hands over his ears and scream. There was only one way to make the demons stop. He had to do as they commanded.

As they walked to the car, she spoke about the meal and how nice it was. 'Nice, was it? You certainly looked like you enjoyed it,' he roared, shaking with a rage he didn't know how to control. She turned to him in surprise and smiled uncertainly, almost apologetically. As if she felt guilty. That was when he knew – the voices in his head were right. She had been interested in the young waiter. It was written all over her face. Just like most women, she was not to be trusted.

Shocked by this sudden realisation, he slapped her hard across her face. 'How dare you flirt in front of me? You have no shame!' he shouted. 'How dare you?' It was as if someone else was moving his hand, making it connect with her cheek, her lovely smile long gone. The demons were forcing him to do things he didn't want to do and he was powerless to resist.

He would never forget the heartbreak on her face. Heartbroken himself, he couldn't believe what he'd just done. He had hurt the one he loved the most. Deflated and lost, all his anger dissipated as if by magic, he broke down in sobs, begging for forgiveness. Bizarrely, it was her who comforted him. 'It's okay,' she whispered. 'It will be okay.'

'I don't know what happened,' he said, his arms around her, kissing her where he'd just struck her, holding her tight and not letting go. Whatever happened, he could never let her go. Because she was his everything. 'I don't know what came over me.'

'It's okay. Don't cry. We'll get through this. It will be okay.' She was a saint. He didn't deserve her.

'It will never happen again,' he repeated over and over, like a prayer.

But it would happen again and they both knew it.

* * *

Why was he telling her this? Did he want her to feel sorry for him? 'You are despicable,' Claire whispered, turning away from him.

As she stumbled out of the room, she heard him say, 'I'm just a human being who has his flaws, just like everybody else. A human being with a loving heart that's been broken too many times.'

As she walked around the house aimlessly, Claire knew she would give anything to have her mother hug her and make everything better. But for now, her favourite photographs would do. To feel sane, she needed to see her mother's face. Halfway up the stairs, her legs gave out and she could no longer walk. She sat on the floor, hugged her knees and shook.

'Please, don't run away from me again,' she heard. She looked up and there Tony was, towering over her. He was moving! Leaning on the banister, pulling himself up with great effort, like a drunk bringing one foot in front of the other slowly, carefully. But he could walk! Why hadn't he said anything? How long had he been pretending to be bedridden? Had everything been a lie?

'I loved your mother. I wish I could turn back time and change things but I can't. Don't think I'm not paying for what I've done. I am, every single day. The worst prisons are those we build inside ourselves, and my prison is a dungeon, without light, without air. I rot in it and suffer, every minute of every day. I pay with sleepless nights, with loneliness and remorse.'

'You took my whole family away from me.' *You took yourself away from me*, she wanted to add. 'I'll make sure you rot in jail for what you've done to Mum and Nate.'

'Don't you dare threaten me. I am still your father.'

Being so close to him, unable to run away, she felt like a petrified mouse backed into a corner. 'Stay away from me,' she cried. 'I'm not Mum. I'm not Nate. You're a cold-blooded murderer. I despise you.'

He was coming closer still, inching his way towards her, his arms outstretched, his mouth twitching. Another step and then another, and soon she could feel his breath on her face. She was shaking, in fear and anger. 'I've been to the police. I told them everything. They are coming for you.'

Suddenly, a light fell on his distorted face and she could have sworn she saw a glimmer of a knife in his hand. Was it her imagination playing tricks on her or was it real? She only knew one thing for sure – whatever it took, she wasn't going to become his next victim.

He was looming over her, dark, tall and skeletal. She could smell his sweat, sense his desperation. In a second, he would touch her. And she knew – whatever happened, she couldn't let him touch her. Rising to her feet, she pushed him as hard as she could. There wasn't much strength in her stupefied body but it was enough to send him spiralling down the stairs. One moment he was leaning over her, the next he was flying. There was a split second when she saw his eyes widen in shock. She saw the look on his face and that was when she knew – he wasn't going to hurt her. There was no knife, only an outstretched hand. It was a peace offering, a beacon. He was going to help her up. What had she done? In horror she watched his hands flail, his body roll, his head loll from side to side like a puppet's as it hit every step.

What was that sound? It was making her ears ring. High-pitched, desperate screaming. Was it him? Or was it her?

Finally at the bottom of the stairs his body twitched one last time and remained still, like a rag doll broken and spent. He was lifeless on the floor but the sound didn't stop. It must be her, she thought. She was the one screaming. She wanted to go to him, needed to go to him, but her body refused to obey. At the top of the stairs she rocked back and forth, watching him and crying for him.

The darkness was closing in on her.

* * *

Blink-blink-blink, went the lights outside. Every year before Christmas, the whole street put up elaborate decorations, garlands, wreaths and nativity scenes. The houses competed with one another for the right to be called the brightest, the jolliest and the most festive. There were Santas and Rudolfs and giant red stockings. How did she know that? She remembered! The memory rose to the surface naturally, without any effort on her part. It just popped into her head as if it had always been there, as if it had never gone away. Paul and her driving home one night not long after they had moved into their home and marvelling at the stunning Christmas lights of the houses on either side. 'I don't know what's more disturbing,' Paul had said, 'the fact they would go into all this trouble or the fact they would do it ten weeks before Christmas. It's not even Halloween.' She remembered laughing and asking whether they were expected to decorate their own place in a similar fashion. They couldn't possibly be the only dark house on the street of light. She didn't want to be *The Grinch Who Stole Christmas*. 'Yes,' Paul had agreed, 'we have to fit in. Our house must be the most well-lit on the street.' But of course, real life intervened and they had never decorated their house.

Now, as she huddled into the corner on top of the stairs, she realised the blinking lights had nothing to do with Christmas. There wasn't anything festive about them. They filled her soul with dread, not joy. It was an ambulance, flashing blue. Who had called them? How much time had passed? Minutes, hours? How long since the push, the fall? How long since she'd killed her father?

She was just like him after all. The daughter of a murderer was now a murderess herself. The apple hadn't fallen far from the tree. Her father had been right all along. *Judge not, that you be not judged.*

Paul was home. She could hear his voice. He was talking to someone. Soon two people appeared. They were carrying a stretcher.

The lights snapped on in the living room. They burned her eyes. She closed them and didn't open them again until she heard their voices. 'He's still alive. He's breathing.'

Suddenly Paul was leaning over her. 'Are you okay?' he kept repeating. 'Are you okay?' She jumped to her feet, pushing him out of the way and running down the stairs. Her father was still breathing. She strained to see him from behind the paramedics. They were blocking him from her view but she could hear his voice. He sounded strained, as if talking was costing him what little life he had left. 'It was an accident, I slipped and fell. I'm just learning how to walk again after a car crash.'

'Please, Sir, don't talk. Try to relax.'

'My daughter needs your help. She's in shock. Please, make sure she's okay.'

He was breathing heavily, like he was taking his last breaths. She wanted to hold him in her arms, to tell him how sorry she was. To tell him she was just like him. Like father, like daughter. But she couldn't get to him. There were too many people.

'We are losing him,' she heard. A flurry of activity followed, someone was running and shouting, and before she knew it, her father was on the stretcher and she was pushed out of the way, while he was being whisked away from her. They were taking him somewhere. She shouted to them, begged them to wait, to let her see him one last time. But no one heard her, no one paid her any attention. Was she shouting or whispering?

The door slammed and she heard the noise of the engine, followed by the sirens. What if he died and she never spoke to him again? She couldn't bear that thought because the last thing she had said to him was that she despised him. The last thing she had done to him was push him down the stairs. But the last thing he had done was lie to protect her.

Hands tried to stop her. Hands, voices. The voice directly over her sounded familiar. It was Paul, trying to calm her down. Pushing him out of the way one more time, she ran outside barefoot, where wet slush was falling from the dark skies. Snow in November? It was an aberration like this day had been an aberration in her confusing, forgotten life. She ran on the snow, not noticing the cold. Over and over she slipped and got up. Was she trapped in her worst nightmare? Any minute now she would wake up and none of it would be real. Her mother would still be alive, Claire wouldn't be a murderess and they wouldn't be taking her father away with the blue lights flashing.

But she didn't wake up. She continued running and soon she lost sight of the ambulance.

The blue lights were gone. And so was her father.

Epilogue

A Year Later

Paul was in the nursery, assembling a cot, so that their little one would have a place to sleep once she finally made her entrance into the world. Exactly one week overdue, the baby was in no hurry. But her daddy was in a hurry. This cot wasn't going to build itself. He was rushing and making a mess of things. Claire, nine months pregnant and loving it, was in her favourite rocking chair, watching him, chanting quietly to her unborn baby, 'Down in the valley, the valley so low, hang your head over, hear the wind blow.'

The baby had her own room, lovingly painted and decorated by her mother, who in the later stages of her pregnancy had become obsessed with building the perfect nest for her little one. The baby had a year's supply of nappies, and more clothes than she would ever need. And she had a name, Angela.

Claire had put on weight. She was no longer a swan, fragile and delicate. Paul called her his hot cross bun. He said the weight suited her. She didn't believe him, even though he seemed incapable of keeping his hands off her.

He was sitting on the floor, surrounded by bits of wood and fabric, but his gaze was on Claire. She could tell he wasn't concentrating. 'Come here,' he called, his eyes twinkling.

'What for?' She didn't stir and only her chair rocked, moving back and forth on the carpeted floor.

'What do you think?' He winked.

Her face stern, she fought laughter. 'There will be none of that. You have a job to do.'

'I might need your help. It appears I have no clue what I'm doing.'

She shrugged, curling up like a pretzel. 'I have mere days left of doing absolutely nothing and I plan to make the most of it! It's a husband's job to build things while his wife is expecting. I'm afraid you're on your own.' There was no way she was leaving the comfort of her chair to sit on the cold floor next to her husband, who was shaking his head in exasperation and swearing at a piece of unfinished furniture.

'Would you like some popcorn while you're watching and mocking?'

'That would be nice.'

He got up then and perched on the edge of her chair, tickling her belly, not letting go of the instruction manual. 'I've never met anyone so . . .'

'Smart? Savvy? What?'

'Spoilt!'

'That's because you've never met anyone so pregnant.'

'Is that so?' His lips were in her hair, his arms around her.

She was short of breath and gasping. Reaching for the instructions, she said, 'See, you're doing it all wrong. It clearly states here, connect point A to point B. That is not point A.'

'So now you want to help?'

'I'm not helping. I'm micromanaging. Nina calls it my backseat driving.'

Paul motioned at a pile of unconnected wooden planks. 'I used to be good at this. I'm out of practice.'

'No, what you are is procrastinating.'

Kissing her on the tip of her nose, he went back to the task at hand. 'You might be right, oh clever and savvy wife. What I don't understand is why they can't deliver the cot in one piece. It certainly cost enough.'

'You were the one who refused to pay for the assembly. When they offered it to you, what did you say? That you want to build it for your daughter.'

'What we need is some inspiration. Music maybe? Queen? Aerosmith?'

'Will music make you more productive? In that case, Mozart. It's good for babies. Makes them smarter.'

'If you say so. But our little girl will be smart and beautiful without Mozart, just like her mother.'

Paul put the music on, then bowed to her and said, 'Dance with me.'

'You want me to dance?' She shuffled uncomfortably.

'The three of us can dance to *The Magic Flute*.'

'At this rate, the cot will be done by the time our baby starts school.' At the look of his mock-serious face, she couldn't help but smile. 'I'd be happy to dance with you. But you might need a forklift to help me up.'

They clung to each other, Paul's hand on Claire's round belly. No longer a graceful ballerina, she swayed and waddled in her husband's arms. He looked so happy and the music was so beautiful, and suddenly she was sobbing into his shoulder while he held her and stroked her back and quizzed her, wanting to know if she was alright. 'I'm fine,' she said, even though she wasn't. She stopped swaying to music and looked up into his face. 'I miss my mother.'

'I know you do.'

'Only now I understand what a mother's love is like. All-consuming. All-encompassing. I remember her, you know. I have memories of her, like movie scenes in my mind. I see her wearing a blue dress. We are at the seaside, Mum and Dad are holding hands and I'm running in and out of the water, giggling and happy. I remember the carousel at Brighton Pier and Dad winning the biggest toy for me. Teddy Bear for my little Teddy Bear, he said.'

'You miss your dad, too.'

'Because of him I have no one. Because of him I'm an orphan. How can I miss him?'

'You know what Nina says? Heart doesn't take orders. You can't press a button and turn off your love for someone. No matter how much you might want to.'

'He lived a monster but died a human being. He died with love in his heart.'

'Yes, he loved you very much.'

She didn't want to talk about her father. Some things were better left unsaid. Things that filled her with dread, thoughts and memories she couldn't face. She did her best to fight them. But still they slithered in, disturbed her sleep and her waking hours, rattled the sharp edges of her heart. No one knew about the suffocating guilt that poisoned her from inside out. No one knew what she'd done. Tony had made sure of it. And she would never tell another living soul, not even her husband. Perhaps she was a coward but she wasn't ready to admit to it, not even to herself. 'I remember Mum taking me to see the ballet when I was five. I think it was *Swan Lake*.'

'Your favourite.'

'I fell in love with the dancers on stage. I was completely under their spell and wanted to be just like them. For weeks I talked of nothing else, begging Mum to take me to a dance studio. And she did. I remember holding her hand, afraid to let go. It was my first time and the other girls had been dancing for months. They had their tutus on and looked like they belonged there. I wanted to run and hide in my T-shirt and a pair of leggings. Mum told me not to be scared. *I'll still be here waiting for you when the class is over*, she said. *Go and be a ballerina. Follow your dream.* Before I knew it, I was twirling like everybody else. And I was no longer afraid.'

There were other memories, too, and each one had her mother in it, so beautiful and kind, the love of young Claire's life. She remembered Angela dressed in striped pyjamas reading a book to little Claire, who was hanging onto her mother's every word, begging her to read more-more-more, another chapter, another page, another paragraph. She didn't want the story to end, even though she knew it by heart. Her mother would read *Cinderella* and *The Little Mermaid*, and her father would laugh and tell Angela to read something about real life, not fairy tales. 'No,' Angela would say, 'little girls need to hear about princesses. How else would they learn about true love?'

And there was Angela cutting her daughter's hair short because Claire wanted to look just like her brother. Afterwards, people would ask if she was a boy or a girl, and she would be so embarrassed, she'd make her mother swear she would never touch her hair again. She remembered dressing up and going out with her mother. Where, she didn't know. Not that it mattered. What mattered was that they were wearing matching outfits and they were happy. She remembered dropping her favourite doll in the river and a young boy (Nate!) jumping in and rescuing it for her, only to spend the rest of the day teasing her mercilessly and threatening to throw the doll back in. Paddling in a boat, the four of them. Only Nate refused to paddle, and their boat was spinning around and around until Claire was too dizzy to paddle herself.

With every new memory, she mourned her mother and brother anew.

But with every new memory, her mother and brother came alive in her mind.

Paul whispered, 'Please, don't cry. Everything will be alright. I can't believe there's a baby in there. Our baby.' Reverently he placed his hands on her pregnant belly, like it was an altar, something to worship and love.

As Paul pulled her close, she knew that no matter what the future had in store for her, she would face it head-on. Because they were together. Because she was finally home.

And then there was water, and it was everywhere – on her legs, on the floor, under her feet. 'Something is happening,' she exclaimed.

'What do you mean?'

'I think the baby is coming.'

She was like the Great Sphinx of Giza, calm and collected. Not so her husband. He was a meteor someone had let loose around the house. He paced and he babbled. 'What should we do? Where is your hospital bag? Do you want anything? What can I get you? What can I do?'

'Call the hospital. We need to go and quickly.'

It was a new beginning. She was ready.

Acknowledgements

This book's journey to publication was a long and difficult one. *Her Perfect Lies* started eight years ago as a short story, hurriedly scribbled on a boarding pass during a holiday in Grenoble. A couple of years later it became a romance novel and then a romantic suspense novel. Finally, it transformed into a psychological thriller. So many people have supported and helped me over the years and I am grateful to every single one.

Thank you to Cara Chimirri for her amazing vision for this book and for bringing the best out of the story. Thank you to Emily Kitchin for guiding *Her Perfect Lies* to publication and to everyone at HQ Digital for making my dream come true.

I would like to thank my family for always being there for me. Thank you to my mum for her wisdom and kindness, to my husband for his love and support, and to my beautiful little boy for filling every day with joy, laughter and cuddles.

Thank you to Salvador Castello for his expertise and knowledge on a variety of subjects and for being the most wonderful father figure for me for the last twenty years.

Thank you to my talented friend and writing buddy Mark Farley for proof-reading, advising and holding my hand through countless brainstorming sessions.

And thank you to all my readers! I hope you enjoy reading this book as much as I enjoyed writing it.

Dear Reader,

Thank you so much for taking the time to read this book – we hope you enjoyed it! If you did, we'd be so appreciative if you left a review.

Here at HQ Digital we are dedicated to publishing fiction that will keep you turning the pages into the early hours. We publish a variety of genres, from heartwarming romance, to thrilling crime and sweeping historical fiction.

To find out more about our books, enter competitions and discover exclusive content, please join our community of readers by following us at:

@HQDigitalUK

facebook.com/HQDigitalUK

Are you a budding writer?
We're also looking for authors to join the HQ Digital family!
Please submit your manuscript to:

HQDigital@harpercollins.co.uk.

Hope to hear from you soon!

If you enjoyed *Her Perfect Lies*, then why not try another suspenseful psychological thriller from HQ Digital?

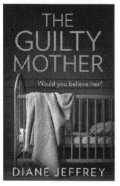
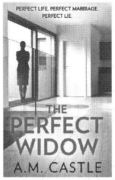

Printed in France by Amazon
Brétigny-sur-Orge, FR